William Henry
IS A FINE NAME

William Henry
IS A FINE NAME

CATHY GOHLKE

MOODY PUBLISHERS
CHICAGO

© 2006 by
CATHY GOHLKE

All Scripture quotations are taken from the King James Version.

Editor: Cheryl Dunlop
Cover Design: Chris Gilbert, Studio Gearbox
Cover Images: Pixelworks Studio, Steve Gardner
Interior Design: The DesignWorks Group, Inc.

ISBN: 0-8024-9973-2
ISBN 13: 978-0-8024-9973-8

Library of Congress Cataloging-in-Publication Data

Gohlke, Cathy.
    William Henry is a fine name / by Cathy Gohlke.
       p. cm.
    ISBN-13: 978-0-8024-9973-8
    ISBN-10: 0-8024-9973-2
       1. Underground railroad—Fiction. 2. Maryland—History—1775-
1865—Fiction. I. Title.

PS3607.O3448W55 2006
813'.6—dc22
                                                         2006021081

We hope you enjoy this book from Moody Publishers. Our goal is to provide high-quality, thought-provoking books and products that connect
truth to your real needs and challenges. For more information on other
books and products written and produced from a biblical perspective, go
to www.moodypublishers.com or write to:

Moody Publishers
820 N. LaSalle Boulevard
Chicago, IL 60610

3 5 7 9 10 8 6 4 2

Printed in the United States of America

For my husband, Dan,
my daughter, Elisabeth, and my son, Daniel—
You are my shining stars.

For my mother, Bernice, and all of my amazing family,
those who walk beside me and those who have gone before—
You are my deep roots.

Acknowledgments

FROM THE MOMENT IN CHILDHOOD that I learned of the Underground Railroad I have been fascinated by that daring race to freedom and inspired by the courageous stories of its runners, conductors, and stationmasters. Because of the danger and secrecy surrounding those journeys and safe houses, little information was documented at the time. But I am grateful for the oral stories and snatches of stories that abound in areas where the Underground Railroad was known to be active.

For believing in this book from the start, for walking with me every step of the way—freely sharing writing and marketing expertise—I thank my dear friend and writing colleague, Tracy Leinberger-Leonardi. It would not have happened without you.

For choosing my book from the hundreds of books you read, and for working diligently with me to make it the best it can be, I thank my editor at Moody, Andrew McGuire.

For challenging me with questions, ironing out details, and fine-tuning, I thank Cheryl Dunlop, my copy editor.

For all manner of valuable contributions, from good advice and the careful critiquing of early drafts to the cheerful exploration of old churches, older cemeteries, and dilapidated houses, I am most grateful to my mother, Gloria Bernice Goforth Lemons; my sister, Gloria Delk; my brother, Dan

Lounsbury; my sister-in-law, Randi Eaton; my daughter, Elisabeth Gohlke; my husband, Dan Gohlke; my pastor, Rev. Karen Bunnell; my writing teacher and mentor, Joan Hiatt Harlow, who pulled the title of this book from its manuscript; my friends and colleagues, experts in their fields, Kathy Chamberlin, Miriam and George Ackerman, Patricia Valdata, Nancy Jennings, and Joan Wilcox.

For help in researching historical details that brought this novel to life, I am indebted to the late Eva Muse, for first placing in my hands an original slave ledger for Cecil County, Maryland, and for introducing me to William Still's book *The Underground Railroad;* Michael Dixon and the dedicated volunteers of the Cecil County Historical Society, who guided me through old census records, maps, and original copies of newspapers; enthusiastic volunteers of the Chester County Historical Society in West Chester, Pennsylvania, and the New Castle County Historical Society in New Castle, Delaware; wonderfully helpful librarians of the Cecil County Public Library in Elkton, Maryland, and of the North Carolina Room of the Forsyth County Public Library in Winston-Salem, North Carolina; the Forsyth County Agricultural Center, North Carolina Cooperative Extension; gracious tour guides at Mendenhall Plantation, Jamestown, North Carolina, at Mount Harmon Plantation, Earleville, Maryland, and at the Hermitage, near Nashville, Tennessee; and Mount Pleasant Methodist Church in Tanglewood Park, Forsyth County, North Carolina.

Many thanks to my church, Elkton United Methodist, in Elkton, Maryland. You daily inspire me by your commitment to sharing God's love through welcoming arms, mission, and social justice. Working on this book while in your fellowship has been a perfect fit.

Very special thanks to my uncle, Wilbur Goforth, for reminding me that a sure way to know if I'm working in the will of God is to ask, "Do I have joy? Is this yoke easy? Is this burden light?"

Last but never least, I thank Dan, Elisabeth, and Daniel, my beloved family, for your love, support, and patience with my passion.

THE YEAR BEFORE I WAS BORN, our neighbor and my father's employer, Mr. Isaac Heath, took up some of the notions of Quakers and freed all his sixty-two slaves, gave them fifty dollars apiece, and provided all that wanted safe passage into Pennsylvania or farther north, into Canada, if they were so disposed. Those who wanted to stay, he gave two acres and a two-bedroom frame house with plank floors and glass windows, ten chickens, one hog, a year's worth of clothes, and hired them on at fifty cents a day. Mr. Heath built them a meetinghouse right on Laurelea so they could walk to church and never leave home. So it's no wonder I grew up not knowing much about the meanness of slavery or the orneriness of greed until the summer I turned thirteen.

CHAPTER

One

June 1859

THE JUNE SUN SMOLDERED uncommonly hot, so hot
that William Henry and I chose to forget our chores, borrow
hot cornbread and cold cider from Aunt Sassy's kitchen, and
take off for Tulley's Pond, home of the best smallmouth bass
this end of Cecil County. By late afternoon we'd swatted a mil-
lion mosquitoes, snagged somebody's old wagon wheel, and
hooked a few sunnies not worth the fat to fry. It was getting
late and we were about to give it up and go on home to chores
and supper when Jake Tulley showed up on the opposite bank.
William Henry elbowed me in the side.

"You boys be trespassing." Jake knew our names as well as
he knew his mama's, but Jake was a year older and calling us
"you boys" made him feel smug.

"Trespassing?" William Henry's eyes opened wide, showing all their white in his black face. He turned to me and in a
voice that held all the shock of a September snowstorm, said,
"Robert Leslie Glover? Is we trespassing? Is that what we're
doing here?"

"I thought we was fishing." I kept my face straight.

Jake pushed a greasy hank of hair off his forehead and
hitched up his pants. "I guess whipping your pa for trespassing

last week wasn't enough, William Henry. We'll see who thinks he's funny when I tell my pa that darkies and white trash is stealing our fish."

I felt William Henry's muscles tense beside me, but his mouth never twitched. "Why, Mr. Jake, we meant no harm! We was just passing the time with these fishing poles while we waited for a fresh crop of ivy poison!" William Henry could talk himself out of a whipping or work, but even I looked at him like he was crazy when he said that.

Jake lifted his chin. "What are you talkin' about, William Henry?"

"I'm talking 'bout ivy poison, Mr. Jake. Last summer when you caught that fearful rash I felt so bad I figured I just had to help find a cure."

Jake eyed him suspiciously. I still kept my face straight, wondering what William Henry was up to now.

"Well, I took myself on down to Granny Struthers. She don't usually get mixed up in white folks' ailments and cures, but she told me that all a body need do not to ever get the ivy poison rash again is to eat a whole handful of fresh young ivy poison sprouts. Mind you, Mr. Jake, that only works if you ever had it real bad—at least once. Like you, sir." The "sir" and "Mr." and the know-nothing smile on William Henry's face reeled Jake right in like he was aching to bite bait.

"You sure about this?" Jake winced into the sun. Everybody knew Granny Struthers had the gift for all kinds of outlandish cures that mostly had to do with plants and mostly worked. Maybe Jake thought he was onto something big—him being white and all. "You sure you're not making this up to get out of being whipped for trespassing?" I felt William Henry's muscles tense again and I knew he was thinking of his pa, who'd only taken a shortcut across Tulley's fallow field.

"Yes, sir, Mr. Jake. I mean, no sir, I'm not tryin' to spoof you. What would I be doin' sittin' in this bed of ivy poison myself if it hadn't worked for me? But I wouldn't want you to try it, Mr. Jake. No sir, I wouldn't." William Henry solemnly shook his head. Jake frowned and strained his eyes toward us. He was squint-eyed and couldn't have spotted ivy poison if he was half as close.

Jake pressed his fists into his hips. "And just why not? I'll be bound it's good enough for me if it's good enough for you!"

"Oh, it ain't that, Mr. Jake. No, sir. It's just that this is a highly scientific experiment and Granny wants to make sure it works on poor folks of color like me before she'd ever try it out on you fine white folks. After a time I reckon she'll take the cure on up to those Philadelphia lawyers, then they'll confer with them kings of England and it'll get to be known all over. Then'll be the time for you to try it, Mr. Jake." William Henry nodded, looking as wise as Judge Mason up in Elkton, and went back to his fishing.

Jake stood, undecided. He shifted his weight from one dusty bare foot to the other. Finally he said, "If it's good enough for Philadelphia lawyers it's good enough for me." He yanked up the nearest handful of ivy poison leaves and stuffed them into his greasy mouth. William Henry feigned horror and I didn't need to pretend at all. I knew we were in for it now. But William Henry shook his head slowly and whispered, just loud enough to carry across the pond, "That Mr. Jake is bound to go down in scientific history."

Jake hitched his britches as he gulped the last mouthful of sticky leaves, then slurped a handful of pond water to aid the process. He swiped his sleeve across his mouth and stood tall. "You boys go on home, now. I won't tell on you fishin' this time. But mind you don't come back here again!"

"Yes, sir, Mr. Jake," William Henry said. "Thank you, sir." We scooped up our string of sunnies and stick poles to head home. William Henry stopped in his tracks and turned. "Mr. Jake? Would you like these fish? It would be our honor for you to have them—you a gentleman of learnin' and all. Nobody need know we caught them. They can be yours."

Jake's mouth watered. His ma dearly loved fresh fish and Jake was no good at fishing. He didn't know how to sit still and never used good bait. "Why, I expect so. I guess it's fittin' since they be from my pa's pond. You don't tell my ma you caught 'em."

"I'd not think on it." William Henry waded straight across, and from waist-deep water handed up the catch of sunnies, pulling us off the hook.

Jake strutted off in his most kingly strut. William Henry kept a solemn face till we'd walked a quarter mile down the road, then we both broke out in rip-roaring, doubled-over laughter.

We whooped and hollered, tripping over each other as we tore through the woods. "That'll teach those Tulleys to mess with Joseph Henry!" William Henry's laugh cut the edge of reason.

"You don't reckon it'll kill him, do you?" I didn't want to be run in for murder.

"No, I'm half sorry to say. I'll go by Granny Struthers later and tell her the Tulleys be needin' her help." He shrugged. "It'll keep him miserable for a time, but Granny'll fix him up." That eased my mind, and we took off running again.

By the time we dropped on the banks of the Laurel Run, tears ran and our sides ached. But ours was minor suffering, all things considered. We knew we'd be late for evening chores and in trouble, but the moss bed under the beech tree called our names. Besides, this was the first time in forever that

William Henry and I had escaped our mothers and outwitted Jake Tulley all in one fine day.

William Henry was my best friend. His ma and pa, Aunt Sassy and Joseph Henry, worked for Mr. and Miz Heath, same as my pa, only my pa was foreman of Laurelea. I taught William Henry to read when we were little. Everything my ma and Miz Laura Heath taught me I practiced on William Henry by scratching it in the dirt behind the barn. Pretty soon he could outread and outwrite me and liked it better. So when Mr. Heath loaned me a book I just passed it on to William Henry, who inhaled it by candlelight. He'd return it a few days later, giving me the gist and a few particulars. Then, when Miz Laura or Mr. Heath questioned me, I could reel off the facts and figures enough to make them believe I was up and coming. I felt a little squeamish about deceiving those I loved, but figured it was the lesser of two evils and that I'd get around to being a genuine scholar someday.

William Henry and I talked about anything and everything. That day I asked a question I'd puzzled over for some time. William Henry might not know the answer, but there was no one else I dared ask. "What do you reckon ladies wear under those hoopskirts?"

"Don't suppose they wear nothin'," William Henry replied. "Why would they?"

"Oh, I think they must wear something. I've seen lots of white things hanging on Ma's wash line that I've never seen her wear on the outside. I reckon they're down underneath, but I can't think why she'd bother."

"My mama don't wear nothin' under her dress. She says that old kitchen's hot enough. I guess white folks wears extra things. Maybe that pale skin keeps them cold."

I knew William Henry was messing with me. "Well, I'm white and I don't wear nothing extra. If I had my way I wouldn't be wearing nothing at all right now, it's so all-fired hot."

"Well, you're different, Robert. I'd say you're pretty nearly colored in your druthers." William Henry lay back against the creek bank, sucked the juice from a reed, and chuckled to himself.

I turned my back on him. He ought not get so uppity and fresh.

"Last one in chops wood!" William Henry screeched. Quicker than a firefly flickers, he stripped down to his sleek black skin and dove headfirst into the run. I was still vexed, and then more so because I had to chop wood. But that was fair and it was hot, and I'd have done it to him if I'd thought about it first. So I stripped down, took a running start, grabbed the rope hanging off the big beech tree, and swung out over the middle of the run. For one glorious moment I stopped dead, straddled the air bowlegged, then dropped straight down into the cold June water. We whooped and hollered and nearly drowned each other before the quitting bell rang outside the Heaths' house. We hadn't finished our chores and now we'd be late for supper, too. William Henry could talk his way out of anything, but my tongue failed me whenever I lied, and I could feel my face heat up like a smithy's fire.

William Henry flew over the ridge, pulling his pants up with one hand while shoving the other through a damp blue shirt.

By the time I reached my back porch stoop, I'd straightened most of my buttons, slicked my hair with my fingers, and was as sweated as if I'd never cooled myself in Laurel Run. I shoved two crusted feet in my shoes and held my breath as I creaked open the back porch door. If there's a way for a half-starved boy to slide unnoticed to a table loaded with steaming cornbread, ham, fried potatoes, and cold canned peaches, I didn't know it.

I slid in and bowed my head to pray. That might soften Ma and give me a minute to catch my breath. The Lord might also appreciate being noticed.

I raised my head to find Pa surveying my shirt collar. His mouth drew a line, but the blue lights in his eyes caught mine. I knew then that I wouldn't get licked and that Pa knew exactly where I'd been. It was lucky Pa remembered being a boy.

"Robert Leslie Glover." Ma used my full name whenever I stepped out of line. "Yes, Ma?"

"Supper was served at six o'clock."

"Yes, ma'am."

"Where are your socks, Robert?" How she knew I didn't have socks on when my feet sat under the table, I didn't know.

"Right here, Ma." I pulled two powerfully dirty socks from my back pocket and held them out for her over the ham platter, thankful I hadn't left them down at the run.

"Robert! Not at the table!" Ma's mouth turned down and her brow wrinkled. It was a shame, for Ma was young and pretty, but frowning aged her.

"Sorry, Ma. I thought you wanted to see them." I stuffed my soggy socks down the insides of my shoes.

"'Mother,' Robert. Not 'Ma.' And I prefer to see socks on your feet, where they belong. Why ever did you take them off?"

"Well, Ma—Mother—you know how Miz Laura likes her flower beds weeded. Well, me and William Henry—William Henry and I—"

"William Henry, again!" Ma was fit to be tied.

"Caroline," Pa cautioned her, but cocked his eyebrows

toward me. He'd understand swimming at the run with William Henry anytime, but he'd not tolerate a lie. Ma, on the other hand, wouldn't understand swimming, especially skinny-dipping in broad daylight. She didn't like me larking with William Henry, and she believed that sticking bare feet in cold spring-water before the middle of July was next to taking your life from God's hands into your own, and that was surely a sin and tempting the Lord ever so severely all at once. I swallowed, felt my face heat up, and started again.

"The truth is, Mother, that it was so hot today that everything I wore began to itch me something fierce and I feared I'd break out in a rash from the heat in my body and the wool in my socks mingling together, so I took them off and kept them safe and clean—clean as possible—in my pocket." Pa picked up his fork. He knew it wasn't the whole truth, but he let me off just the same and I thought well of him for it. Ma studied my face, then tugged with little patience at the tatted edges of her cuffs. Pretty soon she sighed, eased her brow, and passed me the cornbread.

Ma was no ordinary woman. She loved me in her way, but a war seemed to be forever waging inside her, a war I couldn't see.

Granny Struthers, who lived near the bend in the run, told me that Ma was raised at Ashland, a big tobacco plantation in North Carolina, the only child of a well-to-do planter. Ma was just ten when her mother died in a buggy accident. A spooked horse ran wild, throwing the buggy against a tree, ripping the seat apart and crushing Grandmother. Grandfather shot the horse in the head and beat the driver, an old family slave, near to death. After that he gained a fearful reputation with a whip among the slaves, men and women alike. Granny Struthers figured Ma suffered most for losing her mother at such a tender age, but vowed Marcus Ashton may as well have followed his wife to her grave for all the love he gave his daughter after that.

Ma had missed out on family but she'd had everything else in this world. Granny Struthers said Ma grew up talking the most proper kind of southern English and spreading a host of silver spoons and forks beside her dinner plate. She'd been waited on and fussed over by slaves every day of her life. Even Ma said that falling in love with Pa in his military uniform at a Washington, D.C., ball was the first thing she ever did by herself.

But Grandfather wouldn't take a Massachusetts man for his daughter, not even a West Point graduate. He feared all Northerners were "dyed-in-the-wool abolitionists." Still, Pa was smitten, so he wrote to Isaac Heath, a family friend in Maryland, asking for a job. He left West Point and Massachusetts both and took the foreman's job at Laurelea, about halfway between his home and Ma's. Then Grandfather swore Pa was no better than a deserter and dirt farmer, living low. Ma ran off and married Pa anyway. Grandfather disowned Ma, swearing that he was no kin to any Yankee abolitionist and that the day she set her slippered foot off North Carolina red clay soil was the day his only child died. When I was born Ma wrote her pa a letter, begging him to come. He never answered.

That's when Ma settled in at Laurelea. Miz Laura and Aunt Sassy took her under their wing, taught Ma how to cook and get along the way regular folks do. Even so, Ma bristled around anybody of color. She hated being taught how to do by Aunt Sassy. I figured it was just the way she was brought up, owning slaves and all. But sometimes her ways shamed me in front of William Henry and Aunt Sassy. I knew her ways shamed Pa, who'd had to learn a new way of life, too. Sometimes, he took little patience with her.

Granny Struthers told me all this one day when I stopped to see her for herbs for Miz Laura's garden. Granny Struthers is no real kin to me. She's William Henry's granny for real, Aunt Sassy's ma. Granny's as black as the crow that flies, like William Henry. She has a way of knowing things that folks don't speak outside their four walls, and of what's on a person's mind before he speaks it.

The mantel clock bonged seven-thirty. Supper was long cleared. I'd finished filling the wood and kindling boxes, and hauled water for morning. Daisy hadn't liked that I was so late milking her, and let me know with a sharp crack of her tail against my cheek. I'd skimmed the cream for Ma and set the pail to cool in the springhouse. My chores were finally finished.

Sleepy summer sounds of wood thrushes and night owls drifted low on the evening breeze. A Carolina wren sang its lullaby. I stretched long on the hearth rug, my hands locked behind my head, and stared up into the beams of the ceiling. Pa tamped his pipe, lifted his heavy black Bible off the shelf, and sat down by the west window so the light could find his page. Ma folded her mending and placed it square in the basket at her feet. She pushed a pesky curl, the color of chestnuts just ripened, from her forehead, closed her eyes, and gave herself over to listening.

I never minded the evening read. I loved the music in Pa's voice when he took up the Book. Words didn't sit still on the page in black, block letters for him like they did for me. They leaped into the night sky, casting shadows among the fire dancers, conjuring battles and bloody sacrifices. Long, treacherous journeys, spoils of war, and riches beyond anything I could imagine in daylight played through the air while Pa read.

When he read Solomon, I loved a woman with my whole

heart and soul, even though I'd not raised my eyes to a girl in town. In Acts, I believed myself in far-off Jerusalem, breathless from the heat of the mob and bruised by the sharp edges of rocks that stoned Stephen. I lay limp on the floor when the lifeblood and water dripped out of Jesus on the cross.

Some place deep inside me cried over the tenderness of an Almighty God who counts the hairs of my head precious and keeps track of each sparrow, who would search night and day until He found a lone, lost lamb, intent on returning it to the fold.

I wondered how the God of the Bible and the one Preacher Crane railed about on Sunday mornings could be one and the same. Preacher Crane screamed about a God of vengeance, and lakes of fire and brimstone. But when Pa read, I saw a God of peace and mercy, grieved by war and one man's meanness to another. It seemed to me a great, long journal written since the beginning of time, and in it I could learn, little by little, the secrets of life.

CHAPTER

Two

TWO WEEKS LATER I dreamed that William Henry and I and a sea of black bodies with no names and no faces hoed behind the Heaths' house. The sun rode high, bright white above us. The air hung heavy, too hot and too still. The only sounds were the buzzing of mosquitoes inside my ear and the low, in-and-out weaving of Aunt Sassy's spirituals, sometimes loud enough to know she was near, sometimes lost among the hoeing bodies, which couldn't be separated from the soil they turned. A tiny black cloud blew up from the south, so small I might not have noticed if William Henry hadn't laid down his hoe and stretched his arms, calling me with no words, but a deep down sadness in his eyes. The wind rose until it grew into a great black funnel and pulled the green corn from the ground, split the barn, and uprooted the entire Laurelea. The funnel swallowed William Henry and the whole sea of black bodies with no names and no faces, pulling them upside down and backward through the sky. William Henry begged me with his eyes till they lost their color in the distance. His skin split a seam down the middle and peeled off his body in one long sheet that came flying in my face. When I looked down I was wearing William Henry's sleek, black skin, and it felt good and cool and right.

I looked up and there stood Ma, six feet above me, weeping as the world's end came on. I reached up to comfort her, calling, "Ma! Ma!" But she narrowed her eyes in hate and glared on me with shame. She shoved me away, swearing by God Almighty. She whistled a shrill blast on two fingers and set the hounds on me. Then she turned and ran south, away from the storm and Laurelea, and me.

My screams were nothing but spit in the rushing fire and wind. As the hounds bared their fangs and ripped the flesh from my face and arms I screamed and screamed, "Ma! Ma!"

"Robert! Robert! Wake up, Robert!" Ma knelt in her white nightdress, on the floor by my bed, shaking me.

I gulped great swells of air, trying to pull myself up from dream drowning. I jerked upright in bed, the sheet wound tightly around my neck, my heart pounding in its cage, my shirt and hair soaked.

"Robert! You're having another nightmare. You must wake up!"

Ma's voice, urgent, called me up, up out of my dream. She wrapped her arms around me. I clung tight, but still my head pounded. She pulled my head to her chest, like she might comfort a baby.

Time passed until I realized the clock ticked in the next room, my heart beat steadily, and my body was still one long, solid piece. I looked at my hands in the lamplight. They were the color of sand at the bottom of the run, the same as always. That's when I realized that the far-off barking of hounds on the chase was real. My body tensed and my grip on Ma's arm tightened.

"It's all right, Robert. It was all a dream. A frightful dream."

"But the hounds. I hear the hounds!"

Ma's tired sigh came through her nightdress. I pulled

away. "It's Tulleys' hounds. They must be searching for a runaway." Ma sounded worried, vexed, and tired.

Yes. Tulleys' hounds. The Tulleys couldn't make it as dirt
farmers, so they raised a vicious strain of hounds to hire out to
bounty hunters and slave catchers to track runaways. The dogs
were ugly and mean and would just as soon rip the face off a
man as tree him. I shuddered.

"Here, Robert. Wrap this around you. You're taking chill."
Ma stood and pulled the bed quilt across my shoulders.

Daylight rose in the east window of my room, and Ma
smiled on me with love and worry. My dream tugged at me, but
I saw no traces of hate or shame in the corner creases of her eyes.

"Your father's already gone. You may as well get up,
Robert. I'll start breakfast. You and William Henry are to mend
Miss Laura's garden fence today." Ma tried to keep the vexation
from her voice. I knew it was for Pa, not me.

It wasn't uncommon for Pa to go out in the night. I never
figured why a man who worked from dawn till dark as hard as
Pa did would want to go traipsing off in the middle of the
night. He never took the lantern off the hook. Sometimes, if I
happened to wake, I'd hear him lead one of Mr. Heath's horses
or a wagon down the side of the lane. Not on the lane, but
alongside, in the grass, as though he took pains not to be
heard. But who would care? I told myself that everybody has
their odd ways and Pa kept fewer than most.

Ma's hand gripped the doorframe. "Every blessed time
your father goes out those hounds are turned loose! If he isn't
mauled to death it will be a miracle of grace!" She swiped tears
of frustration from her eyes. The next thing I heard was the
breakfast skillet slammed onto the cast-iron stove. What she'd
said made no sense. But it was true. Hound hunts often followed Pa's nighttime ramblings. Why? There were no criminals

or runaways at Laurelea. We kept no slaves at all. And what would bounty hunters, runaway slaves, or no-good white trash like Sol and Jake Tulley and their demon hounds have to do with Pa?

I STUDIED ON MA'S WORDS as William Henry and I mended Miz Laura's garden fence. I couldn't get the sense of it no matter which way I turned the matter. I didn't see Aunt Sassy creep up behind us, never knew she was two breaths away until her sharp voice spoke at my ear. "You boys come on up to the porch when you're done, hear?" I jumped, and my hammer slipped, cracking my thumb wide open. I swore.

"Robert Leslie! Hush your mouth that swearin'! Your Mama hear you she'll wear you out!" Aunt Sassy grabbed my shoulder and swung me 'round in one motion, her tiny face puffed like an owl.

"He's hurt, Mama!" William Henry broke in. "Can't you see he's bleedin'?"

"Hush up, William Henry! Robert, let me see that hand." Aunt Sassy's snap melted. She pulled my bloody thumb from my armpit and cradled it between her palms. "Oh, child. You gonna lose that nail! Come on now Robert, you let Aunt Sassy tend that thumb."

"He's got to spit!" William Henry stood back. My stomach turned over and the green, blue, and purple of the flowerbed yellowed in my head, and I retched. The next thing I knew, William Henry dumped a bucket of cold well water over my head.

"You gonna drown him, for mercy sakes!" Aunt Sassy screeched and snatched the empty bucket from William Henry, just missing my head. "William Henry! Run get me a cup of cider vinegar from the cellar, and bring out that pitcher of lemonade. Go on, now!" She swatted after him, then hurried me toward the front porch, knotting her pocket handkerchief tight around my thumb. When the red stain stopped spreading she unwrapped it and turned it one way, then the other, finally pushing it into the icy golden liquid of a broken-handled teacup. "This will take out the swellin', child." My stomach rose again in my throat but I swallowed it down. "You gonna be just fine."

The lemonade cleared a path down my throat, and I was grateful for the vinegar. The sting finally passed, only to be replaced by a deep, throbbing pain. I pulled my mottled thumb from the china cup, checking for the bruise sure to form around my smashed nail.

I marveled how the vinegar seeped into my thumb and crept toward my palm, turning it the same bronzed color as Aunt Sassy's skin. I wondered if I took a whole vinegar bath if I'd be that same color all over, and would I stay that way for-ever? Was color only as deep as a person's skin, or did it go down inside a person's thinking and dreaming and being? But if blacks and whites were different, why did William Henry and I bleed the same dark red? Does it have to do with a soul? Preacher Crane said that coloreds have no soul. What is a soul? Is it just the person or is it something else that lives inside? Does a soul have color? Is it white or black or red or yellow or some other color, like purple, that could be the same for everybody? William Henry plunked down on the porch step and I peered at him through my wonderings, curious as to the color of his soul.

"How is the book coming that Mr. Heath loaned you last week, Robert?" Miz Laura spoke to me, but I didn't know if she'd just started or if she'd been going on a while. I shifted my seat, trying to get my bearings.

"Ma'am?" I sat up straighter and wracked my brains, trying to remember the name of the book I'd passed on to William Henry the other day. William Henry grinned at me from the other side of Miz Laura's skirts spread over her wheeled chair.

"It's fine, Miz Laura. Just fine, I reckon." I hated that my voice still squeaked sometimes. For the life of me I couldn't remember the name of that book.

"Hmmm." Miz Laura's eyes bore strong upon me. I looked away, pretending to wince from the pain in my thumb.

"And what do you say, William Henry? How do you think Robert is enjoying the book Mr. Heath loaned him?" Miz Laura spoke to William Henry but never took her eyes off me. I felt my face heat up.

William Henry leaned over his toes, intent on worrying a granddaddy longlegs on the step below him. "I reckon he likes it, Miz Laura. He talks about it some." I shot William Henry a grateful glance.

"Oh?" Miz Laura stared holes in me.

"Yes'm. He does."

"And what does Robert tell you about this particular book, William Henry? What does he like most about it?"

William Henry's eyes met mine. Everything grew too warm and too still. "Well, I know he likes it, Miz Laura. But me not being educated, and all, I'm not exactly sure what Mr. Robert likes best."

I groaned inside. William Henry only called me "Mister" when he was trying to pull wool over somebody's eyes.

Miz Laura raised her eyebrows. "I see," she said. I feared

she did. "Suppose you think hard. I'm sure you must remember something Robert said."

William Henry worried the spider some more, then clasped a hand around one knee. "Well, he thought right much of Mr. Longfellow's poem about Hiawatha."

"Go on, William Henry." Miz Laura gave him her full attention.

"That Hiawatha was some Indian, Miz Laura! And that old grandma, Nicomus, teaching him about the birds and animals and trees and the moon, and about how all those creatures be brothers. If everybody thought that way there wouldn't be folks worrying over color. They'd all be looking out for one another and treating each other like family." William Henry, warmed to his subject, might have gone on had he not caught the drop in my jaw and the twinkle in Miz Laura's blue eyes. "I reckon that's what fired Robert up about that book, Miz Laura." William Henry went back to worrying the granddaddy longlegs.

"It doesn't seem to me that Robert is the one 'fired up.'" Miz Laura smiled and laid her hand on William Henry's shoulder, giving him a squeeze more affectionate than I liked to see.

I was Miz Laura's favorite, or so I believed. I was the grandson she and Mr. Heath never had and the boy they lavished hope and affection upon. I wished I'd been the one to bring that twinkle to Miz Laura's eyes. I wondered if she knew I hadn't read that book at all and that William Henry'd read it cover to cover twice.

The sun inched higher, climbing closer and closer to the front porch. I was studying on some way to redeem myself in Miz Laura's eyes and show up William Henry, just a little, when we heard a steady *clip-clop, clip-clop* beating the orchard trail behind the barn. William Henry tore round the house in the direction of the horse's hooves. Miz Laura breathed deeply and whispered, "Thank You, Lord! Oh, thank You, for their safe journey!"

"Who?" I asked, forgetting my thumb. "Whose safe journey?" I scrambled to my feet.

The clip-clops rounded the house then and a sandy haired man, his face bearded with some days' growth, his shirt stained from hard riding, reined in one of the biggest high-stepping horses I'd ever seen. He grasped the reins in one hand and danced William Henry's blue shirt collar in the other, dragging him along like a newly bagged skunk.

"Let me down! Let go!" William Henry kicked and hollered.

The stranger rode to the porch steps and dropped William Henry, sprawling on all fours, at Miz Laura's feet. He stumbled to the far end of the porch, anger and humiliation spitting from his face. I'd wanted William Henry taken down a peg or two, but not like this.

"How dare you! What is the meaning of this!" Miz Laura nearly stood.

The man slouched astride his giant horse, tipped his sweat-banded Stetson, and drawled, "I'm looking for Isaac Heath. Caught your darky running off." He eyed Miz Laura and me, and looked like he figured we didn't amount to much. "If you need somebody to teach him a lesson, I offer my services." He fingered the dark leather whip coiled at his thigh.

Miz Laura's knuckles dug white into the arms of her chair. "I do not know who you are, but you are trespassing. Leave my land by way of the road."

The stranger leaned back in his saddle. "No disrespect intended, ma'am. Like I said, I'm looking for Isaac Heath. This is his place, ain't it?"

"This is Laurelea. Mr. Heath is not available to see you. Now, leave my land."

The stranger stroked the stubble on his jaw. "He's not here, then?"

"He's not available to see you," Miz Laura repeated.

"Miz Heath, I take it. I have reason to believe your husband has some of my property. At least I believe he had it until last night. I'm only here to take what's mine."

Seconds passed. Miz Laura never took her eyes from the stranger's face. "William Henry, tell Sassy to bring my parasol, my blue silk parasol. And tell her to bring in my quilt from the line. It's aired long enough." I looked at Miz Laura, fearful for her mind. Who cared about her blue silk parasol or that old faded quilt on the back wash line at a time like this? That quilt was hung out in all kinds of weather. William Henry stood as though he hadn't heard. "Do as I say, William Henry." She waited. "What is this property you speak of, Mr. . . . Mr.?"

"Slocum. Jed Slocum. I'm overseer for Mr. Marcus Ashton, owner of Ashland, the biggest tobacco plantation in the Carolina piedmont." He lifted his chin.

Miz Laura didn't blink.

"I'm here chasing down some runaways. . . ."

And then I missed some of what he said. Ashton was Ma's maiden name, and Ashland the place she was born and raised. I tried to remember the first name of Ma's father printed in our family Bible, but it wouldn't come to me. Did Ma know this man, Slocum?

"Two of those slaves are my prime field hands. One is near six feet, coal black. The other's a boy, near growed—might try to pass for white. It appears they picked up four or five others as they made their way north, likely bound for the Pennsylvania line. I tracked the lot of them as far as North East before losing them. Met up with a neighbor of yours, man named Tulley. Hired him and his dogs to help track."

While he was talking, Aunt Sassy slipped through the front door, clutching Miz Laura's blue silk parasol with two hands. She carefully laid the parasol in Miz Laura's lap, its point aimed at Jed Slocum. "Did you bring my quilt in, Sassy? I don't want the colors to fade."

"Yes, Miz Laura."

"That's fine. That will be all, now." Miz Laura did not raise the parasol but motioned Aunt Sassy toward the house. "And did you find your field hands, Mr. Slocum?"

"Dogs picked up their scent outside town. Tracked them to a creek near here, name of Laurel Run."

Miz Laura ignored him. From the corner of my eye I saw Miz Laura slip her hand into the folds of her parasol and clasp a small pearl-handled pistol butt. The lump in my throat grew and my heart picked up a beat. I forced my eyes back to Jed Slocum. I'd seen such things advertised in the newspapers that came from Baltimore and over the counter in Eberly's General Merchandise, but never at Laurelea. Ever since Mr. Heath had taken up with Mr. Garrett and his Quaker friends he'd not only freed his slaves, but didn't favor violence or guns of any kind, save for hunting fresh meat or fowl or maybe killing a copperhead. I wondered if Jed Slocum ranked as a copperhead.

"We followed that creek a mile or so, till it branched, then picked up the scent again off the road yonder. Near daylight Tulley's hound kicked up a fuss and ran one up a tree. I wounded one, killed one. I counted one, maybe two white men got away —at least two coloreds. Tulley's boy claims he recognized one of yours."

Jake must have made a good recovery from his ivy poison lunch to be traipsing through the countryside by night. We should have treated him to poison sumac and shut him up for good. Something tugged at my brain—the hounds I'd heard this morning, even in my sleep. And where was Pa? I still hadn't seen him or Mr. Heath, or Joseph Henry, for that matter.

"You missing any slaves, Miz Heath?"

"We own no slaves here, Mr. Slocum." Miz Laura's voice remained steady, but her fingers trembled within the folds of her parasol.

"Blacksmith. Goes by the name 'Joseph.' Tulley's son claims he saw him." Slocum stroked his jaw again. "There's a two-hundred-dollar reward for each of my field hands. Talk in town says this is not the first time runaways been tracked by your place. And then there's this blacksmith, Joseph."

"We have an excellent free blacksmith in our employ, Mr. Slocum, and his name is Joseph Henry. However, it could not be the same man. Mr. Henry hired out this day, which, of course, he is free to do, an arrangement you may one day do well to consider. We have taken enough of your time, Mr. Slocum. Robert, take me in."

Miz Laura's last words may have been lost to Jed Slocum in the barking of hounds, the clopping of horses' hooves, and the swirl of dust that rounded my house at the end of the lane. Aunt Sassy stepped out the door and laid a protective hand on Miz Laura's shoulder. "Robert, Sassy, inside," Miz Laura ordered. Neither of us budged.

My neck prickled as Sol Tulley, his son, Jake, and the county sheriff pounded toward us. The pack of Tulley's demon hounds lunged, barking and vicious, snapping at their heels.

"Down! Down!" Tulley swore and punched the two-toned lead hound with his rifle butt. The dog shrieked, then cowered, whimpering. "Tie up them hounds, Jake. Ain't you got no sense?" Jake obeyed, his face a softer version of the whipped hounds. Tulley turned to Jed Slocum. "We took that live one into the town jail and brung the sheriff, like you said."

"Mrs. Heath. Sorry to bring this ruckus out here." Sheriff Biggs tipped his hat, then turned to Jed Slocum. "I told you yesterday that unless you have proof, there's nothing I can do. It's not against the law to live by a run, and you can't help who uses it, runaways or not. You'd best have something worth bringing me all the way out here."

"Tulley's boy recognized Heath's blacksmith last night," Slocum challenged.

Jake shot a look over me and mouthed, "You and William Henry's good as dead."

"I saw a white man with those slaves. Half the town told me Heath's a slave lover. Him and that blacksmith are both missing." Slocum steadied his horse, still jittered by the hounds.

Sheriff Biggs looked from Jed Slocum to Miz Laura. With his eyes on Miz Laura, he asked, "Jake, who'd you see last night?"

Jake stepped up to the sheriff's horse and declared importantly, "I seen Joseph Henry, Sheriff! I swear I seen him! We treed that other one this morning. Pa whipped him good and made him tell where he got help and he said, 'Down by the creek.'"

"Mrs. Heath? Is what this boy says true? Is Isaac and your man, Joseph, gone?"

Miz Laura folded her hands across her parasol and leveled with the sheriff's eye. "I told Mr. Slocum that my husband is not available to see him, Sheriff Biggs. I don't believe that warrants an arrest."

Sheriff Biggs shifted his hat and turned to Jake again. "Can you swear you saw Isaac Heath and Joseph Henry with that colored in the jail last night?"

Jake hitched his pants, no longer smug. "I never said I seen

Mr. Heath. That was Pa said that. But I seen Joseph Henry. I swear it. I reckon."

"You reckon?" the sheriff repeated.

The upstairs window shot up behind us and Mr. Heath, his hair and nightshirt rumpled, leaned out. "What's going on out there, Sheriff? Can't a sick man have any peace in his own home?"

Sheriff Biggs cast a disgusted eye over Sol Tulley. "So you saw Isaac Heath, did you?" The sheriff shook his head. He looked up at Mr. Heath in the window and raised his voice a bit. "Sorry, Isaac. It seems we have a misunderstanding here. Tulleys claim they saw you and Joseph Henry out helping runaways toward the Pennsylvania line last night. Took some shots at you, and . . . oh, what's the use. Look here, Ike, will you swear you were here at home last night?"

"No better place for a sick man to be, Tom. I'd have quite a time running up and down the roads and through the woods with no privy, if you follow my meaning." Mr. Heath ended in a fit of coughing.

"That's quite enough, now. You're upsetting my husband and he isn't well."

"But, Joseph! I know I seen Joseph Henry, Sheriff!" Jake bellowed.

"Tulley, take this boy home to his mama." Sheriff Biggs tipped his hat to Miz Laura and said, "Beg pardon, Mrs. Heath. If this lot bothers you folks again, send me word and I'll run them in for trespassing. A night in the poke might cure what ails them."

"Thank you, Sheriff Biggs. But I'm certain Mr. Slocum won't be back." Miz Laura smiled, grand lady that she was.

"What about that blacksmith?" Jed Slocum reined his horse sideways, blocking the drive, challenging the sheriff.

Mr. Heath called out of the upstairs window. "If you're looking for Joseph he isn't well, either. I had Charles drive him over to Granny Struthers. Oddest fever we've all come down with."

"Fever, nothin'!" Sol Tulley hollered. "It does seem mighty convenient that they're both down sick all of a sudden, don't you think, Sheriff—especially for a man that 'hired out' today?" Slocum pressed. Sheriff Biggs reined in his horse.

That's when Mr. Heath's wagon pulled in the lane. Pa drove. Granny Struthers perched on the buckboard beside him. The wagon rumbled past our house, bringing Ma out the back door. She lifted her hand, shading her eyes, and called after Pa. He never slowed.

Tulley dragged his hounds across the lane, blocking the wagon's path as it neared the Heaths' house.

"Move aside, Tulley. I have a sick man in back," Pa insisted.

"I'll bet you do, Glover." Tulley sneered. "Sick with a bullet hole!"

"No, suh," Granny Struthers spoke up. "No bullets in this black boy. It's the canker rash."

"Canker rash?" asked Slocum.

"Yes, suh. Canker rash."

Ma caught up as Granny spoke. "Scarlet fever!" she cried, and clapped her hand to her mouth.

"Scarlet fever, my eye!" Tulley spat and stepped toward the wagon. The hounds he held in one hand went wild. He was forced to pull them back. "Fool dogs!" He smacked the lead hound again. "Jake, you climb up there and pull that blanket back. Let's see if this scarlet fever's got bullet holes."

Jake began to climb, then hesitated.

"That's right, honey. You climb on up and take a look to satisfy yourself." Granny beckoned Jake. "It's all right. Come on. Just so long as you done had the fever there ain't no danger. I reckon you did. I know your older brother died of it so you must've had it, too. All but your Pa. He was away them days sportin' himself up in—"

"But, I—I ain't never had the fever," Jake blurted. "Zach died before I was born." A shadow crossed Sol Tulley's face.

"Oh, that's right, Chile. I clean forgot. I nursed your mama and laid out Zach's little body for burial. He be the first-born, wasn't he, Mr. Tulley? Shame you weren't there to see him laid out so fine."

"Stop! Get down, Jake! No darky's worth dying for!"

"You got that right, Mr. Tulley. And this poor boy still weak from his fearful swole-up throat what I nursed that liked to kill him!" Granny shot a vengeful eye over William Henry and me. We backed away. "We got to quarantine this place. Fact is, I be surprised if Mr. Heath's not down with it from what Mr. Charles say." Granny paused. "I hope none of you gentlemen got too close. I had the fever when I was a chile so I ain't scared to nurse it. But if you ain't never had it and then get it when a growed man . . . mmm, mmm." Granny shook her head.

Sheriff Biggs backed his horse away, giving Pa's wagon plenty of room. Sol Tulley, Jake, and Jed Slocum did the same. But the lead hound, recovered from his whipping, sniffed the ground, inching toward the wagon. Suddenly the dog lunged forward, barking madly. Tulley yanked him back. "Get off, you fool hound! If darkies catch the fever I reckon dogs can, too!" The Tulleys dragged their yelping hounds down the lane. Sheriff Biggs tipped his hat to Miz Laura and Ma, then followed the Tulleys.

Slocum stepped his big horse up to the wagon bed and jerked the blanket off Joseph Henry. He pushed Joseph's legs with the barrel of his shotgun. I didn't know if he was looking for a bullet hole or aiming to make one. "This is not over." He looked from Joseph to Pa, tipped his hat deeply to Ma, making her blush crimson, then rode hard to catch up with the others.

Pa pulled the team back of the house, saying to Ma, "Caroline, take Robert home!"

Ma reached for my hand, but I raced after Pa, pretending I hadn't heard. Ma called after me, her voice tight, "Robert, you are to come with me this instant!"

Maybe I should have obeyed, but I rounded the corner of the house just in time to see Joseph Henry jump from the wagon, open a false bottom in the back that I had never seen, and help Pa pull out a coal black man, unconscious and bleeding. Granny Struthers, her voice low and urgent, whispered, "There ain't a moment to lose if the Good Lawd and me gonna keep this man alive."

William Henry held the door while Pa and Joseph carried the man up the back steps of the Heaths' house. A boy about my age, white, or nearly, tumbled from the same mysterious place. I tried to follow them inside but Ma, breathless, had caught up with me and grabbed me by the crook of my arm. Aunt Sassy caught my eye, looked at Ma, shook her head at me, and locked the door. I stepped back in disbelief, jerking away from Ma.

I could still hear Tulley's angry hounds in the distance. It reminded me of my dream and I ran back to the lane. But riders and hounds were gone. Their yelps faded at last. Only then did I reach down to touch the two fresh, red drops of blood in the dirt.

CHAPTER

Four

MA BARRED ME from the Heaths' house and hustled me home. She drove me with yard and garden chores till noon, sidestepping every question I asked about those people from the wagon. The more questions I fired the less she spoke, until she stopped speaking altogether. I couldn't even get her interested in my thumb. Ma banged pots across the stove, burned dinner, and nearly rocked a hole in the floor before she finally set off for a walk in the late afternoon. I figured I'd be turned loose then, but she set me to chopping kindling in the side yard. I piled enough kindling to last us nearly forever.

At supper Ma and Pa barely spoke. She wouldn't meet his eye. When I asked if Granny Struthers still nursed down at the Heaths' and how Joseph Henry and Mr. Heath were faring, Ma shot me a furious glance. Pa mumbled, "Tolerable." Then he barked, "But you know the house is quarantined. You heed that and stay away till those signs come down." I stopped short of asking when that would be or about the man that Pa and Joseph had pulled from beneath the wagon, or why they'd locked me out. Pa skipped the evening read for the first time in my memory and turned in early. Ma rocked late into the night.

Pa took to the fields before breakfast. We carried on like that all day and into the next. By the third day I began to doubt that the Lord would look kindly on blessing the same warmed-over beans and cornbread. But Pa didn't complain and Ma didn't apologize.

Late that afternoon, on a wide detour from the henhouse, I passed the red and white quarantine signs nailed to the Heaths' hitching post and across their back door. I checked every which way, decided to ignore the signs Pa had told me to heed, and slipped into Aunt Sassy's kitchen, hoping for something solid. I filled my shirt with fresh molasses cookies and slipped out, thinking myself clever and lucky until I bumped into Joseph carrying a flour sack up the back porch steps.

"Whoa! Robert! Where you off to in such a hurry?" Joseph's eyes rested on the bulge in my shirt. "You wouldn't be stealin' food from Sassy's kitchen, now, would you?" But the corner creases of his eyes were friendly.

"You don't know what it's like at my house, Joseph! Ma's not cooking—just warming up old beans and such. She's working me to death with no food. My backbone's likely to pop out my belly any day now!" Then I remembered something. "Say, Joseph. I thought you had the fever." A shadow crossed his face. "Granny Struthers said!"

Joseph dropped the flour sack and leaned toward me. "Listen here, Robert. There was good cause to call quarantine on Laurelea. But I heal up real fast and Sassy needs my help. Now, I expect your Mama is looking for you at home. You'd best go on, before you get us both in trouble."

I stepped back. A moan, deep and full of pain, drifted up from the belly of the Heaths' house. I knew it didn't belong to Miz Laura or Mr. Heath or Aunt Sassy. "Who's that? Who's moaning, Joseph? Is it the man you and Pa pulled from that hidey-hole in the wagon?"

"I didn't hear nothin', Robert, and neither did you. Now,

go on, or I'll tell Miz Caroline that you're over here stealing Sassy's cookies."

Joseph brushed past me and disappeared into the house. I backed down the steps. He'd treated me like a toddle baby, and lied to boot. And what about Miz Laura and Mr. Heath? They were the most honest, law-abiding folks I knew. I knew they didn't hold with slavery. They believed it to be against God's will and His plan for men, brought on by this world's greed. They'd freed their own slaves and provided good employment for them that wanted to stay. They treated the Henrys like family. That proved their convictions to my mind. But surely they wouldn't help slaves escape. That was breaking the law, like stealing, wasn't it?

I rounded the side of the house. I felt eyes upon me, but the yard stood empty. Looking up, I saw a boy's face, nearly as white as mine, peering at me from the attic window. My breath caught. It was the same boy I'd seen tumble from the wagon. Our eyes scarce met before he pulled back, dropping the curtain into place. I waited, but the curtain never moved again.

I roamed the long way home, through the fields and by the road, wrestling with my questions and the memory of the boy in the window. Was this the first time runaways hid at Laurelea? Pa's nighttime ramblings had been going on as long as I could remember. Was this why? And where was William Henry? I hadn't seen hide nor hair of him since Slocum came. He hadn't seemed nearly as surprised as I was about that wagon, and they'd let him in the Heaths' house right off. I felt my face heat up. How could Pa and Joseph tell William Henry and not me? How could William Henry keep such a secret from me?

"Fever's not got you down." Jed Slocum stepped from trees lining the road, trailing the reins of his horse. I'd been lost in my thoughts and molasses cookies and hadn't seen or heard him come near.

"No, sir. I steer clear of sick folks." The lie came easily. I hoped it sounded smooth, and that I didn't look as scared as I felt. I tried to sidestep him, but Slocum was faster and blocked my path. I smelled his sweat.

"You know stealing slaves and hiding runaways will land you in jail, or worse."

"I didn't do anything!" My voice came out too high.

Slocum smiled. "But you know something, don't you, Boy?" He circled me, and though he wasn't much taller than me, he was lean and muscled and hard built. He swaggered with a confidence I did not own. "Did your mama tell you who I am? I expect she'd be grateful if you help me. Two of those runaways belong to her daddy."

Now I was in over my head. I'd meant to ask Ma if she knew Jed Slocum and if it was the same Ashland—her Ashland. "I don't know what you mean." I stepped around Slocum, never looking back.

"I'll bet your daddy knows!" I picked up my pace, but he called after me, "I'll be watching you, Boy! I've got time. All the time there is."

When the door slammed behind me Ma looked up from snapping beans. "Robert? What is it? You look ill."

"Jed Slocum. I met him on the road. He's still looking for runaways. He's watching us."

Ma bit her lip. Pa stepped in from the front room. "You stay away from Jed Slocum. He's white trash looking for trouble." I'd never heard my pa call anyone "white trash."

"He said that he works for your pa," I challenged Ma.

Ma stood and set down the pan of beans. She stole a glance at Pa. "Mr. Slocum is the overseer on Ashland Plantation, my father's home—your Grandfather Ashton. One of his jobs is to track down runaway slaves."

Pa stepped closer. Ma continued. "He's not a gentleman, Robert, and I want you to stay away from him."

"What did he say?" Pa asked.

"Nothing that matters. I didn't tell him anything. I don't know anything." My heat was rising, and all they cared about was Slocum.

Pa turned away. "It's best that way," he said.

"Best! Best? Why won't you tell me what's going on around here? The sheriff, the Tulleys with their devil hounds, and now this Jed Slocum's running over the place. They all know more than I do! What about those people in the Heaths' attic?" I heard my voice rise and the panic crawl over my anger, but I couldn't stop. "Slocum said I could go to jail for helping runaways!"

"Nobody is going to jail," Pa said. "You have no part in this, and you don't know anything about it."

"Nor will you ever!" Ma cut in.

"Your job is to stay home and mind your mother. Stay away from the Heaths', and away from Slocum. Do you understand?" Pa's tone brooked no backtalk. Why was he treating me like a toddle baby?

"Yes, sir." I looked away, shamed and angry.

"Caroline, I think we'd best have supper early." It was the first time I'd heard Pa speak directly to Ma since Slocum came to Laurelea. Ma nodded.

Through the rest of my chores and supper I nursed my anger, but dared not cross Pa. Nobody spoke. Ma cooked real food. That was a blessing. After supper I sat on the porch, no longer expecting an evening read. But Pa called me in and lifted down his heavy black Bible. Despite my anger, I felt glad. It was the most normal thing I'd seen in our house in three days.

He pulled a chair next to the western window. The light caught the first traces of gray streaking the hair along his temples, a thing I'd never noticed. He opened to the book of Matthew and read the parable of the talents. When he finished with the sheep and goats, his voice slowed. "Then shall the King say unto them on his right hand, Come, ye blessed of my Father, inherit the kingdom prepared for you from the foundation of the world: For I was an hungred, and ye gave me meat: I was thirsty, and ye gave me drink: I was a stranger, and ye took me in: Naked, and ye clothed me: I was sick, and ye visited me: I was in prison, and ye came unto me. Then shall the righteous answer him, saying, Lord, when saw we thee an hungred, and fed thee? or thirsty, and gave thee drink? When saw we thee a stranger, and took thee in? or naked, and clothed thee? Or when saw we thee sick, or in prison, and came unto thee? And the King shall answer and say unto them, Verily I say unto you, Inasmuch as ye have done it unto one of the least of these my brethren, ye have done it unto me."

Pa closed the Book and rubbed his forehead. He'd read without his usual emotion. Still, the words stood up in my mind. I wondered if the "least of these my brethren" were the two hiding in the Heaths' attic. If Pa believed that, what did Ma believe? Pa raised his face to Ma's. His eyes pleaded and her eyes filled, but her mouth stayed grim. After a time Pa stood, placed his Bible on the mantel, and turned in.

Ma sat in her chair, no longer rocking. It was like being in church, waiting for the preacher to take the pulpit, only he didn't come. Shadows crossed the parlor floor. "Do you want me to light the lamp, Ma?"

She looked up, as though she hadn't seen me before. "No. You go on to bed, Robert. I just want to sit awhile."

I stepped into the half light of my own room and undressed. The sun took longer to sink into the poplars and the wood thrushes stayed up later these early summer nights. The perfume of Ma's June roses, the scent of honeysuckle and Pa's last plowing drifted through my open window. It was my favorite time of year in nature, but I couldn't take joy in it. Something at Laurelea had changed, like the coming of hard frost while peaches still hang on the trees.

I woke when the night was full to the sounds of my parents' voices, heated, rising and falling in harsh whispers on the other side of the wall. I'd heard things through the wall before that weren't meant for my ears, but I'd never heard Ma so angry. I couldn't remember Pa sounding so bone weary or short on patience. My name came in snatches. "It was too close this time, Charles! That man was shot! Killed! It could have been you!"

"But it wasn't me, Caroline. I wasn't hurt. Next time we'll take another route. They won't expect—"

"Next time? How can you throw your life in jeopardy this way, Charles? What about Robert? What about me? What if you are shot, or caught and hanged? Have you forgotten you have a son, a family?"

"Caroline, be fair."

"Fair? You talk to me about being fair? I can't take any more, Charles. I will not have Robert drawn into this. He's almost thirteen. He spends so much time with that colored boy, he's bound to find out. We won't be able to keep it from him forever. He's not a child anymore."

"That 'colored boy,' Caroline? William Henry has been Robert's best friend since the day he was born. After all these years and all we've been through with the Henrys I can't understand why the color of their skin matters to you. And no,

Robert isn't a child. He's old enough to make his own judgments about a good many things. It's time he knows from us, before he finds out from someone else. Then he can decide for himself."

"How dare you suggest such a thing! You promised! You promised that Robert would never be dragged into this. Of all things you must keep your word in this, or I will never forgive you! Color does matter. It matters everywhere but here in this fanciful world that you and Isaac Heath have created. It is high time Robert kept company with his own people."

"If you talk any louder you'll wake him, and then we won't need to tell him. I'm sick to death of fighting you, Caroline. I want peace in our home. I need peace. God knows you mean more to me than my own life, but I'm bound to a God of mercy. You're asking me to be less of a man."

"Mercy? Manhood?" Ma's laugh cut a bitter edge. "No, I simply do not believe God wants you to risk your life breaking the law! You had the audacity to quote Scripture to me this evening! You want Scripture? Paul said we are to be content in whatever state we find ourselves, to know how to be abased and how to abound, to be full and to be hungry, to abound and to suffer need. Do you think there is one Scripture for whites and another for coloreds? Charles, you turn the gospel to meet your own ends. You are breaking the law, and sooner or later you'll be caught or shot!"

I rolled over on my stomach and covered my head with my pillow, trying to shut out their words and the fear growing inside me. I'd heard of people being dragged from their houses and tarred and feathered, of people being whipped or hanged for helping slaves escape, even though they were supposed to be given a fair trial. I remembered hearing Pa read from the newspaper of a man whose barn was burned to the ground for taking up for a colored man. I'd heard whispers at church of families being disfellowshipped and shunned. But those things were far from my world and I'd even doubted they were true—like stories parents make up to keep you from stepping out of bounds. But now I wondered if some of those stories I'd heard neighbors tell were veiled threats for Pa or Mr. Heath. I understood Pa's nighttime rambling and the need to call quarantine. Little things, quirks of Pa's and secrets I'd thought odd from times past, fit together.

But I felt trapped, caught between the things Ma said and the things Pa seemed so sure of, and most confounding of all, my love for them both. Sides were being drawn in the bed on the other side of my wall, and I didn't know where I belonged.

Near dawn I fell into a half sleep. I dreamed that I floated on a flimsy raft in the middle of the swollen run. Ma and Pa stood on opposite banks, both calling my name, hollering for me to paddle toward them. William Henry swam out beside me, grabbed hold of my raft, and tipped it over. Somehow, I'd forgotten how to swim. William Henry smiled with his mouth as though he was my best friend, but laughed at me with his eyes. He chanted the words Preacher Crane quoted every Sunday at the end of his sermon, "Mark 3:25. And if a house be divided against itself, that house cannot stand."

CHAPTER

Five

BY THE TIME the month-long quarantine lifted from Laurelea, we'd missed the Independence Day celebration with all its festivities in town and my yearly birthday trip to pick whatever I wanted from Eberly's General Merchandise. To compensate, Ma gave me the joy of beating every rug we owned in the July sunshine. Then for good measure she had Joseph cart over every one Miz Laura owned. I worked fields with Pa most mornings, then weeded and hauled water and chopped kindling for Ma till I was stooped. I scraped and painted woodwork, washed windows, and did whatever else Ma or Miz Laura dreamed up to keep me busy and away from William Henry. I was thirteen at last, and all it meant was more work.

The one day I snuck off, William Henry claimed he didn't have time for fishing anymore. My world swung off its hinges. Fishing, skunking, skinny-dipping—all the things that made life worth living didn't mean much without William Henry. It was a relief to go to church on Sunday, and that's telling.

Preacher Crane railed all morning about our present miserable journey through this veil of tears, how every decision every day leads us closer to eternity among the blessed or the damned, and how we must stand strong and live law-abiding lives in this world so that the God of justice will crack open the gate to the next. Pa shifted in his seat. I knew he was not comfortable with the pitch of Preacher Crane's ranting or the strain of his doctrine. My stomach rumbled as the noon hour drew near. I stuck my finger between my neck and starched collar, hoping to catch a breeze or at least let my sweat roll down me instead of forming a puddle at my neck. But the air never stirred.

We'd shaken Preacher's hand and stepped full into the sunshine before Jed Slocum rounded the corner of the church. "May I have a word with you, Miz Caroline?" Slocum tipped his hat to Ma. Ma's face flushed and Pa's jaw set. "It's about your father, ma'am. I have a letter for you from Mr. Mitchell."

"Cousin Albert?" Ma looked from Slocum to Pa. Pa stared hard at Slocum.

"I'll bring the carriage around," Pa said. "Robert, come with me." I wanted to stay, but Pa's hand rested on my shoulder, guiding me along. We waited at the edge of the churchyard. When Pa finally helped Ma into the buggy I saw her gloved hand tremble. Pa drove. We held our tongues until she finished reading her letter.

"Cousin Albert says Papa is not well. He urges me to come home, if I hope to see him again in this life." Ma's eyes filled. Pa covered her hand with his own.

"Why did Slocum wait so long to give you the letter? He's been in town a month." Pa couldn't keep the edge from his voice.

"He just received it. Mr. Slocum said it came in his own letter from my cousin. You remember Albert, Charles, from West Point. He writes that things are not going well at Ashland. He thinks Mr. Slocum should return home even if he can't find Papa's slaves. He even suggested that Mr. Slocum offer his services to me as escort." Pa's jaw clenched.

"I would have thought better of Albert." Pa kept his eyes on the road. "Do you mean to go?" Ma stole him a glance.

"I think I must. It may be my last chance—my only chance to see Papa." Ma broke down then, weeping on Pa's chest. We drove home, Pa's free arm wrapped around her.

That afternoon Pa, Joseph, and William Henry disappeared into the barn. I knew I would not be included in their business. Ma combed her hair and announced that she intended taking tea with Miz Laura. I knew if Ma shared her troubles with anybody it was most apt to be Miz Laura.

There was space under the front porch of the Heaths' house, high enough for a boy to sit upright and as long as the porch itself. Yews and hydrangeas shielded the white latticework all around. A few of the slats on one end hung loose—a fact that William Henry and I never mentioned to anybody and never repaired. Under that porch we'd heard many things not meant for our ears. That day I went alone, knowing I was too old for such deceit and nonsense. But I'd been left out of everything by both parents, and I needed to know if Ma really meant to leave us.

I scooted under as Miz Laura's chair rolled above me. Wicker sighed when Ma eased herself into the rocker opposite. Aunt Sassy's soft shoes padded across the porch floor. I could hear her setting out china. "These be my lemon nut cookies you so fond of, Miz Laura." Aunt Sassy's voice came smiling and prideful.

"Sassy, you spoil me so!" Miz Laura's voice reminded me of church bells.

"You ladies enjoy your tea. Miz Caroline, you make sure she eats her fill. She be wastin' away to nothin'."

"Of course, Sassy." Ma's voice came tight and polite.

"Will you pour for us, Caroline?" Miz Laura asked. "I'm so glad you came today. What a lovely afternoon!"

"You're feeling better, then, Miss Laura? We missed you in church. It's not the same without you."

"I'm not up to the ride anymore, Caroline, but I do miss the hymns and the fellowship."

"I'm afraid the fellowship is a bit strained these days, with all the talk of abolitionists and bounty hunters running up and down the countryside." I heard Ma pour the tea. "One lump or two?"

"One, please. Let's not speak of conflict today, dear."

"I'm sorry, Miss Laura."

Neither of them spoke for several minutes and I was getting tired of sitting in the dirt. It crossed my mind to give it up and sneak out the back when my eye caught a slight movement near my foot. Even in the dim light I made out the long diamond pattern as it slid through the dust. I could have kicked myself for not keeping better watch. Panic pricked my spine. The two on the porch above me began to speak.

"Miss Laura, I do cherish your company."

"And I yours, Caroline. I've missed you these few weeks. But I know you've been keeping Robert busy." I heard the smile in her voice.

Ma sighed. Her cup clinked in its saucer. "I have been. He's like a caged animal. But he's done well and needs a rest. I need a rest." Ma spoke softly and I strained my ears to catch her words, not daring to move. I watched helplessly as the snake slithered over my knee. "How are your—guests? Have they gone?"

Sweat beaded my forehead and trickled down the back of my neck. Visions of Pa finding me stone-cold beneath the Heaths' porch made me wince. The shame of Pa knowing I'd died crouched in the dirt, eavesdropping, was even more horrible than the idea of them dragging my lifeless, rotting body from behind the latticework.

"I didn't think you wanted to know."

"I don't, really. I don't. Miss Laura, I don't know what I

want. I'm frightened. It could have been Charles or Isaac shot out there!"

"Or Joseph."

"Yes, or Joseph. But at least he'd be risking his life for his own people! Charles has a family and Isaac has you! Shouldn't that be enough?"

"I know you don't expect me to answer that, Caroline. Here, take my handkerchief, dear. You are upset and I'm sorry. I worry, too. But you know as well as I that they each make their own choices. Were I stronger, I would have done the same."

I closed my eyes, prepared to die.

"I'm just so afraid. I've never been convinced this is right. Not like you, Miss Laura. Perhaps I'm a coward. But even if I believed in—in this cause, I cannot abide the thought of breaking the law. It flies in the face of everything I was raised to believe and practice."

Miz Laura didn't respond.

"There is something else." Ma sniffed, taking time to compose herself. "Mr. Slocum spoke to me outside church today."

"Jed Slocum? I thought he'd returned south!"

"No. He's the overseer on my father's plantation, you know."

"So he said. I wondered if you remembered him."

"Papa hired him soon after Mama died, knowing he'd brook no laziness among the field slaves. Seeing him here last month brought my father so close to me, Miss Laura." Ma hesitated again. "This morning Mr. Slocum gave me a letter from my cousin, Albert. Albert's mother was my aunt Grace, Papa's older sister. He owns the plantation adjoining Ashland. Albert and I grew up together—played together, might have married, except that Charles and I—He writes that Papa—" Ma's voice broke. I heard Miz Laura take the letter and smooth its folds.

It was the first I'd heard that Ma had a suitor besides Pa. I opened my eyes to find the diamondback resting between my kneecaps. I vowed I would never eavesdrop beneath that porch again if the Lord let me live.

"He doesn't mention the nature of the illness. Will you go to him?" I heard Miz Laura's chair roll forward and I imagined she took Ma's hand in her own, as she was wont to do.

"I want to—but I'm afraid. Afraid to go and be rejected by him, afraid that if I don't go Papa will die without things being made right between us. I could live without ever seeing Ashland again if only I knew Papa loves me, forgives me for running away and marrying Charles. I know he'd never understand my life or the work Charles does." Ma sounded helpless. I felt small and helpless beneath her.

"We all crave the approval of our parents, Caroline. It is the most natural of desires, and it comes regardless of our actions, regardless of our age. I think we never grow so old that we can do without their love. Even when our opinions directly oppose."

"I'm not certain that my opinions do oppose Papa's all that much."

Miz Laura ignored that. "Have I ever told you that I often crave my mother's and father's love? Sometimes, at night, when my pain is the worst, I lie awake and search my memory for their smiles. I wish with all my heart that they might lay their hands on me and bless me, just once more. They were from the South, too, you know. They loved me dearly, but if they were alive today they would be terribly grieved and angry to learn that Isaac and I have freed the slaves they willed to me. They believed those people were my inheritance—an inheritance they worked a lifetime to provide for me. But those people were not theirs to give, no matter how kindly they treated them or what bills of sale they possessed. And yet, I hope—someday, when we walk together in that promised land, when all things are understood clearly—that they will bless me for what I've done. In that hope I find peace."

"Papa would never understand hiding another man's slave or condone breaking the law." Ma's footsteps crossed to the edge of the porch. "Papa was wrong to forbid my marriage to Charles. But it wasn't only his pride. He so wanted me to marry Albert. He believed he was protecting me. I find myself forbidding Robert certain company for just the same reason. Perhaps if I'd waited, if Papa had come to know Charles better—if I'd written to Papa before Robert was born—"

"That is all in the past, Caroline. What is it that you want to do now?"

"I'm not sure. But, if Papa could only see Robert—growing so fine and tall—perhaps he might soften."

"And what about Charles? Do you think your father could accept Charles?"

"No. At least not at first. But if Papa took to Robert he might realize that it is time to accept all of us. We could be a family again, a real family."

I held my breath. "Have you discussed this with Charles?"

"It's all so awkward, Miss Laura. Charles and Albert were friends at West Point. But when Charles and I fell in love their friendship became impossible. Now, after all this time, with Albert being the one to write—I don't know what to do. I told Charles I think I must go to Papa. I've not mentioned taking Robert . . . not yet. I want to be certain of myself first. I don't want Charles to dissuade me if I decide it's best. If I bend to Charles now and Papa dies, I may always regret it."

"Do you think Charles would forbid you?"

"No, at least not directly. But he might be afraid that if I returned to Ashland and Papa welcomed me I might not want to come back."

"Does he have reason to fear that, dear?"

I couldn't breathe. Ma didn't answer immediately.

"I don't think so. I love Charles. But we haven't been getting on well lately. I'm so very tired, Miss Laura. I'd like to go home—to be waited on and petted as when I was a child—just for a while. I need time away—time to see Papa and Ashland, time to visit Mama's grave, time to think."

Neither spoke for a long while. A squirrel scolded its mate on the far lawn. The snake still lay, curled in a heap, between my knees. I held my breath and forced myself not to stare into its eyes.

"Perhaps now is best. Summer always means more wagon trips. You and Robert could enjoy the season away, together. Charles, too, if he will go."

What could Miz Laura be thinking? Me leave Laurelea in the summer? Leave William Henry and the run? And with slaves escaping right over our land and me knowing it now, Pa was bound to let me help, to need me before long.

"Charles will never leave. Isaac depends on him to watch over the fields and workers, and we have our own crop to tend. Besides, those—wagon trips. . . . No, Charles won't leave. But I want Robert to go. I want him to know my family—his family—and I don't want him mixed up in any more of this."

Miz Laura drew a breath. "I want only what is best for you and Charles, Caroline. Robert, too. You have my love and blessing whatever you decide, wherever you go. Only, this. Keep close to Charles. Share your worries and your joys with him. Don't let things fester or cause a rift between you. It is easier by far to cross a stream than to take on a river. Untended wounds do not heal."

I'd been so caught up in their talk that I never saw the snake slither away, leaving its slim trail in the dust.

NO AMOUNT OF PLEADING moved Ma or budged Pa. "It is natural for your mother to want you to meet your grand-father, Robert. This trip will be a strain for her and I expect you to help in any way you can."

"Then why don't you go, Pa? You know meeting Grand-father isn't the real reason she wants me to go. She's trying to keep me away from—from helping here!"

"Your mother's wish is all the reason you need. That's final."

I knew Pa was not happy about us going, and I knew my anger grieved him. But I didn't care. Nobody asked me what I wanted.

Pa drove us to the Elkton train station two days later. Ma had washed and ironed and packed every speck of decent clothing we owned. She'd made Aunt Sassy cut my hair. When I complained, Aunt Sassy only sighed and said, "I'll miss you, Robert. But you know the saying, 'What don't kill us makes us stronger.'" I hated that saying.

Pa and I lifted our trunks from the wagon. The engine blew its mournful cry of *Steam! Steam!* The conductor called above the noise, "All aboard!"

Pa held Ma close and breathed in her hair, then handed her up the steps of the railroad car. He shook my hand, a new thing, and said, "Take care of your mother, Son. She needs you now."

"Yes, sir." I wanted to say something more, something to let Pa know that even though I thought he was wrong, even though I was still angry and didn't want to go, he could count on me. But the words wouldn't come.

The whistle cried again. The train jerked, shuddered, then rolled forward. I raised my hand to Pa as long as I could see him. When the last town building gave way to houses, then fields, I closed my eyes, feigning sleep. I needed to clear my head and think on what William Henry had said the night before. It made no sense. Just after midnight he'd hoot-owled outside my bedroom window. "I'm sorry you're going away, Robert."

"I don't believe you, William Henry," I shot back. "You've been shunning me like I was the devil himself."

"You know we not supposed to be together," he whispered. "They're afraid, that's all."

"Afraid of what? I already know what's going on."

"Not all. It's dangerous. But I think they ought to let you help."

That comforted me some. At least William Henry wasn't treating me like a toddle baby. "I don't want to go."

"I know. But keep your eyes peeled. You might give more help there."

"What? How?" But I heard Pa stir in the next room, and the glow of a newly lit lamp danced through their window, across the yard.

"I got to go, Robert. Remember what I said." And then he was gone. I pretended to sleep when Pa brought the lamp to check my room.

What did William Henry mean? How could I help more than four hundred miles away?

Sometime after we crossed the Susquehanna, I really did fall into a fitful sleep.

The cry of the steam whistle approaching Baltimore woke me. I rubbed the sleep from my eyes and pushed away the ache behind them. I lowered the window, but a sharp burning smell made me close it in a hurry. Ma held her handkerchief to her nose as we climbed down. I liked the slap of my shoes on the platform's wooden planks, and was glad to stretch the kinks from my legs. I wanted a good run but Ma took my arm, so I kept myself to a steady stroll, like I'd seen Pa do.

We bought fruit from a fast-talking, plaid-vested platform vendor and added it to our boxed lunch. Starving, I wanted to eat standing, but Ma declared we'd wait until we'd settled on the next train. A four-horse station coach carted us across cobblestone and mud streets to the next line. I admired the pounding of hammers raising new buildings, the whinny of so many horses, and I thought the rattle made by endless bouncing carriages was a fine thing. I'd visited Baltimore two years before with Pa, but even this small part of the city had grown mightily since then. I'd never seen so many people, never heard so much noise in one place.

We were nearly to the new line when we passed a street corner where three colored men, ragged, and dripping from the muck and heat, slumped inside the wall of an oversized cage. There was no shelter from the July sun, and they looked like prisoners in a dog-pen jail cell.

"Ma?"

"Slaves, or will be." A man opposite me spoke before Ma could, as though he'd read my mind. "Some there for debt. Some, maybe, broke the law. When they collect enough of them there'll be an auction. Then they'll start collectin' again."

"If they broke the law, why aren't they in jail?"

"Jail's for white men, Boy, and major crime. Why would you feed and house a colored when they can be sold and fetch a good price? Pays their debt, sends a warning, helps things along."

"There's no water or food in there," I said.

"Keeps them settled."

"All day? All night?" The man didn't answer me. Ma touched my arm, a signal to stop talking. The men in the cage never looked up. One man, his shirt shredded down his back, slapped away flies plaguing his crisscross of sores.

I'd known that free black men could be sold into slavery to pay their debts, but I'd never seen anybody caged. I didn't feel hungry anymore. Settled on the new line, we pulled out of Baltimore. I was not sorry to go.

Mile after mile we rolled on, each more of the same. Closed windows stifled the air, baked the heat, and made breathing hard. But each time we lifted a window, showers of sparks and cinders poured through, covering our faces and clothes. We choked on the black smoke, gave it up, and closed the window again, our throats stinging. I wished mightily for a dip in the run.

By the time we pulled into Washington, D.C., we were done in. Ma kept her spirits up as ladylike as she could, but I knew she was worn and vexed. I'd seen enough sights for one day, and even wished for a basin wash.

We slept over in a hotel as near the train station as we could find, then ate a late supper in the dining room of a fancy hotel a few blocks away. "Your father and I dined here on our honeymoon." Ma smiled, her dimples flashing for the first time in a long while. "We heard Miss Jenny Lind sing that night. What a voice! The newspapers called her the 'Swedish Nightingale,' and with good cause!"

It was hard for me to think of Ma and Pa young and just married, without me.

A colored waiter in a short white coat bowed and asked us for our order. Ma told him what we wanted. I studied on keeping my napkin in my lap. I grinned to imagine William Henry toting one of those large silver trays above his head, swishing in and out through the swinging doors. I imagined him cutting a fancy figure in that dandy white jacket, but could not imagine him pulling such a blank face, at least not for long.

That got me to wondering what William Henry might do when he came of age, or for that matter, what I might do. Stay on at Laurelea? Take a town job? Move someplace far away like my folks did? It was the first I'd thought on such things.

We spent the next night in Weldon, glad to find a room. We made Raleigh the day after. At every stop, posters advertising runaway slaves lined the walls and poles along the platforms. Each one offered a reward and gave a description of the man or woman who stole away. I thought it near impossible to run away with everybody and their brother out looking for you, eager to get that reward and knowing what you looked like right down to your missing teeth or scarred hand.

The train finally left us on the platform in High Point, trunks and all. "I can't believe it's the same place," Ma said. "Things change so much in fifteen years!" I didn't know if she meant for good or ill, but I didn't pester. We stopped that last night in a boardinghouse Ma remembered. Then, in the morning, I found the livery and hired a driver to cart us to Ashland.

Ma drank in every mile. She fretted how things had "gone down," then marveled over new homes built where she remembered fields or woods. When we reached the boundaries of Ashland she complained about the peeling paint on the outbuildings, and there were many. "That's not like Papa to tolerate neglect in any form."

I didn't know about that, but the fields were truly fine. Row upon row of bright green tobacco stood like short soldiers, the leaves heavy, full, and properly curled. Though it wasn't Laurelea's cash crop, I'd grown up planting tobacco. But this looked different. I wondered if it was the soil or if this might be some different strain.

When we reached the drive, the buggy turned down the maple-shaded lane to Ashland. Ma stopped fretting and grabbed my arm, as excited as a toddle baby. "In autumn these trees form a golden arched canopy! Nothing, nothing, Robert, is so lovely in all the world!"

The buggy had barely stopped when Ma pushed her reticule into my hands, jumped down, and flew up the porch steps, past white pillars and through the front door of the three-story white stucco house. I paid and thanked the driver. I'd hoisted one trunk when a white-haired colored man in a dandy suit rounded a porch pillar. Despite a game leg, he hurried down the front steps, bowing to me. "I be taking those, Masta." I stepped back. No one had ever called me "Master."

"Thanks. Where should we take them?"

"No, sir! Old George get those for you." I was of a mind to argue, but thought that might not sound polite and didn't want to start off wrong. It wasn't right, but I set those trunks down by the old man and trailed Ma through the door of the house.

"Nanny Sara! It's so good to be home!" Ma nearly hugged the life from a round little woman the color of molasses sugar.

"It's glorious you here, Miz Caroline! Glorious!" Nanny Sara's deep voice didn't fit her tiny frame. She reached on tiptoe to pull off Ma's bonnet and shawl. "I never thought to set eyes on you this side Jordan, Miz Caroline. And here you be with your baby."

Ma pulled me to her. "This is my son, Robert Leslie Glover."

Nanny Sara bear-hugged me to herself. "It surely is! My, oh my! You surely do look like your daddy!"

"Yes, he does," Ma said, smiling. I felt my face heat up.

"How is Papa, Nanny Sara? The truth, now."

Nanny Sara dropped her smile. "He be poorly. You best steady yourself, Miz Caroline. Masta Marcus not the man he once was. He might not know you."

Ma's brow furrowed. "I wish someone had written me sooner."

"Don't know about writing, Miz Caroline. Masta Marcus too proud. After Mr. Slocum go north Masta Marcus take a bad turn. I don't believe Mr. Troy—that no-account man Mr. Jed left in charge of the fields—I don't believe he writes nothin'. Mr. Albert find your address amongst your Papa's papers and say Mr. Slocum near your backyard door. Then Mr. Albert tell me and Old George to keep an eye in case you come along."

Ma nodded. "I'll send word to Albert that I've arrived." Ma looked around the room. "Where is everybody? Where's Rebecca and Hattie? And Old Zebulon? Is he still alive? And Ruby! Where's Ruby, Nanny Sara?"

Light passed from the old woman's eyes and she drew in her breath. "Rebecca sent to the fields. Old Zebulon, he gone to rest ten winters back. Hattie, two. Masta Marcus sold my Ruby Deep South near fourteen year ago. Just me and Old George in the house now."

"No, no." Ma shook her head, unable to take it in.

Nanny Sara lifted her chin. "Lots of things change since you been gone, Miz Caroline. Masta Marcus took to his bed two weeks past. You go see him, now. I'll brew you and Masta Robert some tea, fix somethin' to eat. I be out back in the kitchen. Let me know when you want it." Ma nodded to the old lady's back.

"Who's Ruby?" I asked.

"Ruby is Nanny Sara's daughter. She is my age. We grew up together. We—"

"Like me and William Henry."

"Yes." Ma didn't even correct my grammar. We stood at the foot of the grand staircase. Ma gripped the banister, then ran her hand over its polished mahogany. The war Ma waged within seemed to be running again. She didn't hurry up the steps.

Heavy drapes in Grandfather's room blocked the fierce summer sun. No air moved. The heat strengthened the smell of years of cigar smoke and lemon oil, added to the more recent odors of unwashed flesh and vomit and something I couldn't name, and it all made me want to gag. I wondered how he breathed.

Ma lit a wall lamp near the bed. Hesitating, she brushed wisps of gray hair from the old man's forehead. A chill ran over me, even in the stifling heat. I'd seen old people before, and sick. But I'd never seen anyone so carry the color of death.

"Papa," Ma whispered. "I'm here." Then, "Caroline," like he might have forgotten her name. His eyes didn't open and he didn't move—only the broken rise and fall of his chest. "I'm home, Papa. I'm here to take care of you." She stroked his cheek. Ma dipped a cloth into the bedside basin, wrung water from it, and sponged his forehead. I shifted my weight and stretched, trying to breathe without taking in the smells.

A good hour passed before Ma straightened and motioned for me to follow her. She pulled the door softly until the knob clicked, trying not to disturb the old man who couldn't hear anyway. She leaned against the paneling. "I had no idea he was so far gone." She cried, soft at first, then sobbed outright. Not knowing what to do I touched her shoulder. She buried her head against mine.

Nanny Sara's supper of jellied tongue and warm beaten biscuits was welcome. The food, sweet tea, and rest seemed to help Ma muster her courage. "Nanny Sara, I want you to send George over to Cousin Albert's with this note."

"He need a pass."

"A pass? But it's just next door."

"Don't matter now, Miz Caroline. Those pattyrollers out day and night. If Old George got no pass they whip him then run him into jail."

"So much has changed."

"Yes, ma'am."

Ma wrote the pass. Old George returned within the hour with my new cousins. The man stood tall, over six feet, broad shouldered, with eyes the same bright blue as Ma's. The girl resembled Ma, perky and pretty, but darker, with brown eyes. She looked about my age. The boy looked a year or so younger, stocky, a little pale.

"Albert!" Ma held her hands out to the man. "It's so good to see you again!"

The man took both Ma's hands into his and kissed her full on the mouth. "Cousin Caroline, a delight! You have not changed since the last day we danced in my father's orchard!" My mouth dropped. Ma blushed, pleased.

"This is my son, Robert Leslie. Robert, our Cousin Albert."

"Why, he's the spitting image of Charles. Welcome to Ashland, Robert!" Cousin Albert extended his hand, clapping me on the shoulder.

"Pleased to meet you, sir." I stretched my manners.

"Caroline, Robert, these are my children, Emily and Alex." Emily dropped a curtsy and Alex nodded, then lifted his chin.

"Welcome to Ashland, Cousin Caroline." Emily searched Ma's face, for what I wasn't sure.

Alex offered me his hand. "Another boy in the family."

"What beautiful children, Albert! And your wife?" Ma blushed. "I declare, I don't even know who you married!"

Cousin Albert's face blanked, then went solemn. "Rose died shortly after Alex was born. It's been eleven years."

"Oh, Albert. I'm so sorry. I had no idea."

Cousin Albert nodded. He smiled, a little less, and wrapped Ma's arm around his, leading her toward the parlor. "We have a lot of catching up to do, Caroline. It's been too long." At the door he turned and said, "You young folks enjoy the summer evening on the verandah. Cousin Caroline and I have matters to discuss."

I stared after them, wondering if I should follow, thinking Ma might need me, thinking that the things they would discuss had to do with Grandfather and us.

"So what do you think of Ashland, the esteemed home of your ancestors?" With the click of the parlor door Alex's voice lost its friendliness.

"It's real nice—grand, even."

"Well, don't get used to it. It will be mine one day. Don't think that because you're Uncle Marcus's grandson that he'll leave it to you. He's never laid eyes on you and likely never will. Besides, he'd leave nothing to the son of a dirty abolitionist."

"Alex!" Emily was horrified. But Alex had already turned, slamming the front door behind him. "I'm sorry, Cousin Robert. That was unforgivable! Alex is spoiled and greedy, though that is no excuse. Please don't pay him any mind."

"I didn't come here to inherit anything," I said, stunned. "I never wanted to come here in the first place. He doesn't even know my pa!" My words slapped Emily and she reddened. Right away I was sorry. I wasn't angry with her.

"It's just the things he's heard Great Uncle Marcus say. I'm sorry, Robert. Truly, I am. I'll leave you alone, if you'd rather."

"No, wait. I didn't mean you—" I stumbled all over the place.

Emily looked up, and the lights in her brown eyes drew me in until my breath caught. I didn't care about Alex anymore, or what he thought or said. I only wanted Emily to like me, and I wanted that very much.

MA AND I WALKED OVER THE RIDGE to the Ashton family plot next day. From a distance the wrought iron fence around the graves looked sturdy and important. But up close, the filigreed gate was badly rusted and swung crooked on its hinges. Ma bit her lip and pulled it open. The gate stuck in a mound of dirt halfway, and I had to force it before we could pass.

"This fence was covered in Cherokee roses when I was small," Ma whispered. "Mama had Old George prune them early each spring. They'd bloom all summer." There were no roses blooming now, only runaway canes and tangled brambles. Crabgrass and wild sweet pea had overgrown the graves. Ma walked straight to her mother's stone and jerked angrily at the chickweed and thistles crowding its base, cutting her hand. I knelt to help, but I couldn't look at her. I knew she'd be crying again. We cleared the plot before and behind the fine granite headstone. Ma had cut magnolia stems, large and perfumed, from trees on the front lawn, and tied them with her hair ribbon. She brushed away her tears and laid her armload of flowers against the stone's base. "There, Mama, your favorites. I'm home at last." The chiseled words read, "Lydia Ashton. Beloved Wife and Mother. Taken too soon. Sorely missed. January 3, 1804–May 18, 1838."

"I wish you'd known her, Robert. She was the most gracious lady I ever knew."

"Sort of like Miz Laura?"

Ma looked up at me and smiled. "Very much like Miss Laura. Only, physically stronger and so energetic! She had brown eyes, like you, and milky skin. She was beautiful." Ma jerked more weeds. "Mama rose by dawn most days and kept busy until the last light burned low. But she never seemed hurried or vexed. I can't understand how. She always had time—and smiles for Papa and me. She lived each day like she knew there would be countless more. There were just too few of them."

We didn't stay long. Ma wanted to get back to Grandfather. But I thought I might come again. I could clear the plots, for Ma's sake.

Late that afternoon Ma came upon Old George giving Grandfather medicine.

"Laudanum! Why, George? Who told you to give my father laudanum?"

"Mr. Slocum, ma'am. He say Dr. Lemly give it to him for Masta Marcus. Mr. Slocum say it cuts the pain and helps him rest easy. Two big spoons twicet every day."

"That can't be right, George. You must have misunderstood!"

Old George drew into himself. "I done like Mr. Slocum told me. He say he send Old George to the fields if I let Masta Marcus down by not giving him the medicine."

Exasperated, Ma turned to me. "Robert, I want you to ride with Old George to Dr. Lemly's. Bring the doctor back with you. Tell him it's urgent, and that I believe Father's been poisoned."

Old George looked up, his eyes wide.

"I'm not blaming you, Old George," Ma retorted. "But this dosage cannot possibly be correct. It's no wonder Father's unconscious. When was his last lucid moment?"

Old George stared helplessly.

"When was he last awake?" Ma reworked the question.

"Couple days ago he wake for a minute. I right away give him more medicine, just like Mr. Slocum told me. Mr. Slocum give me this very spoon, himself."

Ma turned to me. "Go quickly."

When we returned, Old George wouldn't hear of me riding shotgun with him, so I rode in the buggy with Dr. Lemly. Dr. Lemly furrowed his brow and drummed his fingers, but gave out few words. I didn't know either of them any better when we stepped out of the buggy at Ashland than when I'd stepped in.

Ma and I paced the hallway while the doctor examined Grandfather. The brass pendulum of the grandfather clock on the staircase landing ticked off the long minutes. When at last Dr. Lemly opened the door his face was grim. "It is a wonder he's not dead. Months ago I prescribed a teaspoon on occasion for sleeplessness—certainly not for every day and never two tablespoons twice a day!"

"Will Papa be all right?" Ma whispered.

Dr. Lemly lifted his spectacles and rubbed his eyes. He searched Ma's face. "I won't sugarcoat this for you, Caroline."

"You never did." Ma tried to smile.

"Marcus will pull through. He's an ornery old bull, but his body has become dependent on the laudanum, and he craves it. The dosage must be reduced gradually to wean him from it. But I warn you, he won't like it. As he regains his senses he'll become a difficult patient to manage."

Ma laughed unnaturally. "That is not a new state of affairs for my father, Dr. Lemly."

"Perhaps not," he agreed, looking more like a pa to his daughter. "You must remain firm. He'll order you and curse you. He'll slam his fists, but you must not give in to him." Dr. Lemly hefted his bag. "The sooner he is off the laudanum, the better chance he has. I'm concerned about his heart, Caroline. It's working far too hard for a man his age." Dr. Lemly turned to me. "When your grandfather becomes agitated, as he certainly will, you need to help your mother restrain him."

"Yes, sir."

"One more thing. I've known Old George all my life, Caroline. I don't believe for a minute that he made a mistake about that dosage."

"Are you suggesting Mr. Slocum actually . . . but why would an overseer take such a thing upon himself?" Ma demanded.

"That's a question I'd dearly like to ask the man, and one I hope you will have the courage not to neglect. Your father's health has steadily declined for a long time, though he's rarely sent for me. Now I have to wonder . . . Well, let's see how things go. I'll check back tomorrow. Send Old George for me if there's a change before then." Then he softened and placed his hand on Ma's shoulder. "If there's one thing can help Marcus through this, it's your being here, Caroline." Ma tried to look brave.

We nursed Grandfather around the clock in shifts—Ma, Old George, and me. Dr. Lemly came and went as he promised, but there didn't seem to be much he could do. Just as Ma was about to take my place on the fourth day, Nanny Sara tapped at Grandfather's door, and Ma opened it. "Miz Caroline, Rebecca's taken to her bed in the quarters. Her time has come and that baby's still not turned. I got to help bring it.

Can you and Masta Robert manage your supper? I left ham and biscuits under the cloth on the dining room table."

"Of course, Nanny. Perhaps I should send Old George for Dr. Lemly. He watches over Ashland babies still, doesn't he?"

"Not since you went away, Miz Caroline. No, ma'am. It's just me now. Used to be Old Hattie, 'fore she passed. Now, just me."

"But if there is a problem—"

"Mr. Slocum say we got to carry the load ourselves."

"Mr. Slocum? But surely that is Papa's business!"

Nanny Sara clasped and unclasped her hands. "Miz Caroline, Masta Marcus done give the tending of the slaves over to Mr. Jed. Please, Miz Caroline, that baby be breech and Rebecca needs me."

"Go, by all means, go! I suppose if Mother were alive she'd go, too." Ma sounded afraid, but willing.

"Yes, ma'am. Miz Lydia always helped Hattie with the birthin', always had Dr. Lemly check the new mother or come by when there be trouble. But them days is gone long now."

"I've never helped birth, but I suppose—if you need me . . ."

"That's all right, Miz Caroline. Masta Marcus need you now. I manage fine."

Ma heaved a sigh of relief. "Tell Rebecca I'll be down to see the baby tomorrow."

"Yes, Miz Caroline."

"Take whatever you need, Nanny Sara." When Nanny Sara closed the door Ma sank into the bedside chair. "So many things. I can't believe Papa has given over so much control to an overseer, especially a man like—well . . ."

I wanted to tell her that neither Pa nor Mr. Heath would ever have managed anything so shim-sham as Grandfather had, but I held my tongue.

Nanny Sara never left the quarters that night and didn't

show for breakfast the next morning. So Ma stepped up. I gladly followed her to the kitchen behind the big house. It was good to see her cooking again, a starched apron tied over her hoop-skirt. I think even she liked it a little but wouldn't say so. There was no cast-iron stove in the cabin kitchen, and I wondered how Ma would manage with just the fireplace and pots, but she did. Even so, she made us eat in the dining room. We'd just finished our eggs when Nanny Sara pushed open the door, surprised that Ma had cooked our breakfast.

"Never mind that, Nanny Sara. How is Rebecca and her baby?"

"Twins! Strappin' twins, Miz Caroline! 'Bout did Rebecca in. I don't 'spect she'll be up to field work this week."

"Twins! I should say not. She's to stay in bed the week and have the month with her babies."

Nanny Sara's eyes widened. "Mr. Slocum won't like that, Miz Caroline. He say a week too much time off already."

Ma bristled and her color rose. "Mr. Slocum no longer has any say about this."

"Yes, ma'am." Nanny Sara lowered her eyes, but I know I saw a smile play along the corners of her mouth. "I told Rebecca you say you'll be down to see her babies today. She mighty pleased. Her cabin be fourth to the right of the path."

Ma wiped her mouth and folded her napkin. "Now is the best time, before the sun gets too hot. Robert, bring that bundle by the door. It's not much, but I cut a sheet in four and hemmed them while I sat with Papa yesterday."

"They'll be the nicest blankets any baby have in the quarter, Miz Caroline. It be mighty good of you." Nanny Sara beamed on Ma with a kind of pride. If cut-up sheets were the best thing any baby in the slave quarters owned it didn't say much, I decided.

It was my first trip to the quarters and I guess I expected it to be pretty much like the houses Mr. Heath had built for the free coloreds at Laurelea—small four-room frame houses with glass windows, stone chimneys, and plank flooring. I was wrong.

"When I was a little girl Mother insisted these cabins be whitewashed each year and the gardens kept up. Papa saw to that much even after she died. What has become of everything?" Ma fussed as we walked the dirt-packed trail past the kitchen, and beyond the large vegetable garden. Below the garden twenty-one weathered shacks formed three parts of a large square. They looked more like smokehouses than homes, with stick and mud daubed chimneys, no windows, and no porches. On the fourth side of the square, nearest the big house, stood a plain frame house, the overseer's house. From it he could surely see every movement in and out of the slave cabin doors. In the center of the square was a well and three sets of stocks, ringed with shackles and chains. I'd never seen metal shackles up close. Ma paid them no heed. We reached the fourth cabin before she hesitated.

"Do you want me to knock?" I asked.

"No. No, of course not." Ma drew a breath and straightened her shoulders. She pushed open the door and a shaft of light streamed before us. The stench of blood and unwashed bodies and urine rose. I swallowed hard to keep my breakfast down. It took a minute for my eyes to find the black woman huddled with her babies on a pallet in the dark corner.

"Rebecca, Nanny Sara told me you delivered twins last night. I'm here to see them." Ma's voice sounded stilted and awkward, and the pitch ran too high.

"Yes'm." The voice on the pallet whispered, but the body did not move. Ma stepped closer and bent down. She pressed her handkerchief to her nose.

"I brought you these sheets for the babies, but I see you need baskets for them first. Hasn't your man made anything for the babies?"

The woman ducked her head. "No, Miz Caroline."

"Well, we'll see you get some furniture in here. This is not acceptable." The woman raised her eyes to Ma, surprised, then looked away.

"Thank you, ma'am. That be real nice."

Ma smiled. "Now let me see these twins, Rebecca." Rebecca folded back the blankets and Ma leaned in. She gasped, and Rebecca buried her face in their fine black hair. Ma lifted her chin, then stood tall. "Who is the father of these babies, Rebecca?" Rebecca did not look up. "Did you hear me? Who is the father of these babies?"

"Don't know, Miz Caroline." The words came out in a whisper.

"You don't know? You mean you won't say!" Ma's voice rose, scraping a frightful edge.

"Ma," I whispered, sure she'd regret her manners.

"Robert, go outside. Now."

I didn't understand the commotion or the problem. We'd come to see babies and now Ma acted like the babies were cursed.

"You heard me, Robert. I'll not tell you again."

I stomped out the door and stood in the sun. I could not understand Ma. One minute she cried on my shoulder like I was her father and the next minute she shamed me in front of a woman lying on the floor with babies. What had gotten into her? Yelling at a new mother was not like Ma.

Her shrill pitch carried through the doorway. "Don't be insolent, Rebecca. Tell me who the father is." But I could hear nothing Rebecca said. I didn't know why Rebecca wouldn't tell or why Ma cared so much about the father. "We'll see about this, won't we?" Ma's tone trailed a threat as she stormed up the path to the big house.

I closed the cabin door behind her. Rebecca cried quietly, but I didn't look in. I felt shamed for Ma and for Rebecca. I followed Ma at a distance. She raged around to the front verandah, more furious with each step. She nearly collided with Cousin Albert, who'd galloped in by way of the front lane astride one of the biggest, blackest stallions I'd ever seen. He pulled back, and laughing, tossed me the reins of a sleek, saddled bay mare, its mane shining black.

"Meet Marcella—my finest horse next to my own Apollo. It's about time you rode the boundaries of your ancestral land, Robert! What do you say, Caroline? May I kidnap my young cousin for the morning?" His laughter and good spirits faded in the face of Ma's storm. "What is it? What's happened here?"

Ma was so angry she couldn't speak.

"It's something about babies," I offered, shrugging.

"Not just babies," Ma corrected me, her color rising. "One of our slaves has just given birth to twins—mulatto twins!" Cousin Albert nodded with an understanding I did not own, but did not act surprised. "She refused to give me the name of the father, Albert. Such insolence! Father and Mother were always so careful to keep the breeding among the slaves. This is disgraceful."

Cousin Albert studied the reins in his hands. "It's the way things are now, Caroline. If you'll look closely you'll see other mixed children at Ashland."

"But how—"

"Can't you guess?" He searched her face. "Uncle Marcus has lost interest in Ashland. Over the last several years he's turned more and more over to Slocum until Slocum has had free rein in the fields, the quarters, and now over your father."

"Slocum!" Ma sat down heavily on the porch step. "How could Papa let things come to this? He was such an authoritarian!"

Cousin Albert sat down beside Ma and wrapped her hand with his. "Not after you left, Caroline. Oh, he was angry—rash—at first, did things I'm sure he came to regret. Then all the spirit left him. He believed he had nothing left to live for, no one to build Ashland for anymore, no hopes of passing the plantation on to you or your future children. Slocum saw an opening and took it. He fed Uncle Marcus's belief that his family had betrayed him. He even convinced Uncle that I had been party to your elopement."

"You?" Ma couldn't believe it.

Cousin Albert smiled. "I was the one that introduced you to Charles at the ball in Washington, remember? I meant for you to dance the entire evening with William Sherman. I thought you'd like me all the better for the contrast. But the ball backfired. Once I introduced you to Charles you dropped Sherman's hand and never left Charles's side." Cousin Albert picked up a twig and drummed the step. I hardly knew where to look or stand. "Slocum convinced Uncle Marcus that he was the only one to be trusted, the only one he could count on."

Ma shook her head sadly. "I had no idea he'd taken on so."

"Now I wonder if Slocum has been supplying Uncle Marcus with laudanum right along. The more helpless your father became, the more control Slocum assumed. The laudanum would explain why Uncle Marcus never seemed able to focus long enough to be reasoned with or to make his own decisions. It would also explain the steady decline in his health." Ma's eyes filled but she didn't interrupt. "I tried to step in several times. I begged Uncle to let me help him with Ashland, but Slocum convinced him that I was only trying to steal the land from him."

"Papa believed that? Albert, I'm so sorry."

"It's absurd that any overseer could manipulate such control. Uncle Marcus is dependent on Jed Slocum for everything."

"Then there's nothing to be done."

"It's not too late, Caroline."

Ma shook her head again. "Papa may die, Albert. He hasn't even opened his eyes. Ashland is in a terrible state. Slocum has taken control of everything. I don't see how you can say it is not too late."

Cousin Albert put his arm around Ma's shoulder. "You've got to help Uncle Marcus pull through, Caroline. If anyone can do that, it is you. He never stopped loving you. It's just his pride that's blocked his view. Once you make him understand that you are here and will see this through with him, I'm sure you can help him care about his life again. Uncle Marcus's life is Ashland. When he's well enough and has his senses about him, he'll be proud to know he has a grandson like Robert." Cousin Albert looked up at me and smiled. "Any man would be proud to call Robert his own." The words warmed me through and made my heart swell. It was just the kind of thing I longed to hear Pa say to me. "You've got to stay strong, Caroline, for your father and for Robert." He pushed the wisps from Ma's forehead. "You are far stronger than you know, dear Cousin."

Ma sniffed wearily and leaned her head on Cousin Albert's shoulder. I knew she needed him, but their closeness made me uncomfortable and I wished Pa had been there. He should be the one to hold and comfort Ma, the one to tell me he was proud of me. Why couldn't Pa have come? Why did he have to be so stubborn about helping other people when his own family needed him?

"Now, if you can manage, Caroline, I'd like to show

Robert all of Ashland, and then take him over to Mitchell House and show him how a solid plantation is run. You need Robert. He's old enough to be a real help to you and Uncle Marcus. But he needs to see how things can be done with integrity in the South—not Slocum's way."

Ma wiped her eyes. She sat up, drew in a deep breath, and pasted her smile. "I think that is a fine idea, Albert." She squeezed his hand. "I'll expect you gentlemen for the noon meal."

Cousin Albert helped Ma to her feet. "We won't be late."

It was as easy as that! By the time I swung up into the saddle, Cousin Albert and Apollo were already rounding the house at a trot. I dug my heels into Marcella's sides and followed, thrilled to feel the solid power of a horse beneath me. I laughed out loud as soon as we gained some distance from the house, glad to be away from Ma's inner war, gladder still to be away from Grandfather's sick room and Rebecca's sad and foul-smelling cabin.

We rode long to cover the whole of Ashland. "Nearly two thousand acres," Cousin Albert said. "Twelve hundred farmed in bright leaf tobacco—the most marketable and desirable strain there is!" Corn, wheat, and oats took nearly two hundred more, but I was surprised how grass had grown between the rows, and how dry and brittle some of the fields looked. The rest ran wild in woods and stream, apart from the big house, its gardens, the many outbuildings. At the far end of Ashland we found cool shade beside a slow running stream, passing deep for late July.

"This stream boasts some of the best catfish this side of the Mississippi, Robert, and flows directly into the Yadkin River. My land joins Uncle's here. Slaves from both plantations fish it with seines. I'll have one of my boys bring you up some for breakfast tomorrow."

"I'd like better to fish it myself!" I could picture William Henry and me filling a bucket, and Aunt Sassy rolling freshly cleaned catfish in cornmeal, frying it crisp and golden brown. But William Henry wasn't here, and he was half the fun of fishing. "Do you think Alex would want to fish with me?" It was out of my mouth before my head caught on to what I'd said.

Cousin Albert laughed. "I'd like to see it!" Then he sobered. "I'm afraid your cousin is not much of an outdoorsman, Robert. But I'd appreciate it if you'd offer to teach him. He's an excellent one with figures, and his Latin is fine. But he's not much of a practical hand in the world. A man needs to know his land and all that it holds, as well as how to balance the accounts."

I couldn't imagine choosing ledgers over fishing.

"Your mother has asked me to tutor you in Latin and mathematics along with Alex and Emily, just as soon as Uncle Marcus is on his feet again." I groaned inside. Cousin Albert smiled. "Suppose we try that three mornings a week and on the other two you and Alex spend time together—riding, fishing, hunting—whatever you like, as long as it is outdoors. It will do him good, and unless I miss my guess, you are ready to burst from sitting in that dismal house so long."

"Yes, sir! That surely takes the sting out of sitting in lessons three days a week." I shifted in my saddle. "I'd best tell you, Cousin Albert, that I'm not much hand at hunting with a gun."

"Ah, the Quaker influence." Cousin Albert nodded. "Are you opposed to learning?"

"No, sir!"

"Then I'll teach you and Alex together. Perhaps your presence will inspire him with a little healthy competition. A man needs to know how to defend his family and property, Robert. I'm sure your father would agree with that. Charles and I attended West Point together. He was quite a marksman then."

"Yes, sir. Ma told me." But I didn't think Pa would defend us with a gun, not anymore. Pa only used his shotgun for hunting when he couldn't trap. I was sorry to go against Pa, but I wanted to learn to shoot as much as I loved to fish, and that's telling. It made me wonder afresh where Miz Laura got her pearl-handled pistol, and if Mr. Heath knew about it.

"Now I'll race you to Mitchell House, Robert!"

The mare and I pounded dirt and rode the mile hard. But I never caught him. We slowed to a trot when we crossed the property line. Cousin Albert boasted over his buildings and fields, with good cause. The outbuildings were tight and painted, not a sagging roof or cluttered yard anywhere. Every lane was flanked by cut grass. Mitchell House grew the same bright leaf tobacco as Ashland, but Cousin Albert's fields were longer, all the rows unbroken by weeds or grass. I couldn't imagine working that much land, then remembered that the sweat-shined black bodies, bent in their labor, made it possible. I looked at Cousin Albert's smooth, white hands, and knew that he put in no time among the sticky tobacco plants. I could picture Pa's work-rough, tobacco-stained hands, and even Mr. Heath's, and knew that these were two separate worlds.

"And now I'll show you the slave quarters. I want you to see another view of the South and our peculiar institution. I believe you'll agree that it makes sense to keep up the quarters. I respect Uncle Marcus, but I don't believe he treats his slaves properly."

I shielded my eyes against the noonday sun and followed Cousin Albert down the rows of whitewashed cabins. Bigger than the shacks at Ashland, each building was two single-pen cabins joined under one roof. They shared a common center chimney. Each cabin had one window, shuttered, but no glass.

"Notice that the floors are raised, Robert. That keeps the cold out in winter and helps circulate air in summer. You have to watch slave cabins. They can be breeding grounds for disease."

A larger cabin stood at the head of the lane, nearest the big house. At the opposite end, near the fields, was a large garden, maybe three acres, worked by old slaves and children too small for the fields. "This garden produces all the food for Mitchell House. When a man gets too old for the fields he works here. The work is not so strenuous, but he can still be productive. A portion is taken to the house kitchen, and a larger portion kept here for the slaves."

"That's a lot of food."

"Mitchell House has a lot of slaves." Cousin Albert smiled. "Come slaughter time I'll set aside hogs for the quarters. Once they're salted and smoked they're stored in a cold cellar off the driver's house—that large cabin at the end of this lane. My driver is in charge of all provisions—food, clothing, shoes, and so forth—and allots what is needed. Negroes take better to having one of their own in charge. It makes certain that every slave has equal portion with every other slave—no stealing, no hoarding, no selling on the side, no setting aside money for things their neighbors can't have. It takes care once and for all the question of slaves saving up money to barter their freedom. There's no reason to create discontent when all those things can be settled so easily. Remember that."

"But don't they want to buy their freedom or at least earn money to buy things for their families?"

"There's no need." Cousin Albert's jaw set. "My slaves are contented, and so am I, as long as they work hard and bring in a good harvest."

"So, you believe slavery is a good thing?" I saw the folly of my question in the sudden flash of Cousin Albert's eyes.

"Yes, Robert. I believe fully in the good and beneficial institution of slavery—both for master and slave. It is a necessity in the South. It is our moral obligation to take care of these people. They would not, could not manage on their own. We provide them with homes, food, clothing, health care, and moral and spiritual training within their limited understanding. They, in turn, provide us with manual labor for our fields. We could not farm the tobacco and cotton, let alone the rice and sugarcane farther south, without them. The climate and work suits them. The South's agriculture benefits all the states, and slavery benefits all concerned. But just as you would not abuse your horse or neglect your herds, you must not abuse or neglect your Negroes. Neither will perform satisfactorily if poorly treated. That is the lesson I wish Uncle would take to heart."

What could I say? I could not imagine Joseph or Aunt Sassy needing anyone to tend their needs.

Cousin Albert stopped in to see us every day after that, always checking on Grandfather. He whispered with Ma in the corner by the window. I caught the names "Slocum" and "Robert" and "Charles" from time to time. He didn't have much use for Jed Slocum. That, I figured, was in his favor. But I still didn't like how close he stood to Ma or how she smiled up at him so. And I wondered about the sick man in the bed, and how he could let his own land go like it didn't matter. I wondered how a man could take a whip to other men, and even women, as Granny Struthers had claimed he had, and what kind of man would do that.

I was thinking on these things during my shift on the seventh day, beginning to believe I might not like the man Marcus Ashton, when Grandfather opened his eyes and found me staring at him.

"Who are you, Boy?"

"Robert," I whispered, my throat dry. "Robert Leslie Glover, sir. Your grandson."

Grandfather's eyebrow lifted. His blue eyes, the same rich shade as Ma's and Cousin Albert's, grew wide, then filmed over before closing again. And so I met my Grandfather Ashton.

GRANDFATHER GAINED GROUND each day once he realized his own daughter, flesh and blood, had come home to him. But the laudanum didn't leave him of a sudden, and there were times he grew agitated and angry. Old George and I had to bind him once. I hoped he wouldn't remember. It seemed to help Ma get her bearings when she stood against Grandfather, telling him he couldn't have the laudanum, telling him that he would have to trust her and that she was taking over for his own good. Grandfather swore in words I'd never even heard, but Ma didn't back down. I was proud of her. I think she amazed herself.

"I've always been so fearful, so in awe of him," Ma confessed. "I feel like I'm growing up all over again."

I felt like that, too. Only for me it was the first time. As Grandfather gained strength, Ma needed me less. By the fourth week I started mathematics and Latin lessons with Alex and Emily. It was still too hot to sit indoors, but Emily and Alex didn't take notice. Cousin Albert was a fair tutor and worked with me until I caught on. But I couldn't pull anything over on him like I'd done Miz Laura and Ma. Alex snickered at how far behind I was in the simplest studies, but groused when Cousin Albert praised me. In the afternoons I walked out with Emily. She called it "taking our constitutional." She set store by the things I said. Nobody had ever done that. It wasn't like larking with William Henry, but it felt right. I was glad my voice was lowering. Alex was just beginning to squeak.

Every other day Alex and I fished, but he was no good at it. He could sit plenty still, but he always toted a book along and kept at it so that he missed the few times he really got a bite. Those were the days I missed William Henry the most. Still, for the first time in my life I wasn't walking in William Henry's shadow.

"How is your fishing, Robert?" Grandfather wanted to know. Every question he asked sounded more like a challenge, as though I should know better.

"Tolerable, sir. We'll have a mess of catfish for dinner today."

"Have you made a fisherman out of that cousin of yours?"

"He's a mite better at his books."

Grandfather snorted. "Your father taught you a few worthwhile things. I'll speak to Albert about getting you started on some target practice. Hunting should be good in a few weeks. I may even be able to join you by then."

It was the first forward-looking thing Grandfather had said, and I was glad for him and for Ma. But whenever he mentioned Pa I didn't know whether he was trying to bridge a gap or widen it. I wondered how Pa was doing without us. We got a letter from him our third week and I think he missed us, but the letter was about the dry weather and crops, Miz Laura's health, which wasn't so good, and last Sunday's sermon. Ma seemed disappointed. And Cousin Albert was always there, escorting Ma to church, checking to see if she needed anything, helping with Ashland. He even pestered Grandfather to take an interest once he was well enough to reason things through. Ma took Grandfather to task, too.

"Papa, something must be done about the quarters. You know you and Mama would never have let things go like this. The slaves are a disgrace to Ashland. Their cabins are filthy and in need of repair. Scarcely a roof is sound. Their clothes are ragged and they aren't rationed enough food to do an honest day's work if they tried. Most have no shoes, and cold weather is coming. You and Mama always prided yourself on how you cared for our people."

But Grandfather shook his head. "That's Slocum's arena, my dear. I've given him free rein in the fields and quarters, and he's the one kept Ashland going. He'll be back soon and I won't take things out of his hands. I owe him that much. If Jed hadn't been here, Ashland would have gone down into the dust after you left. We all owe him for that."

"Owe him? Papa, he nearly killed you with that laudanum!"

"We don't know that, Caroline. I've needed my medicine for a long time. The dosage was just a misunderstanding. You can't expect darkies to—"

"Old George didn't make a mistake! He was doing as he was told!"

"I won't hear another word against Jed, Caroline," Grandfather boomed. "I told you I'd look into it, but as I said, we all owe him a good deal. He's stayed on through everything. Jed knows how to—handle things."

"I believe Mr. Slocum has been paid handsomely." Ma bristled. "Have you seen the number of mulatto children running around here? Mr. Slocum seems to want for nothing."

Grandfather wouldn't meet her eyes. "Things are the way they are, Caroline."

Cousin Albert stepped between them. "Slocum's last letter said he'd be at least another month following his lead. Let Caroline and me work on a plan, Uncle Marcus—just until

Slocum returns. Improving the conditions of the quarters can't hurt him. If the slaves are healthier and the quarters cleaner, that can only help. I'll even loan you Noah, my own driver, until Slocum returns."

"But Slocum hired someone to oversee in his absence."

"Yes, I've met Troy Jacobs." Cousin Albert said the name like he was sucking lemons. "His greatest accomplishment is raising a liquor bottle. Uncle, the fields are full of grass, and the tobacco needs more water. Jacobs works the slaves all afternoon in the heat with no rest, no water. Let me send him packing and see what we can do to save your tobacco. It would do Robert good to see firsthand a well-run plantation."

"Slocum won't like it." The crease deepened between his eyebrows. He stared out the window. "But I'm not strong enough to fight you both." He sighed. "Just until Jed returns. I know you've always advocated black drivers rather than overseers, Albert, but I just don't see it. Slaves don't have that much sense."

"Mitchell House is doing very well without an overseer. Noah is the best driver I've ever had," replied Cousin Albert.

"Until Slocum returns." Grandfather glared at me beneath bushy white eyebrows. "Did your father teach my daughter this high-handed insolence, or should I be giving the man more sympathy?" For the first time I grinned. I couldn't help it. Grandfather almost grinned back.

Ma and Cousin Albert were as excited as William Henry and me the day we pulled one over on Jake Tulley. They threw themselves into cleaning Ashland, inside out. Cousin Albert brought his driver, Noah, to take charge of the field slaves, as well as six more hands just to help with the hauling of crop water and weeding. He ordered the separation of hogs meant to be slaughtered and salted.

Ma took Rebecca, as soon as she was able, and trained her to help in the house with cleaning and kitchen work and serving. Ma took charge of the storehouse of provisions, wearing the full set of keys on a sash around her waist. It wasn't long before she realized Jed Slocum hadn't ordered the setting by of enough food for winter, either for the big house or the quarters. Ma was fit to be tied. "We'll see about this!"

I didn't tell her about the loose boards at the back of the storehouse and didn't fix them. If Ashland's slaves were pilfering Grandfather's stores it served him right. They looked half starved.

Ma worked me as hard as any of the slaves, but I was used to that. Since Grandfather no longer needed someone in his room at night, she set Old George to working the kitchen garden again and ordered some of the children to weed for him. She pulled two field slaves to prune the Cherokee rose canes and clear the family plot I never got around to clearing, then to get her mother's flower beds in order. "It will take weeks, but we'll make Ashland shine again," she vowed. I never knew Ma could take over and manage like she did. She was a sight to see.

The second week in September a letter came from Slocum saying he'd been delayed. He'd picked up a new trail and hoped to close in north of Philadelphia. He expected to bring home both slaves by the end of September.

We all felt the press for time, fearful our steps forward would end once Jed Slocum returned. It seemed a silly notion, as Grandfather was Slocum's employer and not the other way around.

By dinner of the fourth day I was nearly too tired to eat, but not quite. "Ma, maybe we could take a breather this afternoon."

"We're on a schedule, Robert. Aren't you proud of the work you're doing? Look how those banisters shine! The entire house is smelling better every day, like lemon oil. Nanny Sara and I are going over the silver this afternoon. Can you believe it? It hasn't been polished in two years!"

"No, ma'am. I can hardly believe such a thing."

Ma peered at me to see if I intended disrespect. But I grinned. It was good to see her so perky and pleased. And I admit I was proud.

"The house is nearly in order, the garden is beginning to look like one, and Albert is getting the fields in hand. It's time we took on the quarters."

"We're going to clean the quarters, too?"

"Don't be silly. I'll direct some of the field hands to repair and whitewash those cabins as soon as Albert says they can be spared. When the weather gets cold and all the tobacco is in, we'll set some of the men to building furniture."

"Looks to me like they need food first, and clothes and blankets."

Ma studied me. "A good observation, Robert." Then she reached across the table and squeezed my hand. "I'm glad you're catching Albert's vision. I know he's right about taking care of slaves. They can't care for themselves, and where would plantations be without them? Happy, healthy slaves make far better workers and a peaceful home. It really can be a wonderful way of life for everyone."

I was glad Ma was pleased with me, but I wondered if the slaves shared her notions. I knew Pa didn't. And then, as if she could read my mind, Ma said, "I wish your father could see all we're doing here. He might feel differently—about a great many things." I kept my peace.

Cousin Albert taught me how to respect and care for a gun before he let me fire my first shot. My first target lesson I missed the marker and exploded the hay bale it sat on. Cousin

Albert said things worth doing take time and practice. Alex laughed at me but did no better. In fact, I thought Cousin Albert a brave but foolish man to put a gun in Alex's hands.

"I still don't like you handling guns, Robert, even if it is Albert's idea. Accidents happen so easily," Ma fussed at the dinner table.

"Caroline," Grandfather admonished. "You can't coddle the boy all his life. Learning to shoot is part of his training as a Southern gentleman. You'd have him in sausage curls and petticoats if given a free hand. Let him grow up!" Ma sighed, picked up her silver spoon, and dipped it into her cream soup. The discussion was over. I thanked Grandfather with a grin. He winked. As much as I didn't like the old man, there were times I liked him plenty.

Late the next afternoon, I crept out to the kitchen, hoping for a glass of lemonade. Nanny Sara sat at the table, peeling late summer peaches. She shook her head at Rebecca. "It's nice what they're doing, but Mr. Jed'll put a stop to it. No, no. There will be the devil to pay when he comes back, and that be any day now."

"Jed Slocum doesn't own Ashland, Nanny Sara. Grandfather does."

Nanny Sara started. "You ought not be creepin' up on a body, Masta Robert, and you ought not be in this old kitchen. White folks stays in the big house. Don't you be bearin' tales to Masta Marcus or Miz Caroline what you hear me say."

"I don't bear tales." I plunked myself at the table. I was tired of the suspicious way Nanny Sara kept at me all the time. "All I want is lemonade. I'm dry as those peach leaves."

"Well, say so then." And she poured me a tall tumbler of lemonade. "Hold on, now. Rebecca, get on down to the ice house an' fetch me some shavings."

"No, thanks," I said. "It's not worth the trouble."

"You sure are a funny white boy, telling me it's not worth the trouble." Nanny Sara frowned, the pitcher in midair.

I downed the glass in two long swallows, set it back on the table, and headed for the door. "You sure are a funny Nanny Sara, always giving me trouble about not giving you trouble." Their surprised laughter followed me outside. I missed the easygoing way between Aunt Sassy and William Henry and me. At home the colored workers and I were friends, working together to make Laurelea run and turn a profit. Mr. Heath shared that profit by paying all his workers. Here the coloreds slaved day after day. But they had no hope of owning anything, least of all themselves.

Still, as I walked the path through the quarters and saw the first cabin being whitewashed and two men repairing the roof of the next, I felt glad. I hid myself behind Slocum's cabin when the quitting bell sounded. The slaves ambled in from the fields, singing their end-of-day songs. "I'll meet you in the mornin', I'm boun' for de promised land, on de oder side of Jordan, boun' for de promised land." But the singing slowed as they neared the quarters and went to humming. Then the humming stopped. A little barefoot girl ran up to the cabin and ran her hand over the rough, whitened boards. "Like the big house!"

Her mother slapped her hand away. "Never like that!" And then she rubbed her own hand over the doorsill in wonder. "But it's white and clean, just the same. And that be nice, real nice."

I smiled. It was good to be part of something that brought pleasure. I even wondered if Cousin Albert might be right, if Pa could be wrong about slavery—if it could all be run like Cousin Albert ran Mitchell House.

Late the next afternoon Cousin Albert praised me. "You're

getting pretty good with that gun. We'll be ready for some fine waterfowl hunting this winter."

"I don't know if we'll still be here then," I said, already feeling the regret.

Cousin Albert rested his hand on my shoulder and smiled. "I'm not in any hurry for you to leave, Robert."

I smiled back. I wasn't in any hurry either. And I didn't know if Ma would ever want to leave. A month before, such an idea would have set me in a panic. I missed Pa and William Henry and the Heaths and Laurelea. But it felt good to be wanted and needed, to be treated by men like I was nearly grown. I believe I carried my head a little higher, until the night Jed Slocum came back.

JED SLOCUM HAD BEEN GONE so long that I sometimes pretended he wasn't coming back at all.

Ma and I sat on the verandah, watching the mid-October
sun set, and the slice of new moon climb over the long needle
pines. We breathed in the last of Grandmother Ashton's favorite
magnolias and the first bite of autumn chill. Frost could not be
far·off. Ma wrapped her shawl tight around her, then linked her
arm through mine. "Robert, I'm so proud of how you've taken
hold here. All the—" But she stopped and stood, facing the
drive. "What is that light?"

A ghostly flame danced through the trees to the beat of
horse hooves. The raised torch bobbed closer, growing until its
flickering light fell on a man's face. I made out a figure on the
ground—no, two figures—hobbling behind. Both were shackled
—their wrists and ankles chained together. My neck prickled
as the face of the man on the horse came into view. He rode
directly to the heavy bell in the front yard and rang it wildly.
It was the emergency signal for all of Ashland, slave and free,
to run to the front drive. Ma raised her voice. "Mr. Slocum,
what is the meaning of this?"

Still astride his horse, Slocum held his torch higher, and
the pool of light grew. "Well, Miz Caroline." He squinted
toward us, then rode to the verandah, dragging his prisoners
behind him. "I see you made it to Ashland."

By this time lamps shone through the windows behind us. Lanterns sprang from the quarters. Grandfather opened the front door and a stream of light fell before him. "Slocum!"

"Mr. Ashton. Good to see you on your feet again." But Slocum didn't look glad, didn't sound glad. "Brought back our runaways."

"You were gone long enough." Grandfather's confidence didn't match his words.

"Chased them clean up the Tioga Valley. It's a long walk home."

"You made them walk all the way home?" I couldn't believe it.

Slocum stared me up and down. "Best way to teach a man not to run is to make him remember there's no pleasure in walking home, and then to make sure he can't never run again." Slocum swung down from his horse and thrust his torch in the ground. "You, Boy!" He called to a slave I didn't know by name. "Get me four more torches." Then he called to a boy not yet ten, "Henry, get my axe. Now!"

Grandfather watched as Slocum unchained the prisoners. For the first time I realized that one was dark and older, maybe my pa's age. The other one, farther from the light, couldn't have been much older than me. Unless the night and the crazy torchlight did something to my eyes he was white, or nearly. Something pulled at my brain. Slocum chained the boy to a post and dragged the older man to the center of the ring of slaves. That was when I realized I'd seen them before—the same man who'd been pulled, unconscious, from the bottom of Mr. Heath's wagon, and the boy that had followed him, the one who'd watched me from the Heaths' attic window.

"Jacob!" A woman cried out, pushing through the ring. But Slocum cracked his whip, making her fall to her knees.

"Keep back! Let this be a lesson to every one of you thinking about running. You will never get free. I will track you
down and find you, no matter what rock you hide under, no
matter who helps you, no matter how far I have to go. You will
always come back to me." And then he turned. "Where is that
fool boy with my axe?"

"Ma?" I whispered. "What's he going to do?" And for the
first time I realized that Ma was gripping my arm. The black
woman who had called to Jacob cried and begged, "Please Mr.
Slocum. Please, don't do it. I promise he won't never run again.
I promise."

"Hold her back. You're sure right he won't. Not without a
foot."

The young boy stepped through the parting crowd slowly,
frightened, bearing the axe. "No, Ma. Please," I whispered.
Please stop him!"

"Papa?" Ma whispered. Then louder, "Papa, stop him! This
isn't necessary. It's cruel!"

But Grandfather didn't blink. He stared at Slocum, his
eyes bright with fascination and something else I couldn't take
hold of—something eager and greedy. "This is not your business, Caroline. Let Slocum do his work."

"But Papa! Ashland is your business! You are master here,
not Slocum! This is not how you treat slaves, even if they do
run!"

And then Grandfather turned on her. "I told you Slocum
is in charge of the slaves, Caroline. This is a man's world. Do
what you want with the house slaves, but Slocum handles the
rest. Go inside if you've no stomach for discipline."

Ma started to speak again, but Grandfather's glare cut her
off. He looked down on her like a child he was ashamed of,
and she lowered her eyes. I'm sure Slocum heard, but he didn't

give Ma time to go inside if she'd wanted. He raised his axe to the night sky. The man on the ground trembled. He begged Ma for mercy, but Ma did not look up. His eyes caught mine. The axe fell in one awful plunge and the voice of pain tore the night wide open. The leg jerked as the foot fell away, and blood spurted across the ground. I screamed. But mine was lost in the screams and cries of the circle of slaves reaching toward their fallen Jacob. Slocum wiped his axe on the grass. "Get him out of here." A smaller ring of slaves swarmed the bleeding Jacob and lifted him, trying to bind the wound and stop the flow of blood and life. They were not yet gone when Slocum pulled the younger one, the nearly white boy, to the center.

"No!" screamed Nanny Sara. I hadn't seen her until now, but she shadowed the boy Slocum dragged. She didn't beg Slocum, but ran to Grandfather and fell at his feet, tears streaming from her face and anger in her voice. "You promised, Masta Marcus! You promised! Not my Jeremiah! Not my Ruby's son!"

"He shouldn't have run!" Grandfather spat back.

"You promised! On my Ruby's selling you promised!"

"Ruby's son? What do you mean, Nanny Sara?" Ma tried to lift Nanny Sara from the step, but she would not be moved.

"You ast him, you ast your own papa what I mean!"

Ma looked to Grandfather but he wouldn't meet her eyes. "That's enough, Sara." Then to Slocum, "Fifty lashes. And take it to the quarters."

Slocum, his axe ready, challenged Grandfather. "Lashes won't teach this uppity buck not to run. You'd best let me do as I intend." But something in his challenge woke the sleeping dragon in Grandfather.

"You heard me. Fifty lashes." And he turned, and walked into the house.

"Fifty lashes kill my boy!" Nanny Sara cried. But the door shut and Ma tried to lift the old woman to her feet.

"Ma! Can't you stop this?"

"Obviously I cannot, Robert. Help me get Nanny Sara inside." But Nanny Sara pushed us away.

"I won't go inside! I'm going to the whipping post with my grandson, my own Ruby's boy. I will not leave him. You go ast Masta Marcus. You ast him!"

"Nanny Sara!" Ma called, but the old woman was already stumbling away, following the ring of slaves as Slocum led them to the whipping post in the quarters, dragging Jeremiah with him.

"Ma!" I pleaded. But Ma turned on me.

"Robert! Grow up! This is the way things are here! If a slave runs he must be punished. I don't agree with the severity, but there must be some accountability. It's Papa's decision. If he lets Mr. Slocum do this, we can't stop him. It is better than cutting off his foot or hanging the boy."

"You mean you won't stop him!"

"Robert." She sounded weary and reached for me. But I didn't want her to touch me. A person that weak couldn't be my mother.

"If you won't help I'll get someone who will, someone who's not afraid of Grandfather, someone who can stand up to Slocum! Nobody does this!" I stumbled down the steps and ran.

"Robert! Robert!" she cried. I shut her out.

Run, run, run! My heart beat out the rhythm as I pounded down the drive and out onto the road through the darkness. I ran hard the mile to Mitchell House, gasping for breath, letting the air rush past me, cooling the sweat of fear and revulsion that poured from inside, only to pour it all again. The house was already dark. A single lamp burned in the window of

Cousin Albert's study. I pounded on the door with both fists, but couldn't wait, so pushed it open, nearly falling into Cousin Albert's arms.

"Robert! What is it? Is Caroline—"

But I shook my head, trying to catch my breath to speak. "Slocum—" I gasped. "Slocum is back! Cut off foot—" I couldn't breathe.

Cousin Albert nodded, as if he understood already. "Come in, Robert. Come in and sit with me."

"No!" I gasped. "You've got to come! That man will die! And he's going to beat a boy with fifty lashes! Nanny Sara's grandson! You've got to come and stop him!"

Cousin Albert raised his eyebrows, but shook his head. "I can't, Robert."

"If anybody can stop him you can, Cousin Albert! Grandfather's too weak and doesn't care, but you don't treat slaves that way. I know you don't!"

Cousin Albert sat heavily on the arm of his chair. "No, I don't. But Ashland's slaves belong to Uncle Marcus, not to me. I have no say in how he treats them or how he lets Slocum treat them. They are his property."

"His property?"

"That should not be news to you, Robert," he said quietly.

I backed away from him, disgusted, unbelieving, and shot back, "Pa would never do this. He'd never sit back and do nothing. Pa was right—about everything!" The look Cousin Albert returned was pierced with pain and flushed with anger. I didn't care if I'd hurt him. He was just as bad as the rest of them. They were all weak and full of talk. Talk could not return Jacob's foot or rescue Jeremiah from the lash. I backed out of Mitchell House, tears streaming my face, and spat on the doorstep.

By the time I reached Ashland again, the square in the

quarters was cleared. I wasn't sorry. I didn't want to see. The sound of keening bled through the closed doors in the quarters. I stumbled to my bed and finally slept near morning. The old dream came again. I was in the field hoeing beside black bodies—no names, no faces. Only the field was Ashland, not Laurelea, and the eyes that looked up at me, pleading, the arms that reached for me belonged not to William Henry, but first to Jacob, then to Jeremiah. The wind came up, the funnel grew, the earth spun, and the skin that ripped a seam and wrapped around me was Jeremiah's nearly white skin. I screamed, "Ma! Ma!" Still she stood above me, hate seared in her soul. She whistled for the hounds. This time they found me, jumped, and ripped my life away.

"Robert! Robert!" Ma called. "Wake up. You're dreaming. Wake up, Son."

I sat up in bed, drenched in sweat. There was only love and worry etched in Ma's face, but I remembered last night, and rolled over, pushing her away. No one called me for breakfast or to take Alex fishing.

I kept thinking of Pa, and the Heaths, and the Henrys, and all they'd done to help and protect Jacob and Jeremiah. I thought of how Jed Slocum had done all he could to destroy them. And Grandfather had loved it. My mind could see the misery lust in his eyes as he'd watched Slocum work, and it made me sick. And then I thought of William Henry, and remembered that he'd been allowed in the Heaths' house even though I wasn't—at least that day they first took Jacob and Jeremiah in. I wondered if Jeremiah knew William Henry. I kept seeing Jeremiah's face in the attic window.

Late in the afternoon Cousin Albert, Alex, and Emily came calling. I tried to avoid them, but Emily came looking for me. She found me slumped in a chair in the darkened back parlor. "Robert, Papa told us what happened last night." She sat beside me and reached for my hand. "I'm so sorry. It must have been awful." I wanted to pull away. I could barely breathe, barely hold my anger. But I wanted to punish somebody, so I punished Emily.

"Awful? Yes," I said. "It was awful." How could I make her understand? "A runaway horse would never be beaten or crippled like that. It's awful to own people, to have the power to do whatever you want to them. Slavery ruins people, the people that are slaves and the people that buy and sell other people. I'm sick that I ever came here." I turned away. "I'm sick that any kin of mine own slaves, and I'm ashamed."

Emily didn't move. "What Mr. Slocum did was a horrible thing. But not everyone treats their people that way. Papa never would. You know that."

I stood and walked to the window. "It doesn't matter. He has the power to do whatever he wants with the people he owns. I didn't understand before what that means. Not everybody uses their power in the same way; not everybody treats their slaves or their animals the same. The power to own people is a wicked thing, and it ought to be stopped!"

Emily stood. "Sometimes I've wondered if there was a way to do without it. But I don't see how. How would the land for cotton or tobacco or rice or sugarcane be worked? Papa says that without the help of the slaves we could not survive."

I couldn't help my smirk.

"Maybe that sounds simple to you, but the whole country depends on those things. Where would the mills in the North be without our cotton? Papa says this country couldn't finance itself without tobacco and cotton. How can these things be done without the slaves?"

I turned on her. "Pay them. Free them and pay them—like

regular workers. That's what Mr. Heath's done at Laurelea. He and my Pa work side by side in those fields with coloreds. They are not too proud to dirty their hands. They've given their lives to helping colored people be free, even outside the law. And not just free, but to make a living on their own." And with the talking I grew prouder and prouder of my pa. I wished I'd known it sooner.

Emily shot a worried look toward the door. "I see what you're saying, but you must be careful, Robert. Not everyone would understand. People here fear slave uprisings, and they won't tolerate such talk."

I laughed. "Should I care?"

"Yes." She lifted her head. "If you want to make a difference. If you want to do more than just talk." That hit a nerve. "Robert, don't you see? You are in a position to make change. You are Uncle Marcus's true heir. Someday Ashland and all its slaves could be yours—one of the biggest tobacco plantations in the South, or it once was and might be again. Perhaps you could free the slaves here as your Mr. Heath has done. You could be the first to show a new way of doing things, though I still don't see how you could ever afford to pay them all, or how they would manage. . . . Something my Grandmother Mitchell used to say, and I think it's true—'Change comes slowly, like plants taking root.'"

"You don't sound like Cousin Albert."

"Papa has done the best he knows how. He's good to our people, Robert. He doesn't beat them."

"But he still owns them. He buys and sells them, Emily—human beings."

Emily heaved a sigh and sat down. "I know. I know. But you've got to be careful, Robert. They tar and feather people for such talk."

"Is that a threat?" I wanted to believe that Emily understood, that she was on my side.

"Of course it's not a threat!"

That's when we heard the shuffle by the cracked door. Emily and I locked eyes. "Alex," she whispered. My heart caught in my throat. It would be like Alex to eavesdrop. He'd like nothing more than to make trouble for me by tattling to Grandfather. For all my own big talk of freedom and helping outside the law, my heart beat faster in my chest. I pressed my finger to my lips and tiptoed across the room. But when I flung open the heavy oak door we did not see Alex, only the dark brown of Nanny Sara's skirts disappearing around the corner.

Emily clutched my arm and whispered, "You've got to be more careful, Robert. You can't trust slaves any more than you can trust Alex. They turn on each other for the least favor from overseers and owners. Even Nanny Sara won't hesitate to bring trouble on you if it gains her favor with Uncle Marcus."

JACOB DIED. In all the nightmares running through my head, I hadn't imagined that he'd die. Crippled, I knew he'd be crippled. But after all he'd gone through—working his whole life at Ashland, then running with Jeremiah and surviving Slocum's gunshot wound in Cecil County, and the Heaths and Henrys and Pa all nursing him back to health and getting him and Jeremiah on their way again—I just couldn't take it in. The other slaves did all they could to stop the flow of life, even searing his stump. But it was no use.

Slocum prepared to hang Jacob's body from a tree, as a reminder to all who would run. Ma vowed she'd leave and never return if Grandfather allowed such a thing. So Grandfather stood up to Slocum on that, but only that. Slocum swore he never thought to see Grandfather in petticoats and that he'd see Jacob in hell and take care of it himself. I was living inside my nightmares, and I couldn't get out.

None of the whites from the big house, nor Slocum, tended the body or stood by the burial—nobody but me, that is. And maybe I don't count because I hid in the pine trees, by the slave cemetery next to the river, watching, clenching my fists for what I could not do, for my shame, my hate and fear of Slocum, for the terrible loss in Jacob's family. The slaves, except Jeremiah, who still lay only half-conscious, sang Jacob from grave to glory. I'd never heard singing and praying so wrenching, so full of the Holy Ghost, not even at Laurelea. Slocum was going to be mighty lonesome in eternity.

"Ma," I prodded daily, "it's time we go home. Grandfather's fit and getting stronger every day. The harvest is in. The house and quarters are as good as they're going to get with Slocum here. Don't you miss Pa? Miz Laura might need us."

"Don't pester, Robert. I'm not ready. Mr. Slocum still has far more influence over your grandfather than he ought. If we leave now—"

"Grandfather will never get rid of Slocum!"

Ma looked away. "Perhaps not, but we've made progress." Ma brushed her skirt and clasped her hands. "This is the first time in fourteen years that I've been home. I need more time."

"We'll be home for Christmas," I said. "Won't we?"

"Christmas?" Ma hedged. "Well, yes, I suppose."

But home and travel, and even talk of Jacob or Jeremiah was swept away by the news that came from town. "Blasted Yankee abolitionists! Murderers! Black-hearted devils!" Grandfather stormed from his study, slamming his newspaper against the doorjamb. My heart leaped inside me. Had Nanny Sara told? Pa was no murderer.

"Papa!" Ma hurried from the back parlor. "What is it?"

Grandfather, furious, shook the paper in the air. "Read it! Read it!"

Ma pried the tattered newspaper from his grasp and read, "Yesterday at noon, the whole community was astounded at a report that a band of Abolitionists and Negroes had taken entire possession of the town at Harper's Ferry, including the Armory, Arsenal, Pay Office, and all the other Government property. They cut the telegraph wires and stopped the trains with the mails, imprisoning and pressing into their service all

Negroes found in the workshops and streets, and killing many."

"It was Brown! That bloodthirsty Yankee that massacred innocent people in Kansas! 750! The paper says 750 in his band!" Grandfather shouted, turning purple.

"Papa! Calm down." But Ma was trembling. She took up the paper again. "It says Brown's object was to 'procure arms and money from the Armory, and induce a general stampede of the slaves in this section of the country.'"

"It's war!" thundered Grandfather.

"It's not war, Papa. They've stopped him, surely."

And they had. Colonel Robert E. Lee put a stop to it. Days later we learned that the newspapers had mixed up the facts. It wasn't 750 in his band. It was more like twenty-two or twenty-three. They hadn't damaged the railroads, or the mail, or imprisoned or killed many Negroes, either. But the truth didn't cure the fever sweeping the piedmont.

Planters, including Grandfather, met daily, fearful their slaves meant to rise up and murder them in their beds. Old folks at church claimed it was just like the days of Nat Turner and his slave uprising when no white person was safe. So the planters set their own laws. Slaves were forbidden to gather— no more visiting, no church, no jumping the broom, nothing but work under guards. Grandfather made Ma tote a loaded pistol in her reticule. Pa would have been fit to be tied.

But the real curse, as near as I could tell, was that the planters hired on pattyrollers and vigilante groups around the clock, anybody looking for extra cash and willing to carry a cat-o'-nine-tails, a bowie knife, or a pistol to patrol the roads and streams and woods, or stand guard outside slave quarters at night. The job drew not only white trash, but "gentlemen" with a thirst for misery. Slave beatings became common. Slocum had a heyday.

Finally, according to the newspaper, John Brown was "convicted of treason in conspiring with slaves and others to rebel, and also guilty of murder in the first degree." The judge sentenced him to be hanged in public on Friday, the second of December.

"December 2 can't come soon enough!" Grandfather exploded, throwing the paper across the dinner table. "That trial was a waste of the taxpayers' money!"

"It's the American justice system, Uncle," Cousin Albert said, folding his napkin. "Every man deserves his day in court, a voice to be heard. It's why we fought the Revolution. But I must agree with the verdict. Justice has been served." He turned to me. "Do you understand that, Robert?"

I looked from one to the other across the table. "I don't know. I don't know what to think."

"You don't know what to think?" Grandfather turned the color of ripe persimmons. "The man's a convicted murderer, a traitor to his country!" Grandfather bellowed on, but I closed my ears.

I steered clear of Cousin Albert after that, but not because I stood for John Brown. I didn't know enough to tell the truth of all that. But Cousin Albert had shown me a "code of the South" that left me cold when he refused to help Jacob and Jeremiah. He'd had so much to say about his care and concern for his "contented slaves." But he was caught up in the craziness about John Brown, too, and had clamped down like everybody else. I lost all respect for slave owners and overseers, no matter how they claimed to treat their slaves.

Despite my scorn I walked on a skimming of ice, never knowing when I might fall through, never knowing who might be waiting to take me to task for my loose tongue or my pa's belief in abolition. Emily's warning about slaves tattling plagued me each time my path crossed Nanny Sara's. I wanted to ask Nanny Sara about Jeremiah, to know if he was all right. I wanted to tell her that Pa had tried to help him and Jacob, but I didn't dare.

Ma spent more and more time with Cousin Albert. Alex and I spent less time together as the November days turned colder. He didn't like to fish or ride, and I no longer encouraged him. I preferred loneliness to his company, anyway. Emily and I still walked after lessons, but we were careful not to mention slavery.

"Robert," Ma interrupted my worries late one afternoon, "your grandfather wants to see you in his study." My jaw tightened as I walked toward his door.

"Robert! Come in." Grandfather's voice boomed, but he did not sound angry. "Let me look at you, Boy." I stepped before him. He circled me, searching me up and down with his eyes. I couldn't tell his thinking. "You've come a long way in the time you've been here, Robert. And I'm proud of you." I couldn't believe my ears. Surely he knew of my contempt since the cutting off of Jacob's foot and Jeremiah's beating. "I realize that things are different here in the South than what you might be used to, but I believe that overall you've made a good transition."

My eyes met his then, and he must have read some challenge there.

"Well—adaptation—if you will." He looked away. Grandfather was a boastful man but a weak one. "I think it is time we took another step in your training here at Ashland, Robert. After all, if things continue well, you stand in line to inherit this plantation."

"Papa!" Ma couldn't help her outburst of pleasure.

"Don't sound so shocked, Caroline! The boy is my

grandson, and although you should have married equal to your station, he can't help the folly of his parents. I'm willing to overlook it."

But I didn't want to overlook Pa. I felt the bile rise in my throat.

Grandfather unlocked the gun cabinet behind his desk and removed a sleek new rifle. "This is for you, Robert, the newest gun in town." He turned it over in his hands, rubbing his palm over the barrel. "Sharps New Model 1859. A finer, more accurate rifle was never crafted." He crossed the room and proudly placed it in my hands.

"Papa—" Ma began, the fearful edge in her voice.

"Caroline, marksmanship is part of a Southern gentleman's education." Grandfather ran his palm over the barrel. "Not many men own so fine a gun."

Ma bit her tongue. I swallowed. "Thank you, Grandfather." The stock I held in my hands was polished to a high sheen, and the sleek steel barrel felt solid, cold between my fingers. I knew Pa would forbid it. Ma knew Pa would forbid it. Even Grandfather knew, but he smiled. While the gloat on his face sickened me and I felt like a traitor to Pa, still I held the gun and knew I would keep it.

"There's a black stallion in the stable, Robert. He's yours. I had him brought out from town this morning. Name him yourself." Grandfather delighted in my shock. "It's about time you had a horse of your own—a fine leather saddle, too. Can't have the heir of Ashland running 'round the county on borrowed horseflesh!" I knew he was buying my loyalty, and I didn't stop it. Never had I wanted anything so much in my life. "I know Alex expects to inherit from me, and up until now, I saw no other possibility. But I'm not satisfied with him. A plantation needs a man to run it. Slocum's done the best he could, but he's not Ashton blood." The crease between Grandfather's eyebrows deepened. "Now that you and your mother are home, I believe there's hope for Ashland. I see character in you, Boy, and I'm counting on you to make me proud, prepare yourself for our future here, take your place in Southern society." I didn't know what to say. He waited.

"I'll do my best, Grandfather."

He clapped me on the back. "That's what I ask—what I expect!"

Ma found her voice. "This is wonderful! I know your father will be so proud of you, Robert." But that wasn't true.

"Caroline," boomed Grandfather. "I think it's high time we throw open the doors of Ashland and pull out the mothballs."

"Papa, we've cleaned this house from attic to cellar!"

"No, no, silly woman! A party! I mean a grand party—a ball—like your mother threw in the old days."

"A ball!" Ma exclaimed.

"Why not? Don't you think we've plenty to celebrate? How about a Christmas ball?"

"Christmas is over a month away." Ma looked at me, then added tentatively, "We really should be getting back to Maryland soon."

He ignored her. "It's what we need, Caroline. Have the house painted, if you like. Order new draperies—whatever you want. Invite the whole county! We'll show the town that Ashland is as fine as ever she was. The only thing I insist on is that my daughter be the prettiest belle there! Spare no expense on yourself, Caroline."

Ma flushed in the excitement. I couldn't hold my tongue any longer.

"Pa will be expecting us home before then."

Grandfather turned a look of thunder on me, then caught

himself. "Invite him, too, by George! Let him come and see what I'm offering you both!"

Ma rushed toward him. "Do you mean it? Invite Charles here?"

"Certainly I mean it! I don't say things I don't mean! It's about time we all buried the hatchet and got on with the business of being a family." Grandfather lit a new cigar, drew long on it, and walked out.

"Think what this means, Robert!" Ma hugged me. "I never thought I'd see the day Papa would allow your father across this threshold. We can be a real family, at last! I'm so proud of you, Robert! Your father will be proud, too, once he sees what this can mean for all of us. A future for you, Robert! A real future!" She wiped the tears from her eyes and laughed. "There's so much to be done! A ball! Think of it! I haven't even attended a ball since before your father and I were married!"

Ma tripped out of the room happier than I'd ever seen her. But it was still a lie. Pa would not be proud of the gun or the horse or saddle, or even the inheritance. He would not be pleased with the invitation to Grandfather's Christmas ball. He'd know it all for what it was—a purchase—not so different from the slaves Grandfather bought and sold. I did not doubt that Grandfather would give us all he'd promised, but in return he'd expect our loyalty and service, our obedience and presence every day for the rest of his life.

But when I laid eyes on the spirited black stallion in the stable, I stilled my questions. I'd never dreamed of owning such a horse. The first day I sat on the gate and spoke gentling words to him. The second day I brushed him down till his coat shone and his mane grew fine, like feathers in my hands. I wouldn't let anybody else groom him or feed him. I didn't want anyone to come between us. The third day he let me saddle him and lead him around the drive and pathways. By the end of the week we were racing through the fields and exploring trails along the Yadkin. He was already broken, but we had to get to know each other. I determined we'd be best friends, not master and slave.

I named him Stargazer, for the milk white star blazed on his forehead, and for the comfort he gave me those nights I couldn't sleep, those nights I lay awake, counting and searching the stars outside my window, trying to quiet the rumblings in my mind, aching for the morning when I could ride him again. Stargazer became my closest friend—closer, in some ways, than William Henry. I tried to forget that he was the price of my loyalty to Grandfather. I tried to convince myself that Emily was right, that change comes slowly.

MA INVITED COUSIN ALBERT, Emily, and Alex to dinner the last week in November. We'd just finished dessert when we heard a knock at the front door. A minute later Old George opened the dining room door. "'Scuse me. Miz Caroline? A telegram's brung from town and this boy's got to know does you want to send a reply?"

"Ask him to wait, Old George," Ma said, stepping into the hallway. Ma tore open the paper. Her eyes ran over the words. She moaned. "Oh, it's from Charles." Her eyes found mine. "Miss Laura is dying. We must go home."

Dying? Miz Laura? My inner world fell through ice.

"What do you mean, 'go home'?" Grandfather exploded. "You are home!"

"Papa, Miss Laura has been so good to us—like a second mother to me in many ways." Ma looked up at him, her eyes pleading for his understanding. "And Charles has asked me to come. He's my husband, Papa. I can't refuse him."

"That woman is your husband's employer, Caroline. Surely she's got nurses to look after her, or slaves—at least she could have if they weren't so blamed foolish! Your place is here."

"Papa—"

"I tell you Caroline that I forbid it! If you go this time I'll—"

"Uncle!" Cousin Albert stepped between them, pressing

Grandfather's arm. "Don't threaten things we'll all regret. We've come so far. Caroline is not leaving for good—are you, Cousin?" Ma shook her head uncertainly. "As long as you don't scare her off with your vile temper!" Cousin Albert tried to make light.

Grandfather bristled, but backed down a mite. "I don't understand why you think you need to go, Caroline. It's foolishness. But you'll leave Robert here."

"No!" My voice came louder than I'd expected. "I'll come back when Ma wants to come, but I need to see Miz Laura, and my Pa. Ma, I have to go."

"Caroline must have an escort at any rate, Uncle—now, of all times." Cousin Albert broke in again. "Certainly Robert must attend her."

They followed Grandfather, blustering, into his study, arguing, trying to make arrangements. I left Emily and Alex and ran outside. I couldn't take it in, Miz Laura dying. I guess some part of me knew that she'd been doing just that for months, but I wasn't ready. Of all the people I'd ever known, Miz Laura was surely the best and most unselfish. It didn't seem fair that she should be called so soon. What did God want with her anyway? Couldn't He see we needed her?

I took to the barn, needing my best friend. Stargazer and I beat a path to the Yadkin, galloping for miles along its bank. I wasn't praying exactly, more like arguing—with God. We rode until we both were spent.

On the way back I walked Stargazer by the river, past the slave cemetery. Jeremiah was there, draping an old quilt over Jacob's marking stone. "What's the quilt for?"

Jeremiah tripped over the stone beside him. He swore in his fright, then told me, "You scarier than a haint!"

"Sorry," I said. "I thought you heard me coming." He rubbed his shin. "How are you feeling?"

"I'll do." He looked away.

"What's the quilt for?" I asked again. "Was it Jacob's?" It looked like something more than most Ashland slaves could boast.

Jeremiah looked me in the eye, something few slaves do, I'd learned. "Just an old thing with crooked stitches." I knew it wasn't "just an old thing" to people so poor. I must have showed I didn't believe him. "Crooked stitches on a quilt keep evil spirits away." He let me take that in. "Evil travels in a straight path—can't follow a crooked line."

"Oh," I said. "I see." But I didn't. I wondered if he was messing with me like William Henry sometimes did, or if he was saying something more that I should understand.

"No need to tell Mr. Jed I out here." Jeremiah sounded like he didn't much care, but I knew better.

"I won't say anything." He nodded. I stepped over to the quilt and ran my fingers over the patches. "Miz Laura's got one almost like this. It has that same deep blue center patch. She hangs it out on her wash line lots of the time. I don't know why she does that."

"I remember." Our eyes met and I knew he told the truth. I also knew he remembered that day when I saw him in the Heaths' attic window.

"Jeremiah, if I could have stopped Jed Slocum from cutting off Jacob's foot or beating you, I would have." My hands shook, and I couldn't still them. "I didn't know how." Jeremiah looked at the ground. I wanted him to say something—anything.

"Those people that helped us up where you live, they were fine people."

"One was my pa. He'll be grieved to know Slocum caught you after—"

"Don't you tell him!" Jeremiah's eyes flashed.

"What? Why not? He'll want to know."

"He done his best. They all did. That was the best I ever been treated outside of Granny Sara my whole life. That the first time I ever had me a good friend—that William Henry." Jeremiah looked away. I felt jealous all of a sudden. William Henry was my friend. "He'd come up to the attic with a checkerboard. Taught me how to play. Taught me letters and how to write my name."

"You have friends here, don't you?"

Jeremiah looked back at me. "Who gonna be my friend here? I not black enough for the other slaves to take to. Who gonna be my friend? Your mama or your granddaddy? Jed Slocum? No." He shook his head. "William Henry the first don't care about my color, the only time I had me a real friend."

I understood; that was like William Henry. "William Henry's a good friend to me, too." And then, before I'd thought it through, I said, "Maybe we could be friends."

Jeremiah grimaced. "I don't see how. Nobody here gonna let that be."

He spoke the truth. I picked up Stargazer's reins. "You might want to know . . . Miz Laura's dying. We got word today."

"The white-haired lady in the chair?" Jeremiah looked stricken. I nodded. He looked away. "She a great lady—the kindest white lady I ever knowed."

I couldn't talk anymore. "I'd best get back."

"Me, too."

I didn't look to see what trail Jeremiah took. I didn't want to know.

Dusk had fallen by the time I'd fed and brushed Stargazer's coat to silk, his mane and tail as fine as feathers. When I reached the front lawn Alex stepped off the verandah, blocking my path.

"So you really imagine that you'll inherit Ashland one day and run it to ruin by 'freeing the slaves.' You're stupid. More stupid than I even imagined."

"Leave me alone, Alex." The hair raised from my neck. I tried to brush past him, but he pushed me back and I tripped on the step. Alex was on top of me in a moment, his knee in my chest and his mouth against my ear.

"I know all about you and your yellow-bellied weak stomach for whipping slaves, your 'run-cry-to-Mama' over things you have no business meddling in. Well, I have no such qualms, and I mean to make sure Uncle Marcus understands the difference between us."

"Get off me, you lunatic!" I pushed Alex as hard as I could, but my arms were weak against his weight above me.

"Lunatic!" Alex cackled as he rolled to the grass. "I'm not the crazy one, Cousin. Wait until I tell Uncle Marcus. Maybe he'll have our good Sheriff Grady telegraph the sheriff in your one-horse town. 'Arrest Charles Glover stop Stinking abolitionist stop Helps runaway slaves escape stop.' Do you think that might get their attention? Maybe I should send the telegraph on December second, then your father could join John Brown. I think they're calling such thieving the 'Underground Railroad' in the newspapers now. Is that what they call it at your house, Robert? Are you part of it?" Alex's voice rose to a fierce whisper.

"Shut up, Alex! You don't know what you're talking about." But he could smell my fear.

"Shut up? Possibly, Cousin. For a price."

"A price?"

"The gun Uncle Marcus gave you. I'd like a gun of my own. And stay away from Emily."

"Emily?"

"You are stupid! You repeat everything I say!" He was enjoying himself. "Uncle Marcus and my father are already playing matchmaker between you and Emily. I won't stand by and watch you two marry and inherit everything that belongs to me."

"That's insane, Alex. Nobody's thinking of such things." But I heard the ring of truth in what he said. It would be like Grandfather and Cousin Albert, even Ma, to concoct such a scheme.

"The Sharps. And stay away from Emily—no explanations, just stay away."

I didn't mind so much about the gun. The guilt of owning it against Pa's convictions carried a heavy weight. But Emily. I hated doing that to her. But the price of refusing was too high. I couldn't risk Pa and Mr. Heath or William Henry's family getting into trouble, all because I'd confided in Emily, or boasted to her. Had Emily told Alex? The thought of her betraying me stung like a punch in the stomach. Had Alex overheard us sometime, or had Ma told Cousin Albert?

"I didn't come here with a plan to inherit anything, Alex."

"And you won't. The question is, what are you willing to lose?"

"You can have the gun. I'll bring it over before we leave for home. But Grandfather won't understand why I gave it to you."

Alex smirked and mocked a bow. "My silence for hire. And Emily. Stay away from her."

"That will happen anyway when Ma and I leave."

"Not good enough. You make her understand that you don't want anything to do with her—not ever."

I stared hard at him. How did someone so young get to be so mean? I stood and brushed my pants. His smug face sickened me and I wanted to punch him, cut him down, but I didn't dare. I turned my back and walked inside.

Upstairs, I closed and bolted my door. Moments later a knock came. Emily whispered, "Robert? Are you in there?" She knocked again. "I saw you come up the stairs, Robert. Let me in."

"Go away, Emily."

"I just want to say good-bye. Papa has worked it that you'll be leaving tomorrow. I'm sorry about your friend, Miss Laura. She sounds like a great lady. Cousin Caroline told me about her." I didn't answer. "I may not see you again before you leave."

I leaned into the door, feeling the cool wood against my sweating forehead. "I said, go away."

"Are you ill, Robert? I know you're upset about your friend—"

"I don't want to see you anymore, Emily. Now, I'm going to bed." Her footsteps backed away from the door, hesitated in the hallway, then sounded slowly down the stairs. I unbolted the door. I'm not ashamed how much I wanted to run after her, but I'm mightily ashamed of the way I treated her. Stretched across the bed I counted over in my mind the people I'd let down—Emily, Pa, Ma, the Heaths, even Jacob and Jeremiah. It was a miserable recitation and a miserable night.

Finally, I fell into a half-sleep. Long after the house was quiet for the night, I dreamed that a squirrel scraped at my head. I woke to a soft tapping outside my door. Nanny Sara crept in by moonlight and pulled my door behind her, her finger to her lips. I pulled up on my elbows, wondering if I was still dreaming, trying to push the sleep from my eyes. She sat down beside me. The ropes of the bed groaned.

"You leaving tomorrow, Masta Robert."

"Yes, Nanny Sara."

"But you be back before Christmas."

"Maybe. I don't know. It depends on Miz Laura, and my pa."

"You know your way north by yourself?"

"What? We'll go on the train."

"Not then. You know your way? By the drinking gourd and the moss on trees?"

"The drinking gourd? You mean the North Star?"

Nanny Sara's white teeth smiled in the moonlight. "The moon be right Christmas week and the drinking gourd shine bright."

"What are you talking about, Nanny Sara?" She was starting to scare me.

"You know Moses? 'Cause we need Moses here now. We need a deliverer bad."

I tried to shake the fog from my brain. "I don't know any Moses. I don't know what you're talking about." I could feel Nanny Sara staring hard at me. Finally she rose from the bed. "Maybe you just a boy—a boy with big talk." Then she crept from the room, as quietly as she had come.

I stared at the closed door, wondering if I had dreamed her visit. The clock downstairs struck eleven. I'd told Nanny Sara that I didn't know what she was talking about, but that wasn't true—at least not altogether. She wanted me to help someone find their way north. But who? Her? Jeremiah? It was true that I didn't know anyone named Moses. Was Moses a real person, or was she asking me to deliver somebody to freedom like Moses in the Bible delivered the Israelites from Egypt? I could hear Pa's voice in my mind, reading that story, bringing Moses and his serpent staff to life. I wished Pa were here now to tell me what to do, to let me be a boy again and not have to make these decisions. I'd let everybody down and I needed Pa to set things right. Didn't I?

IT WAS THE LAST WEEK in November. The leaves had long fallen. Gnarled, bare trunks stood stark against gray skies. The rain-wet wind blew through bones and set teeth on edge. If a person was going to die, nature marked it a fitting end.

Saying good-bye to Stargazer was the hardest. I nuzzled his nose into my chest and whispered in his ear, "I don't know what will happen when we get home. I don't know how long it will be before I can come back. But I love you, Stargazer. With all my heart, I love you."

Cousin Albert drove us to the train himself. He and Ma parted tenderly, more so than cousins ought, it seemed to me. It was good we were going home. It was time.

I checked my watch. I'd done it twelve times in the hours since Grandfather had given it to me. "I know it's early for Christmas presents, Robert, but I want you to have this now," he'd said. I'd opened the box and inside, on a blue velvet lining, lay a scrolled, solid gold pocket watch. I opened the case and read the engraving, Robert Glover, 1859, from Grandfather Marcus Ashton. "This is to remind you, any time of day or night, of the family and stock you come from. Make the Ashton family proud, Robert." He pressed my shoulder. I didn't shrug him off. It was a special gift, a man's gift, and I took it, though my loyalties churned inside me.

"We'll try to be back before Christmas," Ma had told Grandfather. "With Charles."

"You'd better be!" Grandfather had bellowed. "You've a ball to host!" But he'd held Ma close and then blown into his handkerchief. I knew he wasn't worried about the ball.

Nanny Sara did not speak to me or show me her eyes. It was as if her late-night visit had never taken place. Despite everything, I left Ashland with some regret. I wanted to go home, to see Pa and Miz Laura and William Henry. But I'd been treated more like a man here and was given freedoms that I'd not dreamed of at home. I didn't want to step back into my old shoes.

The days settled into a blur of jerking trains, stops and starts, of coaches shuttling us from train line to train line, boardinghouses and hotels. We either sweltered too near the stove in the car or our feet froze too far away. Still, Grandfather had seen to it that our tickets were first-class—better seats on the train than when we'd gone south, better hotels, good food. I tried to imagine Pa traveling to North Carolina on the train with us for Christmas. I couldn't make the picture stick.

At last our train pulled into Elkton. Pa stood, waiting for us on the platform, hat in hand, broad grin across his face and new worry lines etched in his forehead. I waved from the window. He raised his hat to me. I stepped off the train first and turned to help Ma, but Pa squeezed my shoulder and pushed past me. He swept Ma off the bottom step and into the air, twirling her three times around. Her bonnet went flying. I didn't mind. From the laughing color in her cheeks I don't think she minded, either. Pa looked tired and thinner, but happy to have us home. "You've grown, Robert! You're nearly as tall as me!"

But our spirits settled when the talk turned to Miz Laura.

"Her body's just giving out. She can't get out of bed anymore and can't bear the pain of being lifted. Doc's been out from town a number of times, but told Isaac there's nothing more to be done. He leaves medicine to cut the pain, but you know Miss Laura, she doesn't like missing anything. She'll only take it at night when she thinks she ought to be sleeping anyway. Trouble is, she needs to sleep most of the time." Pa squeezed Ma's hand. "I'm glad you're home, Caroline. She'll be glad, too."

I turned away. Why did things have to change? Why couldn't we go back to the way things had been last summer?

"Something else you should know." Pa studied the reins in his hands. "Sol Tulley caught Joseph on his property and set his hounds on him, tore his leg up pretty bad. Then he strapped Joseph to the hooks in his smokehouse and beat him unconscious. Joseph's just now sitting up."

"Was he trespassing with illegal company?" Ma asked, her voice cold.

Pa didn't look at her. "The Tulleys had a poor crop this year. Joseph was delivering an offer from Isaac for a wagonload of corn and potatoes."

Ma looked stricken. "I'm sorry, Charles. I spoke out of turn."

Pa squinted into the afternoon sun. "When Joseph didn't come home Isaac got worried, sent me looking for him." Pa swallowed hard. "There's not much left of his leg. The Henrys have had a hard time of it."

We drove straight to the Heaths' house. Aunt Sassy was out carrying the noon meal to Joseph. Mr. Heath had gone to Elkton for the doctor again. The wasted body in Miz Laura's bed looked nothing like the woman who'd clutched the pearl-handled pistol in the folds of her parasol five months before, nothing like the Miz Laura I'd known all my life who reigned over all of us with courtly grace and good humor. She'd lost most of her soft, white hair. Only her eyes and the soft lines creeping from their corners looked familiar.

"Robert," she whispered and smiled, reaching for my hand. I held her blue-veined hand and tried to return her smile. I chattered to her of our time in the South because I couldn't think what to say, but her pain soon grew too sharp for her to listen. Ma sent me out so she could tend to Miz Laura's needs. I was glad to leave the sick room. I couldn't get my mind around the idea of Miz Laura dying.

"What you wearing that step out for?" William Henry's voice found me slumped on the back step of the Heaths' house.

"William Henry!" I stood to shake his hand but he didn't respond at first, and I realized that I'd never shaken William Henry's hand. We both laughed uneasily. When did I get such high and mighty notions? "It's good to see you, William Henry. How have things been here?"

"You seen Miz Laura?"

I nodded.

"Then you know how things been." We both looked away. "It's not right. It's just not fair and doesn't seem possible."

"Not much fair in this life."

"I heard about your pa. Is he any better yet?"

William Henry shrugged, his jaw clenched. He buried his fists in his pockets. "Better, maybe. He always carry a limp now." I waited. "Jake's the one set the dogs on my pa. He begged his daddy to let him do the beating. Sol Tulley said no, he wanted the pleasure for himself. The Tulleys be out to kill my pa." I didn't know what to say. William Henry rubbed the back of his neck and looked at the ground. "What you do all day in North Carolina?"

My first thought was of Jeremiah and Jacob. But I'd promised Jeremiah that I wouldn't tell. I'd almost told Pa already. It was a hard thing to keep. So I stepped up to the question. "Been getting to know Ma's family. Grandfather Ashton gave me my own horse, a black stallion with a white star blazed on his forehead. I named him Stargazer. I ride every day. You'd love him, William Henry." But William Henry didn't answer, so I rattled on. "I learned to shoot. Grandfather and Cousin Albert say I'm a fair marksman. That's the good part. Cousin Albert's been teaching me Latin and mathematics with my cousins, Alex and Emily—but I get equal or better time fishing." William Henry looked at me like I was talking Latin.

I couldn't bring myself to tell him about the saddle or the gun I'd already lost or how much I liked Emily. I fingered the gold watch in my pocket, but left it there. "You'd like it. The Yadkin River is full of catfish and you can fish long into the fall, easy."

"Your granddaddy own slaves?"

"Yes." Now I looked at the ground.

"Then I don't reckon I'd like it much."

"Not everybody treats their slaves bad." But the words sounded false, even to me.

"Those slaves wait on you and say 'yes, massa and no, massa'?"

"Sometimes. But only because I'm Grandfather's kin." William Henry shook his head and turned away. But I wanted him to understand, so I spun him back to me. "I might inherit Ashland someday, William Henry. Then I can free the slaves just like Mr. Heath did here." I wanted William Henry's approval like I wanted air.

"They wait on you because they're slaves, because you are white and free. Because your granddaddy keeps a bill of sale in his pocket saying he owns their bodies." He turned again to walk away.

"It's not my fault, William Henry. I didn't start slavery."

"No, but I don't see you doin' anything to stop it, either." William Henry kept walking. I watched him go and felt sick to my stomach. What had happened? Why had everybody changed? I walked back to my house, hoping to see or feel something familiar and comforting. I hadn't even seen Joseph or Aunt Sassy or Mr. Heath, and yet part of me dreaded that, too.

My room looked smaller, and bare. I lay on the handmade crazy quilt and stared at the beams in the ceiling. I could see why Ma had missed Ashland—long summers, people waiting on you. Even the house was a world apart from our home at Laurelea. I realized for the first time all that Ma had given up to marry Pa and live here, and knew firsthand that she must not have known what she was getting into. Still, I loved Ma and Pa both. I hoped they didn't regret their life together.

Ready to shed my traveling suit, I pulled open my drawer. Inside I found my old coat and a pair of britches I didn't recognize, brown homespun and ragged. I emptied the drawer. The pants I was looking for were gone. Who would trade ragged pants for my blue stained work pants? I looked around my room, seeing it again. Some of the furniture had been moved, just a little. Pa would not have bothered. Runaways. Pa must have hidden runaways in our house while we were gone. I stuffed the brown homespun into the bottom of my drawer and sat down to think. I hoped the boy who'd taken my pants was getting good wear out of them. I hoped he'd made it to freedom, wherever that was. I wished that boy could have been Jeremiah, with Jacob.

I heard Ma and Pa through the wall that night. They

sounded happy to be together, and I breathed a little easier. Maybe things would turn out right after all. Maybe we all just needed time to settle into one another again. Maybe that was true for William Henry and me, too.

I dreamed that a hoot owl was pecking at my head and woke, realizing that the pecking was a soft tapping at the window in Ma and Pa's room. I could hear the muffled voices of Pa and William Henry, then Ma, angry and urgent. Their window closed and William Henry's voice was gone, but Ma's rose.

"You can't mean it, Charles! Miss Laura is dying, and now you're off running stolen slaves across the countryside! I can't believe you'd leave me on our first night home!"

Pa's boots hit the floor. "It has nothing to do with your being home, Caroline. You know I'd stay if I could. But we've got to move them tonight. It's too dangerous to keep them here with the doctor and all the people coming and going to say their good-byes to Miss Laura. I'll be back before daybreak if all goes well."

"Pa?" I stood in their doorway. "Pa, I want to help, if you'll let me."

"I forbid it!" Ma screeched. "Not another word! One more word and we'll pack for Ashland and leave on the morning train."

Pa looked at Ma, then at me. He didn't speak and I couldn't tell the meaning of his look. He tried to take Ma in his arms, but she pushed him away. He walked out the door, giving my shoulder a squeeze, but not speaking the forbidden word. Ma threw herself on her bed and cried. I felt knots roll in the pit of my stomach. I couldn't go to her. How could she let Pa go out on a trip that dangerous with such anger between them? I sat on the edge of my bed again, not knowing what to do.

Only minutes passed before a pounding came on the front

door. I flew to open it and Aunt Sassy nearly fell in my arms. "Robert! Robert! I'm so glad you're here. Where is your mama? Where is Miz Caroline?"

Ma appeared in the doorway, frightened, trying to compose herself. "What is it, Sassy? What's happened to Charles?"

Aunt Sassy was still fighting for her breath and shook her head. "Miz Laura. She's taken a bad turn and I don't think she can last long. Come. Please come, Caroline."

Ma's hand flew to her mouth. I found Ma's shoes and pulled her shawl off the peg and wrapped it around her. Aunt Sassy took Ma's hand and led her out by her pool of lantern light.

I sat down on the rocker and held my head, praying hard for Miz Laura and for Ma and Pa. The mantle clock swung its pendulum with maddening regularity, and the sound stretched my nerves to the breaking point. I couldn't wait it out. I pulled on my clothes and shoes and pushed into the night. Maybe I could just see if the wagon with the false bottom was missing. At least I'd know if Pa and his cargo had gotten safely away.

The wagon was gone and the barn door stood open. I closed it softly, glad to do even a little thing. I pulled Grandfather's watch from my pocket and held it up to the moonlight. Two o'clock. If they'd be back by daybreak they must not be going farther west than the Susquehanna or farther north than the Pennsylvania line in Chester County. A noise behind the barn caught my attention and I tiptoed around the corner. Clouds gave way again and the moon shone down on William Henry, bagging a skunk pelt from the barn wall. "William Henry, what are you doing?"

Startled, William Henry dropped his bag. "What you sneak up on a person like that for, Robert?" He swore under his breath.

"Well, what are you doing? You going skunking now? Whew! Why'd you save such a smelly pelt?"

William Henry turned back to his chore. "Never you mind. You go on back to the house. Your ma'll be worried and come looking for you."

"Both of our mas are up with Miz Laura. Aunt Sassy said she can't last long."

William Henry stopped his task then. I couldn't see his black face in the dark, but he whispered, "You go on home, anyhow."

"Stop treating me like I'm some stranger, William Henry! Does this have anything to do with where Pa went?" He didn't answer. "Tell me! My pa is out there, William Henry! If you're doing something to help, I want to help, too." Still he didn't answer. "Don't you trust me?"

"I don't know who to trust, Robert. I don't know what to think. You been off down south living high on the hog in the golden land of slavery. You seem to think it's mighty fine, like maybe you'll live there and 'inherit' your granddaddy's plantation, slaves and all. How do I know what you think?"

"I'm the same person I always was, William Henry. Only now I know about slavery from both sides. And even though it cuts Ma's heart, I know it's wrong. Even if I didn't, my pa is out there and I want to help him any way I can."

William Henry stared at me in the dark, surely taking my measure, and I wished I could have seen his face. At last he handed me the burlap bag. "Hold this." He unpinned two good pelts, dumping them in the bag. "Smokehouse." I followed him to the smokehouse, anxious to know his plan. We pulled open the door. William Henry felt his way through the hanging meat and finally lifted something from one of the ceiling hooks. "This should be big enough. No sense throwing away more than we need to." In the moonlight he wrapped skunk pelts loosely around the ham, the stinky one inside the other two, then tied it together with a rawhide strip. Still, the stink overpowered the smell of the ham for me.

"What are you doing with this?" I couldn't stand the suspense any longer.

"What's needed."

"Don't fun me, William Henry. Let me in."

"You've helped some, now go on home. If you get in any deeper your mama will have my hide and she'll send you packing, south."

I grabbed his arm. "She won't know. I need to help."

This time William Henry didn't hesitate. "As soon as the word goes out those slaves are gone, trackers will go for Tulley and his hounds. I'm making sure Tulley's hounds won't be smelling nothing for a while, least of all your pa."

"You sure it will work?"

"They'll go after that ham like Jake went after that ivy poison. Tulleys are all stupid. They want quick glory, even the hounds."

I knew William Henry hated the Tulleys, and with good cause. I wasn't sure they were all as stupid as he said. But it seemed like a good plan. As long as we didn't get caught it might help Pa, bide him some time.

"Mr. Heath's out there, too, you know."

"Mr. Heath? But what about Miz Laura?"

"She told him to go on, that she'd said her good-byes and he should help those folks for her sake." William Henry hefted the sack. "So we got to make this work. For Miz Laura."

"For Miz Laura." It was my solemn pledge.

We kept to the fields and woods. Tulleys' place was just over Laurel Run and a mile beyond. We made good time, even in the dark. The hounds picked up our scent a good thirty feet away. They barked wildly and lunged against their pen. William Henry lifted me up on his shoulders. I meant to empty the burlap sack over the pen wall. But my pants caught on a stray wire from the fencing, and between the dogs lunging against the fence and William Henry about to drop me, I was lucky to throw the whole bag over the top of the fence before Sol Tulley stepped out on the porch and raised his shotgun in the moonlight. A lantern lit up beside him. "Put that fool light down, Jake, I can't see! Who's there? Speak up or I'll fill you full of buckshot!"

We fell backwards on the ground, scrambling to find our feet as the dogs went wild, tearing open the sack. The shotgun exploded over our ears. We tore through the trees, then out toward the road so he'd not think we came over the run. Those dogs would be too busy for a while to try to track us, and with any luck, their noses would be so full of skunk perfume they wouldn't be able.

We ran until our lungs felt they'd burst, then dove in a stubbled cornfield, and let out our rip-roaring, doubled-over laughter. It was almost like old times.

By the time we reached the back porch of the Heaths' house we'd gotten a little control over ourselves, mighty little. William Henry set a lantern with only one slat open so we could wash the stench from our hands with strong lye soap and a jar of Aunt Sassy's tomato juice. We stuffed our heehaws in our armpits and did all we could to keep the noise down. Aunt Sassy appeared in the doorway. "You boys finished?"

We sobered. "Yes, Mama," William Henry said. "Those dogs won't be worrying nothin' for a while."

Aunt Sassy nodded and glanced at me. She put her hand on my shoulder. It felt good. "You boys come on up and speak to Miz Laura. She going fast."

"Did Pa and Mr. Heath get back?"

"Not yet." Aunt Sassy looked worried. "But don't you let Miz Laura know you worried. You done your best for them, now do your best for her."

I couldn't think of Pa being caught. How long had they been gone? I reached for my pocket watch to check the time. It was gone. "My watch! My watch is—"

"Come on, Robert. Hurry, now." Aunt Sassy pushed me toward the downstairs bedroom they'd made up for Miz Laura when it hurt her too bad to be carried up the stairs. I tried to push my panic down. I tried to forget my gold watch, but the fear nagged at my insides. Ma sat on the bed, cradling Miz Laura's hand. Joseph sat in a chair alongside. It was the first I'd seen him and I nodded. He looked pained and older. The soft glow of candlelight cast a halo all around the room, lighting the faces of the people I loved. If angels attend death, I know a host stood guard that night.

We knelt on either side of Miz Laura's bed. Ma made room for us, but she looked at William Henry and me, then gave me a look I don't like to remember. I wondered if Aunt Sassy'd told her where we'd been. Miz Laura opened her eyes, looked at us, and smiled. She whispered, "By the smell of you both you did your job well."

We smiled back. Miz Laura was a great lady. She opened her palms and we each placed a hand in hers. In the light I saw the difference between our skin colors. Miz Laura's was white, not much darker than the sheet beneath them. Mine was the color of sand at the bottom of the run. William Henry's was the sleek black color of a raven's wing, almost blue. I was surprised I noticed that now. I expected Miz Laura to speak to me first and was surprised again when she didn't.

"William Henry, I am more proud of you than ever you

will know. Mr. Heath has books for you that you are to read and own, with my blessing. You are fulfilling your destiny, and I love you for it." William Henry buried his face in the sheet and Miz Laura placed her hand on his head. In that moment I didn't feel equal to William Henry in Miz Laura's eyes, and I could not understand it.

Then she reached for me. "Robert, my dear Robert. I know you are searching for your purpose. I know you will find it. Go, with my blessing, and—" But she couldn't finish, for a spasm of pain racked her body and Aunt Sassy pushed me away to support her back as she arched it upward. Mr. Heath and Pa ran in then, tired, dirty, and so afraid they would miss her. They nearly did. Mr. Heath fell to his knees beside his wife. Her last look, her last smile forced through a struggle with pain, was for him. Her blue eyes closed, and she was gone.

Pa reached for Ma. We all knelt to pray. Aunt Sassy's spiritual began softly and rose near to a keening.

"Swing low, sweet chariot, comin' for to carry me home.

Swing low, sweet chariot, comin' for to carry me home.

I looked over Jordan, and what did I see, comin' for to carry me home?

A band of angels, watchin' out for me, comin' for to carry me home."

Pa and Joseph and William Henry and I left then. Ma and Aunt Sassy stayed to wash and lay out the body. Mr. Heath, broken, and looking older than I knew he could grow, remained on his knees by Miz Laura's bed. Ma said he prayed there all night, and that the candles burned till dawn.

MA AND AUNT SASSY laid Miz Laura out real nice in the front parlor. Joseph Henry had already made the casket weeks before: solid mahogany, polished to a fine sheen and fitted with brass hinges. It was a thing to behold and I realized that they'd all known a long while that Miz Laura wouldn't last. That morning, as soon as word got around Laurelea, the workers poured through the back door, knelt for prayers and good-byes around the casket, then spilled onto the front porch and lawn. Thirty dark heads bowed, thirty pairs of hands clasped in prayer, and thirty voices rose and fell in sweet spirituals, singing Miz Laura over Jordan. It was somber, but not sad. Miz Laura was free from pain and had died in her own bed, among her own people. We all knew she'd have a mansion in God's house.

By late afternoon, word had reached neighboring farms and the houses of other church members. People started coming from as far away as Chesapeake City, from below North East, and even some from Wilmington, Delaware, to pay their respects. Some stayed in the parlor and dining room all night and held a sort of wake, waiting for the morning burial. Aunt Sassy and Ma and the ladies of Laurelea fed everybody. It was good to be together. The lines between color were not so clearly drawn in the Heaths' parlor. I noticed it more now than

I ever had before, and for the first time, appreciated it.

One person I never expected to see at Miz Laura's burial the next morning was Jake Tulley. He came by just as Pa and William Henry and I finished digging the grave and were going to wash up. William Henry took one look at him and marched away. Jake pulled me aside when Pa walked ahead, and he whispered in my ear, "Can't you get your darkies to do that dirty work?"

I swiped at the sweat streaking my brow. "Digging Miz Laura's grave is a privilege; it's not dirty work."

"You won't talk so high and mighty to me when I turn you and your pa in to Sheriff Biggs and watch you dance off the end of a rope."

I pulled away from him. "Get away from me, Jake. I've got no time for you. If you want to pay your respects you'd best go inside. The service'll start shortly."

Jake laughed. "Pay my respects?"

My dander was rising. "That's what this day is about."

"Not mine. Recognize this?" Jake pulled my gold watch from his pocket and flipped open the case, showing the inscription. "Know where I found it?"

I did not breathe.

"Outside our dog pen, yesterday morning, after our hounds got skunked the night before by some weasel in the henhouse."

"Give me that." I reached for my watch.

Jake pulled his arm back and grinned. "I know your pa helped those slaves run t'other night. I know because he took that wagon out you keep locked in the barn. The one with the hidey-hole in the bottom."

My face must have betrayed me.

Jake smirked. "You and William Henry and your pas ain't

the only ones run around the county at night. I coon hunt and I see many things." He circled me.

"You think you know so much." I stalled for time, trying to think what to do.

"You say right. I do know so much. I know enough to make all of you and Mr. Heath swing. One little word to my pa and that is just what will happen. He'd love to see that uppity Joseph Henry dancin' off the end of a rope. But there is one thing I don't know that I'd give this gold watch and all that knowing for." Jake paused, dangling the bait. Still I didn't breathe. I knew he'd get wherever he was going. "I've heard talk about this Underground Railroad. Jed Slocum reckoned you all are in on it. I heard my pa say that he can't imagine such a thing being real, but if our hounds can't track those runaways he don't know where else it could run but underground."

"That's stupid."

Jake spun me around, grabbed my collar, and spit in my face. "Don't ever call me stupid again. I've checked every cave and holler around here, and I've not found any underground railroads." He pushed me away. "I never been on a train, and I mean to ride that one."

"Give me back my watch. You probably stole it." I tried to keep the panic from my voice.

Jake laughed. "We both know I didn't. I believe I'll just hang on to it—until tomorrow. Because if you don't show me that railroad underground I'll have to turn this pretty ticker over to my pa and tell him all about that wagon sitting in Mr. Heath's barn. I expect Monday morning would be a fine day for a hanging." Then he pulled a sober face. "You and that coal-faced William Henry made a big mistake the day you messed with Jake Tulley. I just been bidin' my time, and my time is now!"

"Listen, Jake, you—"

"Robert?" Ma stood by the cemetery gate. "It's time you washed up. The service starts in twenty minutes. Jake, if you want to come in and pay respects, you'd best come now."

Jake stood back and pulled a humble face I'd never seen. "Thank you, ma'am. I'll wait here for the burial."

Ma nodded, eyeing Jake's dirty clothes. "That's fine. Robert? Come along."

"Meet me tomorrow," Jake said, as I walked away. "Meet me here tomorrow." I did not dare look back.

It was hard keeping my mind on Preacher Crane's words as he preached Miz Laura into heaven. I didn't think she needed his help. But I needed help. I needed to talk to Pa, but he did not have a free moment between helping with the service and the burial, tending Mr. Heath, and helping Ma with all the guests. There was a big feed afterward where the good memories of Miz Laura ran freely as water washing over brook stones.

But I dared not tear my mind or eyes off Jake. Jake helped himself to the loaded table, then mingled with the mourners who carried their plates to the front lawn, enjoying the mild December day. I realized with a start that it was Friday, December 2, the day set for John Brown's hanging. But nobody mentioned it. There was sadness enough this day.

Once Jake caught my eye. He pulled my watch from his pocket, fingered the case, then grinned and held it to his ear as though listening to the tick.

"What's ailing you, Robert? Miz Laura wouldn't want you to pass up a feast like this." William Henry stood with a heaped plate beside me.

"It's Jake Tulley."

"I know. I wanted to run him off, but Pa said Miz Laura

wouldn't have wanted us to do that. He said she always felt sorry for him the way his daddy beats him."

"I wouldn't feel too sorry for Jake if I were you," I whispered. "He knows."

"Knows what?"

"He knows about the skunk pelts and the wagon with the false bottom. He knows that your pa and my pa and Mr. Heath are all part of the Underground Railroad and that Pa helped those slaves escape last night."

William Henry held his fork in midair. "He knows about the wagon?"

I nodded, our eyes locked. "Said he coon hunts, and he sees lots of things. He knows I skunked his dogs."

"He's guessing."

I looked beyond William Henry, at Miz Laura's freshly dug grave on the hillside. "My Grandfather Ashton gave me a gold watch. I kept it in my pocket, but it went missing after we skunked those dogs. Jake has it, said he found it beside the pen yesterday morning." I could feel William Henry's eyes on me.

"Nobody'd believe him, except for the wagon. They'd think he stole that watch." William Henry set down his fork. "We can't lose that wagon."

"I don't think he's bluffing. He said we made a big mistake the day we messed with him. He says if he tells we'll all hang. He said to meet him at Miz Laura's grave tomorrow. I'm supposed to show him the railroad underground."

"That's stupid. There ain't no railroad underground. It's all routes. Nobody knows all of it, just how to get from one safe house to the next."

I nodded. William Henry had just given me the fullest explanation I'd ever heard. "I've got to talk to Pa."

"No. Don't do nothin' yet. Just let me think a minute."

I closed my eyes. "This is too big for us, William Henry. We might hang."

"No. It's all right. I'll take care of it."

I opened my eyes. "What are you scheming?"

William Henry smiled. "We have to be smarter than Jake Tulley, that's all. That can't be too hard, now, can it?"

The pit of my stomach tossed and flipped the rest of the day. I ached to talk with Pa, but there was no chance to get him alone. As dusk came on, the last of the neighbors left, and the food and plates were cleared away. I helped Ma and Aunt Sassy set the parlor to rights. Pa and Joseph Henry, who'd been up and limping, were gone. I don't think Ma noticed until darkness fell. She and I, tired to the bone, walked home by lantern light.

I changed into my nightshirt and lay on my bed, waiting for Pa. But when he came home, Ma met him at the door. "Where have you been, Charles? I've been worried sick!"

"Joseph and I had some business to take care of for Isaac, that's all. I'm sorry I worried you, Caroline."

"Business! You can't expect me to believe it was so innocent on this of all days. Was it the same business that carried you off while Miss Laura was dying?"

"Caroline, not now." Pa sounded tired. They carried their argument into their bedroom.

A tap came at my window. "Meet me on the front porch!" William Henry whispered. I closed the front door softly behind me and stepped out into the darkness. The temperature had fallen and I shivered in my bare feet. I couldn't see, but William Henry placed something squarish in my hands. "I want you to have it. It's one that Miz Laura gave me. It's my favorite, that one about Hiawatha I read this summer, front to back, twice." I remembered with chagrin that I was supposed to have read it. "It's the first thing I ever owned in my life, free and clear, and I want you to have it, Robert." William Henry sounded anxious, earnest, and talked too fast and low, too close for comfort.

"William Henry, I can't take this. It's yours. It's right that it's yours. I don't read near as good as you, and Miz Laura knew you loved it. That's why she left it to you." I pushed it back into his hands and clutched the sides of my nightshirt. Why did William Henry have to be so forward?

William Henry ignored me and reached for my hands, placing the book squarely in them, locking his fingers around mine. I couldn't see his eyes in the dark but could feel his ragged breath in my face. "You'll read it someday, Robert, and understand what it means to me to be free, as free as the animals or the wind. You'll read it," and his voice smiled, "someday when you get around to being a genuine scholar." He let go of my fingers and I felt my face flame in the dark.

"That's not likely to happen soon," I said, even though I knew I'd made a lot of progress under Cousin Albert.

He ignored me again. "Remember, if you need help on the railroad and can't get to your pa or mine, go to the Quakers. They won't all help, but they're likely."

"Why would I need help on the railroad?"

William Henry rushed on, as though he hadn't heard me. "Before we was born Mr. Heath freed all his slaves. Each family got to choose a last name, something they'd never owned before. My daddy chose 'Henry.' Do you know why?"

"No. William Henry, it's cold out here. Let's—"

"Because Mr. Heath told Pa about a man named Patrick Henry lived last century, back when America fought the War for Independence against England. Patrick Henry wanted freedom. He wanted it so bad that he made a big speech to get his

Virginians to fight the British. He said, 'Is life so dear, or peace so sweet, as to be purchased at the price of chains and slavery? Forbid it, Almighty God! I know not what course others may take; but as for me, give me liberty or give me death!' That's how important freedom was to him, Robert. That's how important freedom is to me, as important as life. Henry is a proud name. I don't ever want to be without it."

"Nobody's gonna take your name away from you, William Henry. What are you so fired up about? Take your book back and—" But I didn't finish because Ma's voice rose from inside the house and now she was crying. "Look, I better get back inside." William Henry slipped something hard and round and cold into my palm. I knew exactly what it was. "How'd you get this?"

I could hear the smile in William Henry's voice. "A trade. Jake wants to see the Underground Railroad. I'll show him."

"But you said—"

Ma opened the front door. "Robert? Robert, are you out here?"

"I'll be there in a minute, Ma."

"What are you doing out here? It's the middle of the night. Who's with you?"

"I gotta go," I whispered, trying to return the book to William Henry. He wouldn't take it. The smile left his voice.

"Remember, you are my best friend, Robert," he whispered and squeezed my arms that held his book. "Remember what I said, 'William Henry is a fine name.'"

"Robert!" Ma called again.

"Coming," I said to her, then whispered into the night, "William Henry—William Henry?" But he and the moment had gone. There was something more that should have been understood or said, something my mind couldn't get hold of, but I didn't know what, and I had no choice but to step back into the lamplight and heed Ma's scolding.

That night my old dream returned. William Henry and I were hoeing in the field amid the sea of black bodies with no names and no faces. Aunt Sassy hummed and the mosquitoes buzzed too near my ear. The tiny black cloud blew up from the south. This time, when William Henry set down his hoe and reached his arms to me I saw he held a book in one hand and my gold watch in the other. His dark eyes pleaded with me, his mouth opened, but no words came out. "What? What is it, William Henry? What are you trying to tell me? What do you want from me, William Henry? Tell me!" I screamed.

Then the funnel came on and on, just like always, pulling up everything and everybody but me. This time I grabbed for William Henry and tried to hold him down. His eyes still begged, but the wind and the fire and the storm ripped him away. I was on the ground, weeping. I looked down. Again I wore William Henry's sleek, black skin and it felt good and cool and right.

When I looked up, there stood Ma, weeping all the louder, six feet above me. I stretched for her, calling, "Ma! Ma!" But she looked on me with hate and shame. This time I knew it was because William Henry's black skin covered my soul. She raised two fingers to whistle, but I knew it meant the hounds would come and I couldn't bear it. So I squeezed my eyes tight shut and covered my ears while the shrill whistle blast on her fingers screamed on and on.

Voices, urgent and loud, called me from the next room and brought me up out of my dream. I pulled the sheet from my neck and stumbled, my heart racing, to the doorway. Pa was pulling on his boots as Ma lit the lantern. Still the shrill whistle blast screamed on and on, stopping only for air.

Pa looked up and saw me standing in my nightshirt. "Something's happened to the train. They must need help to whistle so long. I'm going up to the trestle. Pull on your pants and boots, Son. Follow me. They'll need all the hands they can get if there's been a wreck."

But I couldn't move. My feet would no more lift from the sanded floorboards than my hands could pull away from the paint-peeled doorposts. I knew in my soul that they wouldn't need many workers that night. I wondered why I hadn't seen it coming, or if, in fact, I had. It was not a wreck, and it would not take many hands to lift two young, mangled bodies from the tracks—one white, and one black.

The wind and the fire and the storm had passed, but the nightmare was real. I looked at my hands. In the mingled shadows of midnight and lantern light they were black, the sleek black color of William Henry's skin.

CHAPTER

Fourteen

FORGETTING IS A BLESSED THING. My mind won't remember all I saw or did that night. I don't know how I got to the trestle. I don't remember when the train whistle stopped its piercing cry. But I remember my breath standing in frozen clouds before my face. I remember Joseph Henry's unbroken stream of shining tears when the lantern light found him on the ground, rocking and cradling his dead son's body.

I remember picking up William Henry's shoes, which had been yanked from his feet and thrust down the tracks by the force of the train. I held them next to my chest, breathing the smell of William Henry's fear, or was it mine, wondering why I couldn't sense him near me. I followed Joseph as he carried what was left of his son, his only child, down the hill and across the meadow to Laurelea. I stood on the doorstep as Joseph, burdened and bloody, carried William Henry in to Aunt Sassy. When her scream rent the night like a wounded animal I backed away, still clutching my best friend's shoes. I don't remember that Pa found me, crouched in the yard, and walked me home. I only heard about it later.

Jake Tulley was buried late the next day.

"I won't go to Jake Tulley's funeral."

"It's only decent," Ma insisted. "He was our neighbor."

He wasn't my neighbor, and I considered that he as good

as murdered William Henry. I knew William Henry had lured Jake there. I could imagine him telling Jake to look closely at the tracks, under the speeding train, to catch a glimpse of the Underground Railroad. I wondered if William Henry had intended to go on that ride all along or if Jake pulled him down with him.

"It might help the Henrys more for you to go, Son." Pa placed his hand on my shoulder. "Sheriff Biggs is questioning everybody, trying to find out why the boys were at the trestle that night. We don't want to give him any hurtful ideas."

So I went, for the Henrys' sake. But I couldn't bring myself to speak to the Tulleys.

"I'm so sorry for your loss, Mr. and Mrs. Tulley," Ma said. "If there's anything we can do . . ." But there wasn't anything, not beyond the fried chicken and cake Ma did up for them, and maybe, they suggested, Pa could donate a wagon of straw and a hog or two for winter. The Tulleys never missed a beat.

Ma didn't push me. She told folks I was in shock. Pa didn't push either. I think he wondered what I knew but didn't probe. Sheriff Biggs probed. I was careful not to say much. He finally figured it was two boys tried to jump train in the dark and got pulled under. Jake and William Henry were the least likely two boys to run off larking together, and everybody knew it. But nobody had another explanation. Jake Tulley was buried in the woods behind his house, next to his older brother, Zach. Charcoal-scratched slates marked both brothers' graves, but you could no longer read Zach's. Preacher Crane came and said words. There weren't many there. The Tulleys had kin but didn't make friends.

William Henry was buried in the colored cemetery at Laurelea, beside the church Mr. Heath built. Preacher Crane didn't come and I was glad. Mr. Heath and Pa and several of the workers from Laurelea prayed and said words. Joseph Henry held Aunt Sassy, who in three days had lost her world. Granny Struthers sang. Her old voice cracked, but the spirituals she sang came from a deep well. There was a goodly crowd, but no gathering afterward. Nobody had the heart for eating or visiting. A long life well lived is one thing. But a young life snuffed out of time is nothing to celebrate.

The weather had turned overnight. Before the last shovel of dirt covered William Henry's pine box, the freezing rains started. They whipped our coats and hats, beat through the trousers against our legs and stung our faces, then poured and whipped some more. We walked home through the swelling storm and sat till dark.

Pa gave the evening read. I felt no power in it. Why had God let this happen? Why did William Henry have to do such a fool thing? Had he committed murder? William Henry was my best human friend, and now that he was gone I felt more alone than ever. Why hadn't he thought ahead to what it would be like for the rest of us? Had he meant to die? Did he feel he had to give his life to take Jake's? Those questions haunted me like Tulley's hounds. If it hadn't been for my watch, maybe—but what was it that William Henry had said? Jake knew about the wagon. The wagon couldn't be explained away.

"I think our going is for the best, Charles," Ma said. "I only wish you would come with us now, too. There is just too much sadness here." My ears came alive.

"I can't leave now, Caroline. It makes sense for you and Robert to go. But I can't leave Isaac or Joseph or Sassy. They are as much my family as your father is yours. And there may be more that needs to be settled with Sheriff Biggs." I felt Pa's eyes on me.

"We need to be together, Charles. We are a family, too,

and we need to start behaving like one. I understand your loyalty to Isaac and the Henrys, but what about your loyalty to Robert? To me?"

"I'm not saying I won't come. Just not now. Stay here with me, and we can all go together later."

Ma shook her head. "Papa needs me. But I want you to promise me you'll come by Christmas."

Pa looked at Ma and then into the fire. "I'll do my best. Let's see how things go here." Neither spoke after that. I didn't care if I stayed or went. What mattered, anyway?

Ma helped Aunt Sassy some, but mostly it was the colored workers at Laurelea that gathered 'round the Henrys and drew them in, forming a protective net, a small shield against the world. I knew how flimsy that shield stood in a white man's world. I knew Sol Tulley longed to take his anger out on Joseph, even though he didn't know why Jake had been with William Henry that night. Except for Mr. Heath there would have been no protection from people like the Tulleys.

We hadn't been home a week when our bags were packed and loaded on the wagon. Ma spent her last hour before leaving for the train at the Heaths' house with Pa and Mr. Heath. I spent mine in the freezing drizzle at William Henry's grave. "I don't know what you're doing now, William Henry," I whispered, "but I sure hope you're all right. I hope there's fishing holes in heaven. . . . Why'd you do it, William Henry? Why?" I swiped my tears with my sleeve, as I pulled away some leaves that had blown against Jake's grave.

"I guess Jake never told his pa about the Underground Railroad or the watch or the wagon or any of it. You saved us all. And I reckon I ought to be grateful, but I'm mad as a hornet. I miss you, William Henry, and I'm not ashamed to say it." I pushed back the hot tears that kept coming, angry with myself for crying, angry with William Henry for dying, and above all, angry with God for letting it happen. A twig snapped behind me.

"William Henry gone to a better place, Robert. Gone to a better place." It was Granny Struthers cradling her basket of herbs and flowers beneath her dripping shawl.

"Yes, ma'am." I turned a little away from her so she couldn't see my face and tried to get hold of myself.

Granny crumbled some dried herbs over William Henry's grave and chanted. "Go 'long home, William Henry. Go 'long home. No need to tarry 'round here. No need to tarry 'round here. Ooooh—ahh. No need to tarry 'round here. We'll carry on, William Henry. We'll carry on. Go on over Jordan, William Henry. Row your boat. Go on now. Go on." Granny kept on.

I wasn't sure she knew I was standing there anymore. I took a good look at her as she chanted, something I never did when her piercing black eyes were turned on me in daylight. She wasn't more than four and a half feet tall, withered and bent like a bare tree branch, her blue-black skin wrinkled like winter-dried apples. Coarse white hair escaped the calico turban wound around her head, reminding me of the wool Aunt Sassy spun. Granny's hands, small and gnarled, dove in and out of her basket like sparrow claws. She crumbled different herbs for different parts of her chant. I didn't know what they meant. She spoke to me, at least I thought she did, but it still sounded like a chant.

"Work's not done. Work's not done. You know moss grows on the north side of trees? You know the star paths? You know when the moon be right? You know where the drinking gourd shines? You know to walk in the river to kill scent? You know onions rubbed in the feet kill it, too? Tell me, now, do you remember Moses? Moses be our deliverer. You go on back to the land of Egypt and you lead my people home. That's what William Henry be tellin' you. That's what he be crying from the grave in this rain for." And then she began to sing a song I'd heard all my life but never gave meaning to. "Go down, Moses, way down in Egypt's land. Tell ole Pharaoh, let my people go." And all her words made me think of Nanny Sara and her talk of Moses and star paths.

"Granny Struthers, you hush that kinda talk. Robert not needing to hear that now." Joseph Henry limped between the graves. "You say your prayers and go on home. Sassy'll be down directly to see you 'bout some herbs."

Granny Struthers lost her trance-like stare. "I expect her. Sassy be all right. She strong. You drink what I give her. It make you sleep when sleep won't come."

"I appreciate it, Granny. You'd best go on home now and mind the slick path. This cold rain be no place for you."

Granny nodded. She didn't look at me, but toddled away, leaning on her cane, whispering to herself.

Joseph and I stood by William Henry's grave. I knew there were things to say and this was my chance to say them. "Joseph," I began, not sure how to go on. "I'm sorry about William Henry dying." Joseph nodded but did not speak. He stared at the mound that covered his son. Joseph Henry was one of the tallest, straightest, smilingest men I'd ever known, black or white. But he wasn't so tall now, and he didn't carry himself proud. He surely wasn't smiling. "He was my best friend."

Joseph placed his hand on my shoulder, but kept his eyes on the mound. "I know, Robert. I know." And then the work of holding it there seemed too heavy. His hand slid from my shoulder.

"It's my fault," I whispered. "It's my fault William Henry

got killed by that train." And then the story poured out. I told my best friend's father about skunking the dogs and dropping my watch, about Jake Tulley's threats, and how he knew about the wagon with the false bottom, having seen it while coon hunting one night. I even told him about William Henry coming to me the night of the accident, and that I should have guessed what he was up to, and about the horrible dream I had that very night. I didn't tell him that the dream had come before, so many times before. I clutched my hands to still their trembling. Joseph wrapped his arm around me and pulled me to his chest.

"No, Robert. It ain't your fault. It was William Henry's calling." He held me until he had to pull away to blow his nose. "It's good you told me. I just wished he'd come to me. I figured it had something to do with them dogs. I been blaming myself 'cause I was the one told him to skunk them dogs." He shook his head. "But if Jake knew about that wagon, William Henry'd done it anyhow. I know him. I know my son." He shook the drizzle from his hat and pulled his collar up the back of his neck. "But why them railroad tracks? I been puzzling on that, but can't make it out."

"That was William Henry's trade," I said. "Jake wanted to see the railroad underground. William Henry showed it to him."

Joseph looked at me like I'd grown antlers. "Showed him the what?"

"Jake didn't understand that the Underground Railroad is a route of safe houses. He believed it was a real railroad under the ground and he meant to ride it, said he'd never ridden a train before but he meant to ride that one. William Henry promised Jake that he would show him the Underground Railroad if Jake wouldn't tell what else he knew, and if he'd give back the watch first."

Joseph Henry looked at me a long time. He nodded slowly, the realization of what had happened unfolding in his mind. Gradually, lines crept from the corner creases of his eyes. One side of his mouth turned up in a smile, and before long he chuckled. Pretty soon we were both belly laughing and crying at the same time, so hard we could barely stand, slapping the rain from our clothes and one small layer of sorrow from our souls. Even in the sadness and the horror of it all we realized that William Henry had skunked Jake Tulley one last time.

THIS TIME THE MILES ON THE TRAIN passed without me knowing. I kept picturing William Henry. In those pictures I lived all our growing-up-together years over and over in my mind. Always, at the end, was that plot of ground in the cemetery, and his marker. Pa wrote the letters and Joseph Henry carved them. Joseph and I set the finished marker in place, near William Henry's head. It wasn't enough, but this way nobody'd ever forget William Henry's name or that he lived—not them that knew him, or those that come after.

Our last night of travel we stopped in a boardinghouse in Jamestown, a small town in Guilford County, North Carolina. The plain clothes and large bonnets of Quakers lined the streets. I wondered if these Quakers were abolitionists or if living in the South had changed their views of slavery. I remembered what William Henry had said about going to the Quakers if I ever needed help on the railroad. I knew he meant the Underground Railroad, but I swore never to go near it, ever again.

We hired a coach to drive us to Salem and arrived about noon on Friday. We knew there'd be somebody from Mitchell House in Salem to pick up the weekly edition of the *People's Press*. Cousin Albert and Old George met us by the newspaper office. Pa had telegraphed ahead.

Ma acted as though we'd never been away. She fell right in with Grandfather and planning the meals and running the house. She and Cousin Albert spent even more time together, giddy as children, planning their Christmas ball. Grandfather had asked that it be hosted at Mitchell House, since he didn't know how long Ma and I would be away. Both houses were full of Christmas smells—pine and cedar garlands, plum cakes and gingerbread and sugar cookies in all shapes. Ma and Rebecca paraded the hallways, new clothes, gifts, and ribbons in tow. It was as if she didn't remember that Miz Laura and William Henry had just died. But I could not forget, and all the smells made me sick. Everything tasted like tin. I only wanted time with Stargazer, and to be left alone to spend my grief. But Ashland and Mitchell House had been turned upside down, and Ma kept at me till there was no time and no place to be alone, inside or out, anywhere.

The only person who might understand was Emily, or Jeremiah. But I'd hurt Emily with my snubbing. Besides, Alex watched us closely and the risk of his telling all he knew or guessed was too great. I'd learned that the hard way through Jake Tulley. And how could I tell Jeremiah that William Henry was dead—the only friend he'd ever had?

Ten days before Christmas I made my way outside to Nanny Sara's kitchen. Ashland was quiet for a few hours. Ma was at Mitchell House supervising the tree trimming. Grandfather was napping. At last I could be alone and quiet. In all contrariness, I didn't want to be alone.

Late afternoon light filtered through the kitchen window and cast a glow around Nanny Sara as she rolled piecrusts. Rebecca tended meat sizzling in the Dutch oven in the fireplace. Something about the light or the kitchen smells or the hard wooden bench pulled up to the plank table reminded me of Aunt Sassy and her kitchen in the Heaths' house at Laurelea. I sat down across from Nanny Sara. She didn't look up from her work but cut me a slab of warm hoecake, slathered it with butter and molasses, and pushed it across the table toward me.

I tasted it and relished the warm sweetness. It was the first thing that had tasted good to me in a long while. I drank the glass of milk Rebecca quietly set before me. "This reminds me of home and Aunt Sassy." I realized Nanny Sara didn't know who I meant. "Aunt Sassy cooks for the Heaths at Laurelea." And then I remembered, and the hoecake stuck in my throat. "Now I guess she just cooks for Mr. Heath. Miz Laura died just lately."

I traced the wood grain in the table with my finger. "Aunt Sassy is William Henry's ma. William Henry is—was—my best friend." The hoecake nearly spilled out, but I pushed it down. "He got killed just before we came back here. There's others there, too. Pa and Joseph, that's William Henry's pa. And there's Granny Struthers, Aunt Sassy's ma. She's an old midwife and herb doctor. She knows more about folks than sometimes they know about themselves." I talked faster, trying to run over my pain. "Granny Struthers talked to me about star paths and Moses, like you did. Is it the same Moses?" But Nanny Sara wouldn't answer. She just started humming as though she'd not heard. "Is it?"

But still Nanny Sara hummed. Rebecca looked from her to me and back again, but didn't say anything, either. After a while I pushed my plate away and walked out. What was the matter with everybody? Why wouldn't she answer me?

Ma nearly ran into me in the front hallway. "Oh! Robert! I'm glad you're here. Call Rebecca for me. I want her to make up the north bedroom. We're having company! Rev. Andrew Goforth is coming from Wilkes County to preach our

Christmas Eve service, then he's to fill Rev. Cleary's pulpit on Christmas morning. But he will be back here to stay through New Year and to preach our Watch Night service on New Year's eve—the first one our little church has had in years! And he's staying with us! Abuella Cooper wanted him to stay with them, but I insisted. This will be our first real company and I hear he's quite young, so you and he might have a good deal in common. Hurry, now! He'll be here before supper!"

Ma turned us all upside down giving orders right and left. Company might be good for the grown-ups, but I didn't relish having a preacher under the roof. I was mad at God, but didn't want to talk that out with anybody. I couldn't pretend to have the Christmas spirit.

A banging on the back door and cries from the quarters stopped our work and called us outside. Jeremiah, Nanny Sara's grandson, was tied with leather thongs to the whipping post in the quarters. Jed Slocum, vengeance on his face and the bright light of drink in his eyes, cracked the whip across Jeremiah's back.

Nanny Sara ran to Slocum and pulled at his clothes. "Please, Mr. Jed. Don't do it. Not again. Please!"

Slocum pushed her away. "Get off me or I'll lash you, too, Sara. This young buck will learn one way or another who he answers to!"

Slocum laid the lash on three more times. Three more times I stood frozen to the ground, seeing what William Henry must have seen Mr. Tulley do to his pa, seeing what William Henry had died to stop. Jeremiah didn't cry out. It was the slaves around him that screamed for mercy. When Slocum raised the whip a fifth time something snapped inside me.

I barely remember grabbing the whip from Slocum's upraised hand. I saw him trip, and must have forced him, with all my weight, to the ground. I remember raising the whip to beat him into the dust, and his wide eyes, the stark white fear there. I remember the catch of breath around me. I wanted to beat him like Sol Tulley had beaten Joseph. I wanted him to feel the bleeding pain that William Henry had felt when the train hit him. I wanted him to know what it was like to be Jeremiah. But Ma pushed between us.

"Robert! Robert!" Her face was a blur to me. "Get hold of yourself!" She came into focus. I held the whip in the air. She pried it from my fingers. Jed Slocum wiped blood from his mouth and stumbled drunkenly to his feet. She turned on Slocum. "Robert is right, Mr. Slocum. This is not the time. We are expecting an important guest momentarily and I do not want an uproar. Tend to these matters later, if need be."

I saw the humiliation and white-hot anger war in Slocum's face. I jerked away from Ma, ashamed that she'd spared Slocum, ashamed that she could even think about her house or guest now. Still shaking, I untied Jeremiah.

"Jeremiah! Oh, my Jeremiah!" Nanny Sara wailed as she helped me lift him.

"I'll tend to you later, Boy!" Slocum threatened. I think the threat was for me as much as for Jeremiah.

"Nanny Sara!" Ma called. "I need you in the kitchen now."

"Just as soon as I tend my grandbaby, Miz Caroline."

"Let someone else do that. Rev. Goforth will be here any minute, and I want supper on the table."

My mother's selfishness made me sick, but I knew better than to push her. "Go on, Nanny Sara, I'll take care of Jeremiah. I've seen it done." Nanny Sara's eyes filled as they looked full into mine.

Jeremiah leaned heavily on me and I wondered how many lashes he'd taken before we got there. I laid him as gently as I could on his pallet. One of the quarter slaves found a candle for me and another brought clean rags and a basin of water. Gently, I peeled Jeremiah's shirt from his back. Some of it pulled unwillingly in strips, already glued to his flesh by stripes of his own blood. I ground my teeth to keep the wail from escaping my throat. I'd seen Aunt Sassy tend Joseph Henry's back after the first time Sol Tulley beat him, but I wasn't prepared for the crisscross of old scars plastered across Jeremiah.

"Why you helpin' me?" Jeremiah whispered, when at last he could talk.

How could I answer? Suddenly everything that Pa and Joseph Henry and Mr. Heath and William Henry had done to help runaway slaves became clear to me in a way that I hadn't seen, even after Jacob's death. It wasn't just important. It was life and death. Liberty or death. And that is what William Henry meant. I said aloud, "You'd best steer clear of Slocum. He's got it in for you."

Jeremiah gave a wry grunt. "He won't stop till I'm dead or sold. Doesn't matter which to him."

I couldn't figure it. It went without saying that the mixed children running around Ashland's quarters belonged to Slocum. Why would he want so much to hurt his own son? "Isn't Slocum your father?"

Jeremiah turned slightly to catch my eye, even though he winced in pain. "No."

"But all the other—" I stopped.

"All the other mulatto babies is Slocum's. All five years old or younger. That's about the time he figured he could have his way and Masta Marcus not bother with him."

"But you must be my age, or older. If not Slocum, then who?"

Jeremiah pushed himself up and looked me fully in the eyes. "Who you think? Who else be white on this plantation?"

And then I knew why the brown eyes looked out of place in Jeremiah's face. Because the oval face with the chestnut hair should have had blue eyes, like my mother's, like Grandfather's. "When?" I whispered.

Jeremiah lay back down on his stomach. He recited a story he'd long known. It sounded like a litany from church. "When Miz Caroline run off to marry Mister Charles. My mama helped her get away. Masta Marcus go crazy. He beats his slaves till he learn it was Granny Sara's daughter, Ruby, what helped Miz Caroline get away. He take Ruby that very night, no matter that she never been with a man. He take his way with her. He lock her in the attic and do her over and over again every night for ten days, and there ain't nobody to stop him. Then he send her back to the quarters and vow he never want to lay eyes on her again. Nearly killed her. Nearly killed Granny Sara. When the birthin' time came he swear Ruby a whore until I come out near white as him."

I wanted to throw up, but the bile stuck in my throat. "What does he say now?"

"Say now? He don't say nothin'. He won't lay eyes on me if he can help it. Soon as she could walk again he sold my mama away. I don't even know what she looked like. Gave me over to a wet nurse and Granny Sara to raise."

I sat back on my heels. "So that's why Grandfather promised Nanny Sara—promised her what?"

"To let me live and that I not be sold. That's why Mr. Slocum hates me so much. He know I the one slave he's not allowed to sell off or kill. It eats at him. But I question Masta Marcus remembers his promise."

"He remembers," I said, thinking of the night Slocum returned with Jacob and Jeremiah. And then more pieces of the puzzle fit together. "Your name is Ashton."

Jeremiah grunted. "I don't want that name. My name is Jeremiah. What a slave need two names for anyway?"

I thought of William Henry. "A last name is a proud thing. William Henry, my best friend—your friend—always went by two names. When his pa was freed he had to choose a last name for his family. He chose 'Henry' because of a man named Patrick Henry that made a speech once. In that speech he said that life was too dear to be bought with the price of chains and slavery. He said, 'Give me liberty or give me death.' He wanted freedom that much."

"Was Patrick Henry a colored slave?"

"He was white. But he wasn't really free. They had to fight a war before he got free."

"We got no war, and Masta Marcus ain't never gonna free his slaves like your Mr. Heath." And then he softened some. "So that why William Henry go by two names. I wondered. He the first free Negro my age I ever knowed."

I knew I had to tell him. Jeremiah was William Henry's friend, too. "He's dead." Jeremiah lay still, but rigid, like a cat ready to spring. "What you mean, he dead?"

And so I told him everything, just as it happened—about the runaways and the dog skunking, and the watch, and Jake Tulley, and William Henry and the Underground Railroad, and my dream, and the train—every word.

Jeremiah went limp. His tears fell silently. In all his hard time since I'd known him, it was the first time I'd seen him cry. But he cried for William Henry. And that made me cry for all the evil—the Jake and Sol Tulleys, the Jed Slocums, the Marcus Ashtons of this world. I despised them all and I could not understand how a God of mercy could let such wickedness go on. Jeremiah sighed long and winced from the pain of it. "Well, I ain't free and I ain't dead, but I'm gettin' close."

"Don't say that."

Jeremiah shook his head. "Slocum won't give up till—"

"Then you have to work on getting free." The words came out of my mouth before I knew what I was saying. It was as if Jeremiah and I both knew I'd gone too far. I cleaned the rest of his cuts and patted in the salve someone had pushed inside the door. But we didn't say another word.

My head pounded as I climbed the steps of the big house. I let myself in the front door quietly. I couldn't face Nanny Sara just now, or Ma. I needed to think on all that had happened, on all that I'd learned.

Voices raised in argument came from Grandfather's study. The door stood ajar, and even though I didn't want anything to do with Grandfather just then, I couldn't resist the pull of the other voice, Jed Slocum.

"Selling Jeremiah makes sense, Mr. Ashton. There's a buyer in town now. He's making deals and will run a coffle south just after New Year's. The boy is nothin' but trouble. He riles up the other slaves." There was a pause. "We're running short after this year's poor tobacco harvest. A good price on him could help square things."

"That north field wasn't tended, Slocum. If you'd spend as much time watching over the fields as you do in the quarters chasing every skirt—"

"That's not the problem. It's those lazy—"

"According to my nephew it's a good deal of the problem! But we're getting off the point. I promised Sara I would never sell Jeremiah. He's not just any field hand."

"All the more reason to get shed of him. Sara's gotten too mouthy for anybody's good. She makes it hard to keep the others in line." Slocum hesitated. "I'd best ask you, Mr. Ashton, does Sara run Ashland, or do you?"

"Don't be impudent, Slocum. Sara doesn't run Ashland, and neither do you!" I heard Grandfather slam something on the floor. "It is a worry what with that Harper's Ferry affair. It has us all spooked. Thank God those slaves can't read! We need to keep a firm hand just now." Grandfather's footsteps echoed across the floorboards. "Well . . . I have wanted to give Caroline a little something extra for her house decorating."

"He'd fetch a good price, long as nobody knows how uppity he gets."

"I'll think on it."

"Don't think too long. We'll miss the opportunity."

I couldn't listen to any more. I went to my room, leaned out the window, and threw up.

THE STRIKING OF the downstairs clock dragged me from my pit of sleep. Three o'clock? Four o'clock? The stench of vomit on my shirt and the sour taste in my mouth jerked me awake. I remembered Ma shaking me, coaxing me awake for supper, then telling me to rest. Like a black bell tolling against my head it came back to me: Slocum's beating of Jeremiah, and me grabbing the whip to beat Slocum to the ground, the revelation that Grandfather had violated Jeremiah's mother and sold her south after Jeremiah's birth, all for helping my own mother elope with Pa, and Grandfather's plan to sell Jeremiah, his own son. I needed to talk with William Henry. Then I remembered that William Henry was dead, and a mountain of pain crushed my chest all over again. I needed Pa and Mr. Heath, who worked every day to stop this kind of craziness. I wanted the world turned right side up.

I pulled myself up and reached for the water pitcher. Empty. The burning in my throat matched the pounding in my head. I slipped out my door and felt my way down the staircase, trying not to wake anyone. I wondered if every room in this God-forsaken house held ugly secrets, then pushed the thought away because even if they did, I did not want to know them.

I pulled the back door behind me and found the well in

the dark. Lowering the bucket, I willed it not to knock against the stone sides. Frozen grass blades and pine needles shot prickles through my bare feet, but I welcomed the pain as a rival to the one in my head. I gulped the icy water too fast. It burned my throat and I heaved in a fit of coughing.

That's when I looked up and saw the light from Grandfather's study window. I imagined him sitting there, smoking one of his expensive cigars, drinking his brandy, and making plans to sell Jeremiah, his own blood—my own blood—so he and Ma could decorate this stupid house. The fear and disbelief and grief that had numbed me fell away. Anger and shame for my grandfather exploded in its place, plugging every hole burned in my heart. I did not try to harness the red-black rage eating my body, my fingers, my mind. With no plan in my head except to tell the old man just what he was, I rounded the house, stumbled through the front door, and threw back the door to Grandfather's study.

"Yes? May I help you?" The voice wasn't Grandfather's. I blinked in the lamplight that shielded the face.

"Grandfather?" I stammered, taken off guard.

"Ah. You must be Robert," the voice said, followed by the rising of a figure from behind the desk. "I've looked forward to meeting you." Hesitation. "I'm Andrew Goforth."

I came stupidly to myself. "I was expecting to find my grandfather here."

"At four in the morning? I didn't realize he was such an early riser. I mustn't presume to use his study if he might be down."

"No—I mean, no, he isn't an early riser." I pushed my hair from my face. "I saw the light and thought—I meant to speak with him."

"I see." But he didn't.

"Sorry. I—sorry." I turned.

"Before you go, Robert, I want to say something. I heard of the—events—in the yard just before I arrived yesterday." I didn't turn around. I was in no mood for another Southern "gentleman's" lecture, especially a slaver hiding behind the Word of God. He hesitated. "I simply wanted to offer my hand and commend you for your act of mercy. It was a brave thing you did, and compassionate."

I turned to face him, not sure I'd heard right. I met his out-stretched hand and mumbled, "Thank you." My armor of anger cracked.

"It is rarely easy to live obedient to our conscience or our calling."

There was that word, *calling*, again. "Are you the preacher?"

"Yes." He smiled. "I've practiced law these last few years, and have only recently heard the call of God." He hesitated. "Perhaps you have your own calling?"

"I don't know what you mean."

"I don't mean anything, particularly. Only that it is re-freshing to meet someone so young with strong convictions and compassion for his fellow man. I was trying to encourage you, but I gather I'm bungling the job."

"No. I'm just not—not used to—" I stopped. I looked him square in the eye. "Do you believe that it is right to break laws that hurt people?"

"I've spent much time with the law, Robert. And now I spend much time with God. I can only repeat our Lord's words, that we render unto Caesar that which is Caesar's and unto God that which is God's."

"What if we're not sure what belongs to God and what belongs to Caesar?"

He removed his spectacles and polished them on his vest.

"Ah," he sighed, "there is the dilemma. I think we can only pray to be led of the Holy Spirit for that, and perhaps, to rely on the leading of those we trust as God's instruments."

"Like you?" I challenged.

"No. I am an instrument in training." Rev. Goforth walked to the window and pulled back the curtain. Lamplight reflected in its dark glass. "I believe your ear is as finely tuned to the Spirit's leading as mine, Robert. 'Be still,'" he quoted, "'and know that I am God: I will be exalted among the heathen, I will be exalted in the earth.'" Then he returned my gaze. "Ask yourself if the voice you hear exalts God or belittles Him."

I felt that a blindfold I didn't know I wore was being pulled from my eyes. Maybe it was the early hour, or the strangeness of finding this man, so different from Grandfather, in his study at just this time. But a little of the creeping in of wonder and strength I used to feel when William Henry was beside me, egging me on, returned. I stepped up. "I had a friend—my best friend. He was colored." Rev. Goforth didn't flinch, so I went on. "But I have to know—do people with colored skin in this life go to the same heaven as those with white skin? Does God make a difference between colored and white once He's looking at our bare souls? What is a soul, anyway? And if color doesn't matter then, why does it matter now? Does slavery end with death? Then, is death a good thing?"

Rev. Goforth didn't answer. He knelt on the carpet between us and reached for my hand. Dizzy, I went down on one knee. "Loving Father," he prayed. "Robert and I come to You, broken by this life. We long for that promised day, when there will be no more death or sorrow, no more crying or pain, when things as we know them are passed away. We are ready, Lord, to be instruments of Your peace, soldiers for Your kingdom. Show us the way. Bind Robert's broken heart, Lord. Cast out his sorrow and the dark spirit of fear. Fill him with Your Spirit of power, and of love, and of a sound mind. Make Your will clear to him and give him strength of character to go forward in Your name. Give him a thirst for Your Word. Guide him by the examples of the faithful found therein. Through Jesus Christ our Lord, Amen."

Small shards of anger fell away, like broken panes of glass. I felt, for a moment, like Moses, standing on Mt. Horeb, staring into the burning bush—as though Grandfather's study had turned into holy ground. Rev. Goforth stood, placed his hand on my shoulder, then turned away. "I'll be here at five every morning. If you want to join me for prayer, you are welcome."

I couldn't speak. I walked to my room, feeling strange in my own body. I didn't have answers to my questions, but for the first time it seemed like maybe there could be answers, and that maybe Rev. Goforth could help me find them. I felt like I'd walked through fire these last weeks, that nobody could ever take anything away from me again, nothing that mattered nearly as much as what had already been taken. So, I got down on my knees and prayed. For the first time since William Henry's death, I talked with God without fighting Him. And I believe He heard me.

I kept my distance from Grandfather and I kept my early morning meetings with Rev. Goforth over the next few days. We prayed together. Sometimes I prayed. That was new to me. At home, Pa had always prayed out loud. At night, when I was little, Ma made me recite prayers. But now I came to the God of heaven alone, and we talked.

Rev. Goforth didn't answer my questions straight on. But he gave me things to read, and more to think about. Once I asked him if the Lord might ask me to do something that He might not ask of somebody else, and he said, "Abraham was asked to leave his country for a new land. Moses was asked to lead a nation from bondage. Joshua challenged the Israelites, 'Choose you this day whom ye will serve . . . but as for me and my house, we will serve the Lord.' The Lord does not require us to be obedient on behalf of our brothers, but He requires us to choose for ourselves. We are responsible before God for our actions, or our lack of action—no one else's."

One afternoon Grandfather spoke of the South's "peculiar institution" of slavery at the dinner table and how it benefited both the owner and the owned. "It is what has enabled this country to grow agriculturally. It's God's gift to these United States and to the heathen people of Africa."

Rev. Goforth placed his fork across his plate. "It would, indeed, be difficult to imagine the South without slaves. I wonder how they've managed in the North?" Things like that confused me. Which side of the fence did he come down on? I wanted to ask him directly, but something held me back. I was beginning to heed the stirrings in my own soul. That was new, too, and the feeling that I could trust myself.

"Robert." Grandfather broke my wondering after Rev. Goforth left the dinner table. "I hear you're up before dawn with the preacher. I hope you're not going soft in the head, Boy. A little religion is a dangerous thing. Remember you have a future here ahead of you. No good getting your head in the clouds."

"Oh, Papa. I think it's wonderful that Robert has taken to the Reverend. Commitment at any age is a noble thing." Ma glowed, and I realized she was looking younger and prettier lately.

"Excuse me, Mr. Ashton." Jed Slocum stood at the dining room door, hat in hand.

"I'll thank you not to interrupt my dinner, Slocum," Grandfather spoke gruffly.

Slocum didn't like the rebuke. "I'm on my way to town and wondered if you wanted me to have that bill of sale drawn up."

"No hurry."

"January first will be here before my next trip to town."

"Step into my study, Slocum. I'll be there directly." Grandfather waited until Slocum left the room, then rose from his chair. Rebecca cleared the plates.

"Mr. Slocum still has difficulty keeping his place with you, Papa. I'm surprised you tolerate his insolence. I saw Dr. Lemly in church on Sunday. He asked if we'd taken Jed Slocum to task for the mix-up in your laudanum dosage."

"Hang Dr. Lemly and hang the laudanum! You're both to stop meddling. I spoke to Slocum, and it was just a misunderstanding."

"A misunderstanding! Papa, it nearly took your life! Mr. Slocum—"

"Not another word, Caroline. It's over. I can't do without Jed, and I'll not accuse him further. Let me remind you that I'm perfectly capable of looking to my own affairs." Grandfather spoke low, in his "this is final" voice.

Ma sighed. "All right, Papa. As you say." She folded her napkin and rose from the table. "I'm off to Mitchell House. Will you need me for a few hours?"

"No, my dear." Grandfather seemed glad to change the subject. "Enjoy yourself. It will do you good to get out of the house for a bit. Robert might like to go along."

"No, thanks. I need to work on my lessons."

Ma raised her eyebrows. "I'm delighted to see you so industrious, Robert. But a little fresh air and sunshine might do you good." I looked down at my plate. "Another time, then," she said.

As soon as they'd left the room, I shucked my shoes and crept toward Grandfather's study, pressing my ear to the door.

"I'll see Stephen Bailey to draw up the papers. The buyer's planning to run this coffle of slaves to a plantation in Louisiana January first. Jeremiah should fetch near twelve hundred dollars, and being shed of him will be a good lesson for the rest."

"I suppose," Grandfather said. "I don't want to know where he's going, and I don't want any word of this getting past these walls, Slocum. I'll not have Sara throwing fits before Christmas."

"I could take Jeremiah into town now. Jeff Dawson could hold him until New Year's Day. That would cut off the commotion."

"No, no. Let them have Christmas week together. I'd like to keep peace as long as possible. I want to make this a special Christmas for Caroline and Robert. If Sara gets her dander up she'll spoil the meals."

"I could take care of that."

"Keep your hands off my house slaves, Slocum. You have free rein in the fields, but not in the house. This is Caroline's domain."

A door closed above me, and I ducked behind the stairs, tugging on my shoes. Slocum came out a moment later, and Grandfather closed the door to his study. The pit of my stomach heaved, but I swallowed it down. I had to warn Jeremiah and Sara, or I had to stop the sale. Grandfather had no right to sell his own son like he was some of the livestock, and I didn't know if Ma even knew she had a half brother.

"Rebecca, bring my hat and muffler. I'm off to Mitchell House." Ma's voice came from above me. I met her on the stairs. "Robert!"

"I'll walk you to your carriage, Mother, and—I need a word with you."

"I'm so pleased with the fine manners and speech you've developed, Robert. I believe this stay is doing us both a great deal of good."

I held the front door for her. "Mother, I need your help."

"Of course, dear. What is it?" She seemed anxious to help. I dared hope.

"Grandfather is planning to sell Jeremiah."

"Jeremiah?"

"Nanny Sara's grandson." She lowered her head. "Your half bro—"

"Robert, that is no concern of mine, nor should it be yours. I can't imagine Papa telling you such things, and I trust you have not reduced yourself to listening at keyholes. Papa must handle his slaves in the way he sees fit. They are his property." I winced. She swept her eyes past me and continued. "You heard Rev. Goforth at dinner—it is the way things are in the South. Slavery and the discipline and orderliness of slaves is crucial for the development of the land, and the running of happy homes, safe for all."

"Andrew—Rev. Goforth didn't say all that, Mother. And Jeremiah is not just any slave. Do you know who his father is?"

Ma's face froze and her back grew rigid. "That is a rumor, Robert, and I'd like to know where you heard such filth. I'll thank you not to repeat it."

"It's true, isn't it?"

Ma tugged sharply at her gloves, pulling them over her wrists. "Such is the grief of every Southern woman, and the sin and shame of every Southern man. Sometimes life is ugly, Robert, but it is life just the same." She stepped up into the carriage and was gone.

I TRIED TO REACH JEREMIAH all the next day, to warn him. But Slocum was on a rampage. He'd taken to drinking more, followed by fits of temper, uncoiling his whip every chance he got. He worked Jeremiah like a mule and watched me like a bird he planned to shoot and stuff for Christmas. I couldn't go directly to Jeremiah for fear Slocum might become suspicious or trump up some excuse to beat him again. Jeremiah might lose his chance to run. I saw no other way to save him. And if I didn't save him, if I didn't try, I'd be as guilty as when I let William Henry go off with Jake Tulley.

It was December 21, four days before Christmas, eleven days until Jeremiah's sale. I made my way to the kitchen, waited until Rebecca had taken her basket to fill in the root cellar, then told Nanny Sara.

"You are setting a snare for me and my boy, Masta Robert. A snare, just as sure as you're standing here. Masta Marcus done promised me on my Ruby's selling that he always keep Jeremiah—never sell him."

"You can't trust my grandfather, Nanny Sara. I know what I heard. He's not going to keep that promise unless we can think of a way to make him."

"He promised." Nanny Sara drew into herself.

"Nanny Sara?" She didn't seem to hear me. As soon as

Rebecca returned Nanny Sara started humming to herself. "Nanny Sara?" But it was no use. She shut me out. Why did I think she'd be of any help, anyway? I slammed the kitchen door behind me.

That night I dreamed that a hundred white rabbits ran over my room. But I woke with a start to find Nanny Sara standing over me in her nightdress and shawl, whispering. "Next time you got something to say, don't say it in the kitchen. That Rebecca has big ears and a bigger mouth on her if she thinks it help her along."

I rubbed my eyes awake. "I thought you could help Jeremiah if you knew."

Nanny Sara shook her head. "Nothin' I can do. But you can take my boy to freedom."

I sucked in my breath. Somehow I'd known this would come, ever since I'd spoken to Jeremiah about getting free. I wished mightily Pa was here with me, or Joseph or William Henry. They'd know what to do. "I can't."

"You can take my boy to a safe house and maybe they send him on with Moses. It no good him running off by himself. It be better, two together. Besides, anybody catch sight of you they think you two white boys runnin' off. Nobody care about that."

"How do you know about safe houses?"

Nanny Sara smiled. "Old Nanny reads tea leaves. I read yours sometime."

"You don't read about safe houses in tea leaves." But she didn't answer. "I don't know any Moses. I told you what Granny Struthers said about Moses, but I don't know who that is."

Nanny Sara frowned. "Your daddy know?"

"I don't know." I knew so little about my pa or his work. "There's not enough time, even if I wrote to him."

"Then you do it. You take him."

"I can't do that!"

"If you can't help, my Jeremiah be sold." Nanny Sara waited, then said the thing I'd been thinking for three days. "He be your blood."

"I know. I know. Let me think." And that was why I could not understand my grandfather. Even though he held to slavery, how could he sell his own son? How could he live on the same land fourteen years and not even know him, not want to know him, not see the boy he'd grown into?

"Christmas Eve be the time Masta Marcus give out the slave bundles, next year's cloth and shoes, before dinner. After supper he go to church. After that only house slaves work Christmas week. By dark Mr. Jed be drunk in his cups. That be the time to run."

"But that's the day after tomorrow. I wouldn't know where to go!"

"There's them that know. They can tell you how to get away to the first safe house."

"Who?"

She shook her head. "It's better I don't know, or you, either. But I can pass the word of need. After you get to the first place they'll help you there. Don't nobody know all the way. It's too dangerous."

"That's what William Henry said." I wondered if that was true for Pa and Mr. Heath. I wondered that they were willing to risk everything time and again with so little to go on. "Let me think on it. Give me some time to think."

Nanny Sara squeezed my arm and padded away. I tossed and turned all night, frightened, worried, half dreaming, half praying. Five o'clock finally came. I washed and dressed by candlelight and met Rev. Goforth in Grandfather's study.

"You look as though you didn't sleep well, Robert." Rev. Goforth lit the lamps.

"No, sir," I said. I couldn't tell him. I didn't know if I could trust him with this. I didn't know where he stood on slavery, or if he'd understand stealing away.

The next two days tortured me. I didn't want to do it. I was scared, more scared than the night William Henry and I skunked those dogs. I knew that if I did this thing there was no turning back. Grandfather would disown me. Ma would live in shame, and there was no way I could explain it to Cousin Albert or Emily. I'd probably never see them again. Beyond that I was afraid to run all the way north, hungry, and through the dark, not knowing where I was going or how to get there, trusting to the goodness of strangers. It was winter, and although the snow hadn't started yet it would surely come soon. Our tracks would be plain as summer berries swimming in cream. I was afraid of the pattyrollers, of the hounds, of what might happen if we were caught. I was afraid for me and terrified for Jeremiah. What if I failed? What if Jeremiah was killed because of me? The talk at the dinner table didn't help.

Grandfather slammed his fist, making the crystal jump. "Hang those abolitionists! Murdering, thieving scoundrels!"

"Papa! Please! We have a guest." Ma tried to calm him down.

"I'm sure the good Reverend has heard that sentiment before, Caroline. Look at this newspaper! They've discovered that lunatic, John Brown, had a whole network of criminals at his disposal. Men in high places financed him and his band of cutthroats! Who knows what they'll find next?"

"But he's dead!"

"Hanging was too good for him! They've made a martyr out of him. They should have dragged his body through the streets and hung it on the courthouse wall. Let it be a lesson to those scoundrels!"

"Papa, you can't mean that. Please forgive him, Rev. Goforth. He's overwrought." Ma was close to wringing her hands. Rev. Goforth smiled feebly.

"I am not overwrought! And the other planters feel the same. We'll not take chances."

"What do you intend to do?" asked Rev. Goforth.

"Increase the pattyrollers—give them more liberty. We'll teach these uppity nigras not to run or hope that some misguided white traitor will 'steal them away to freedom.' Freedom! They wouldn't know what to do with it if they had it." Grandfather waved the paper in the air. "If they got hold of this foolishness, no telling what they'd do."

Ma probed the brooch at her neck. "I don't believe our slaves would turn against us, Papa." I looked at Ma and wondered what world she was living in that she could think such a thing.

"Not if I can help it. We'll increase the patrols starting Christmas Day. Fools won't go anywhere till they get shoes and a good meal in their bellies. Then we'll keep watch over our own and guard the roads and riverbanks. I'll send Slocum out for a turn."

I felt sick. What chance did Jeremiah have with or without my help? But Nanny Sara watched me from hooded eyes, waiting, I knew, for a sign that I was willing to help.

Just before bedtime on December 23, I stepped out onto the front verandah. Stars danced in their patterns and the cold December night only made their white lights burn brighter, icy cold and beautiful. I thought I was alone and leaned my fevered head against a pillar, glad for the frost. "What do I do, Lord? What do I do?" I prayed out loud.

"Robert?" It was Rev. Goforth, rising from his seat on the steps. "I heard your voice and didn't want to startle you. Beautiful night, isn't it?"

"Yes, sir," I said, glad that I hadn't prayed all my heart out loud.

"Robert," he began, hesitantly. "I've noticed that something seems to be troubling you. I don't want to pry, but if there is anything I can do to help, I'd be honored."

"Thank you, sir. It's just—" Just what? What could I say? What dared I say? "Have you ever wondered what God wants of you? I mean, have you ever felt that God asked you to do something you weren't ready for, that you were afraid to do?"

"Almost always." I heard his sad smile in the dark. "I think that's how God gets us to grow. He gives us tasks beyond our ability. And then He says, 'My grace is sufficient for thee: for my strength is made perfect in weakness.'"

"But how does He give me that strength? How do I know I can do it?"

"You can't do anything alone, Robert. You have to trust. Trusting is the hard part. Paul said, 'I can do all things through Christ which strengtheneth me.' He never claimed to do great things alone."

I sighed. I wasn't feeling strength from anybody. "What do you think of slavery, Rev. Goforth?"

He didn't say anything for a minute. We both knew a great deal hung on his answer. "Slavery comes in many forms. Some people, like the Negroes here, are slaves to other people. Some of us are slaves to sin, or worldliness, or greed. I aim to live as a slave to Christ, because only then am I free."

"That didn't exactly answer my question."

"We're all in some kind of bondage, Robert. Most of us have the freedom to choose that slavery, whether we realize it or not. Are you free to love, to help your neighbor?"

"I am. But who is my neighbor? My cousins? My grand-father? Ma? The slaves here at Ashland? Helping one gets you in trouble with helping the others."

"They are all your neighbor. Do you remember the story of the Good Samaritan? He helped the neediest of them all, the man who had been robbed and beaten. He ministered to the desperate need, saw to it that others helped when he couldn't, then came back to check on his progress. That has always been a tremendous example to me. He continued his giving until the entire need was met."

"The entire need," I repeated. "That means you have to choose who to help, and that might be different people at different times."

"Remember Isaiah's words, 'Is not this the fast that I have chosen? to loose the bands of wickedness, to undo the heavy burdens, and to let the oppressed go free, and that ye break every yoke? Is it not to deal thy bread to the hungry, and that thou bring the poor that are cast out to thy house? when thou seest the naked, that thou cover him; and that thou hide not thyself from thine own flesh?'"

My heart beat faster. Did Rev. Goforth know what he was saying? "'Let the oppressed go free' . . . my 'own flesh,'" I whispered. "What if helping the people who need you most gets you into trouble? If it's against the law?"

"Remember Queen Esther? She knew that by approaching the king without permission she might lose her life. But the lives of her people were at stake. Her uncle reminded her that she may have been placed in that position for 'such a time as this.' I think all of us have defining moments in our lives, when we are allowed to make a choice that carries us down one path or another. Sometimes they are choices between good and evil, right or wrong. But they are choices that change our lives forever. They decide who we will be or what we will do for a long time to come."

I turned away. I remembered thinking once that the Bible was like a great, long journal written since the beginning of time, a hiding place for the secrets of life. Maybe Rev. Goforth believed that, too.

"I know you are struggling, Robert. Let the Lord prevail. Ask Him to show you the way. He will not fail you." I could not see his face, but I felt the hands of my friend reach for mine. It reminded me of William Henry, reaching for my hand the night he spoke to me in the dark, the night he'd said more to me than I'd understood at the time. That night I slept straight through, a dreamless sleep. Early Christmas Eve morning I made my way to the kitchen. I asked Nanny Sara for a cup of chocolate, and whispered, "I'll do it."

The house buzzed with Ma's excitement. She bustled in and out of every room, sometimes singing, sometimes shouting orders. She'd spent a fortune on her crimson ball gown, and Grandfather and I had been fitted for coats with tails. All our clothes had been brushed up for the holiday round of parties and outings. Ma fussed over every little thing, anxious that all be "perfect" for her first ball since she was a girl. So when it came time to give out the annual Christmas bundles to the slaves, Ma tapped her toe and clearly resented the time taken.

Just before the noon meal, Slocum and all of Ashland's slaves were called to the front lawn. Grandfather stood between Ma and me on the verandah steps. "I thank you all for the service you've rendered to me and my family this year," Grandfather began. "Some of you proved to be good workers. I trust you'll all work harder in the new year. Enjoy this Christmas week with your families, and thank God that you can look forward to a home and food in your bellies for another year."

Grandfather motioned for Old George and Nanny Sara to carry the bundles down the steps. "The bundles aren't quite as big as I'd expected, but y'all get your shoes and cloth enough for a shift or shirt. You know that north sixty acres didn't harvest well. I'm sure you all can improve that next year. George, you go on now and hand out those bundles. You all have a Merry Christmas."

A chorus of "Thank you, Masta Ashton! Thank you, Miz Caroline," and "God bless you, Masta Marcus" followed Grandfather and Ma into the house. I felt ashamed to sit down to my rich dinner.

"Robert, you're not eating!" Ma protested. "You'll need your strength for the midnight ball!" Before I could answer she chided, "You should have let me teach you those dancing steps. Emily will be expecting a waltz."

"One thing you'll learn, my Boy, is that it is not wise to disappoint the ladies!" Grandfather twinkled as he spoke, a rare thing for him. "Don't you agree, Rev. Goforth?"

Rev. Goforth's color flared. "It is not something I have much experience with, Mr. Ashton."

"Oh! I beg to differ, my fine young Reverend. By refusing to join us at the ball you are gravely disappointing our lovely young ladies. Every belle in the county will be decked to the hilt and ready to dance until dawn," Grandfather wheedled.

"I meant I don't dance. I—"

"And for that I will extend your sincere apologies to the ladies, Reverend. I know how you members of the clergy frown upon our heathen customs. But do you really think such hardness of heart is in keeping with your calling, in keeping with the spirit of this season—this Christian season?"

"Oh, Papa! Hush! You are embarrassing us all! Don't pay him any mind, Rev. Goforth," Ma fussed. "But it is true, the ladies are anxious to get to know you better."

Rev. Goforth ignored them both, and didn't fall into a fuss about dancing. I thought well of him for it. "Rev. Cleary is expecting me to fill his pulpit tomorrow. I would not go back on my word."

"Of course not!" Ma sputtered. "Papa just means we'll all miss you. But you'll be back soon. You'll be able to make better acquaintance of our young ladies after your Watch Night service, New Year's eve."

Rev. Goforth smiled uncomfortably.

"I'm not sure I'm up to the midnight ball," I said, holding my stomach.

"Whatever do you mean, Robert?" Ma asked.

"I'm not feeling so well."

"You do look a little green around the gills," Grandfather observed. "You're not frightened by the prospect of a ballroom full of pretty girls, too, are you, Boy?"

"No, sir," I lied. "It's just my stomach."

"Nothing a little rest and a good nip of brandy won't cure."

"Yes, sir." I grimaced.

"Really, Papa! We'll enjoy a light supper at five and then dress for church. If we leave by seven thirty we can easily reach the church by eight," Ma said. "Rev. Goforth, after the service Albert's driver will take you to Rev. Cleary's. Mrs. Cleary wrote saying their housekeeper is staying on to welcome you."

Rev. Goforth nodded. He looked grateful to talk about something else.

"The rest of us will go straight to Mitchell House. I'm having our evening clothes delivered there so we won't have to come back through the weather. Old George says he feels snow in his bones, and he's never been wrong."

I passed my hand over my forehead, as though I were tired.

"Maybe you'd better lie down, Robert. You've barely tasted your food, and I so want you to enjoy this evening."

"Yes, Mother. Please excuse me." I rose, and my fine manners alarmed Ma more than my poor eating.

"I'll tell Nanny Sara to send you up some mint tea. That might settle your stomach."

"Get some sleep!" Grandfather boomed. "I have a surprise this evening. You don't want to miss it!"

I nodded weakly and walked from the room, glad to set the stage for my coming illness, glad to get out of their view, hoping to think through all I needed to do. My biggest worries were for food, warmth, and money—in case we needed help. I could dress in layers and wear a blanket. I didn't have much money, and there was no one to ask for it. I trusted Nanny Sara to come up with directions, at least to the first safe house.

Nanny Sara brought me the mint tea herself. Inside her apron she'd slipped a chicken leg and a large piece of cake. "You need your strength this night, Masta Robert. You eat up now."

"Did you send the word of need out?"

She nodded. "Your black, Stargazer, be fed and saddled to go just as soon as the others leave for services."

"And Jeremiah?"

"He be ready."

"What about Jed Slocum?"

Nanny Sara smiled. "We take care of him. He be asleep in his cups by then."

"But what if he isn't?" I was more afraid of Slocum than of the unknown things that lay ahead.

"Old George still have some of Masta Marcus's laudanum. Enough in his drink and Mister Jed won't wake up till Christmas Day." She grew serious. "But you and my boy have to be mighty far from here by then." There was a sound outside the door. Nanny Sara pressed her finger to her lips. Louder, she said, "You let Nanny Sara know what else you need, Masta Robert. We gonna get you well for that ball." Then she whispered, "Dress warm."

I nodded and tried to breathe as Nanny Sara padded down the stairs. The fear in my chest kept it tight. I ate, then stuck my finger down my throat. I left the mess in my chamber pot. I needed to convince Ma that I was too sick to go to church and the ball. Even with all my worry, I slept through part of the afternoon. Ma knocked softly and woke me.

"Robert, I thought you'd be dressed for supper. Nanny Sara just rang the bell."

I didn't have to feign sleepiness. "Sorry, Ma. I'm so sleepy."

"What is that foul smell?"

"I spit up. I'll carry it down later. I just don't feel so good."

"Don't be silly. I'll call for George to take it out. What's ailing you, Robert? Do you have a fever?" She laid her hand across my forehead. "It doesn't seem so."

"My stomach. I don't think I can eat anything. I just want to sleep."

"Well, you can't miss church or the ball. It would spoil Christmas Eve!"

"I'm sorry, Ma. Maybe I'll feel better later."

"I just can't believe it. Rest during supper and I'll check on you after. I do hope you're not coming down with anything serious. Maybe I should send for Dr. Lemly."

"No, Ma. I just need to sleep."

She tucked me in and brushed her lips across the top of

my head. "Sleep on, then, dear. I'll check on you in an hour or so."

I felt bad for deceiving Ma, but guessed that was mild compared to what else I planned to do.

Ma, Grandfather, and Rev. Goforth all stood over me an hour later. "I can't abide the thought of leaving you here on Christmas Eve, Robert. I'll simply have to stay home with you."

"Nonsense!" Grandfather boomed. "You can't miss your own ball, Caroline! Besides, I have a surprise waiting for you at the church. You must go! I insist! Robert's not a babe in cloths. Leave him to sleep until we get back."

"But the ball doesn't even begin until ten! The banquet starts at midnight and the guests may not leave until dawn— not then if we get snowed in!"

"The snow is already falling. I was just outside," Rev. Goforth said. "If I wasn't expected in Rev. Cleary's pulpit tomorrow morning I'd be glad to come back and stay with you, Robert."

"No," I said. "I'd feel bad about that." Rev. Goforth could have no part in this.

Grandfather clapped Rev. Goforth on the shoulder. "No, you must go on, Reverend. Nanny Sara and Old George are both here if Robert needs anything."

"I just don't know what to do." Ma sat on the bed and fussed with my covers.

"Go on to church and Mitchell House, Ma. I'll be all right once I get more sleep. I'll probably be up again sometime tomorrow. If I need help I'll call Old George."

"It's settled then." Grandfather pulled Ma to her feet. "You've got to get well, Robert. The surprise I have is for you as well as your mother. Perhaps it's just as well she get first sight of it. But you must be up and about by tomorrow—Christmas Day—my orders!"

"Yes, sir." I smiled weakly.

"All right, then," Ma relented. "Sleep well, dear. I'll be home early tomorrow morning or surely by tomorrow noon, even if the snow is deep. Albert has more than one sleigh, doesn't he, Papa?"

"I'm certain he does. Now let's get dressed for church and give this boy some peace!"

On their way out the door Rev. Goforth took my hand. His eyes probed mine. "I'll pray for you, Robert."

"Thank you, sir." But I looked away, afraid my eyes might say too much.

An hour later I heard the front door close and the carriage horses trot away. I raced to the window and tried to catch a glimpse as it passed up the drive. "Good-bye, Ma. I love you," I whispered. "I hope someday you'll understand and forgive me." But I didn't believe she would.

I DRESSED IN TWO LAYERS of warm clothing, topped with a vest, a coat, a muffler, riding gloves, and a warm cap. On my way downstairs I crept into Ma's room. Moonlight spilled through the open curtains and across the floor. The air smelled like Ma—like her new toilet water—and it made me miss her already. Ma's everyday drawstring reticule lay on the dressing table. I'd never taken money from anyone. I wondered if the Lord looked kindly on this action, but I couldn't stop to ponder. The little gold clasp of her change purse came undone easily, and I poured the gold pieces into my palm—ten gold pieces, each worth twenty dollars. It must be Grandfather's money. Ma never had so much at home. I laid the purse down.

My hand was on the door handle. I couldn't do it. I couldn't go off and take Ma's money and not let her know that I was all right. I couldn't go without telling her again that I loved her and not to worry. Who knew if I'd even make it home alive? I lit the lamp at her writing desk and drew a sheet of paper from the drawer, then penned this note. "Ma, I love you and am sorry to take off like this without telling you. But it is Christmas. We've never been apart from Pa at Christmas and we are all he has. I'm going home and will see you when you come home. Don't worry about me. I took money for the trip from your purse. Love, Robert."

She'd figure out soon enough that I'd helped Jeremiah run. But at least she'd have another story to tell if she wanted one. And at least she'd know I was the one that took her money. I didn't want to get Old George or Nanny Sara or Rebecca in trouble for stealing. I folded the paper and left it beneath the gold watch Grandfather had given me. She'd see it, and I doubted Grandfather would want me to have the watch now. I surely didn't want to risk dropping it while helping Jeremiah like I'd done with William Henry. It could be the end of us both.

I met Nanny Sara in the dark saving room behind the dining room. "Jeremiah and Stargazer be waiting on you in the barn. Listen careful, and remember the way. Take the road to the church. Keep to the woods till the doors close and the singin' starts up. Then follow that road till you come to a fork. Take the right fork, what runs along the Yadkin. Stay close on its banks till you make sure they's no pattyrollers out, then go on to Mount Pleasant. They be a white Methodist church up the hill there. Make sure everybody gone. Then you boys hide in the bell tower. They's a man will come and take you the next way."

"Who?"

Nanny Sara shook her head. "Don't know. Don't need to know. Put this tin of lucifers in your pocket. Keep it dry or they be no good. Look in your saddlebag for food; the other one totes oats. They be a gourd of water, too. Fill it fresh, often as you can." She nodded in the moonlight. "Be fast. Watch your tracks. Come morning they be looking for two boys traveling together."

I swallowed. My heart beat faster. What hadn't I thought of? "Slocum?"

"Dead to this world. Dead to this world. He drank that

whiskey and laudanum like a baby sucks milk. Don't you worry your head about that man. We keep him fed and drunk." On impulse I hugged Nanny Sara good-bye. "God bless you, Masta Robert. I know my boy be in good hands. You your father's son."

I hoped she was right. "Are you coming to the barn to say good-bye to Jeremiah?"

She shook her head. "My grandbaby and I done said our good-byes. Once more'll break this ole heart. You go 'long now and watch that you not be seen."

"If there is any way we can get word to you that we're safe, we will."

She shook her head again. "Not hearing is good news. Not hearing means you on the freedom train and nobody's draggin' you back." Gently, she pushed me out the door. The frigid air caught in my throat. Powdery white snowflakes brushed my face, and I looked up, searching for stars. No stars tonight. But the moon was a pale light, and the fine layer of white powder on the ground helped me see.

The scene in the barn was something out of the Christmas story. Old George held the reins of Stargazer, saddled and ready to ride. Jeremiah, wrapped against the cold, clutched a lantern and his small bundle of clothing, which could have been a baby in the lamplight. How sacred, how holy this mission looked to me, and how dangerous.

Old George wrapped me in a bear hug and breathed a prayer over me. I swung up into my saddle. Jeremiah grabbed my arm, swinging up after me. Stargazer pawed the floor. Old George put out the lamp, lifted the bar, and pushed open the heavy wooden door. He swatted Stargazer on the rump and we were off.

It felt strange, riding off with Jeremiah behind me. But

Stargazer didn't flinch, and I wondered if he sensed the danger. We kept far from the quarters and the drive, finally coming out on the road a quarter mile from the house. I knew the postings of the pattyrollers. I'd overheard Grandfather giving Slocum orders for the extra men he'd hired. I just hoped they'd keep to their routes.

By the time we neared the church, the snow fell in earnest. The large white flakes became smaller, drier, stinging our eyes and cheeks as we rode into the wind. I reined in Stargazer. We stood for a moment at the edge of the woods. Horses, tethered with their buggies to the hitching posts, pawed the ground in front of the little church. The whitewashed doors were closed and wreathed with pine. Lamplight glowed from the windows, inviting weary travelers, but not us. As we walked past we heard the chorus of "Oh, come all ye faithful, joyful and triumphant . . ." Part of me wished I was inside, safe and warm, singing beside Ma. And part of me tingled with the daring and excitement of what we'd begun.

Just beyond the church's glow, I dug my heels into Stargazer, and we began a cautious trot. Ahead of us a horse pounded the road. Before I could pull into the ditch we nearly collided with the charging horse and rider. Stargazer reared and kicked the air. I clung to his neck. Jeremiah clung to me, and we both nearly tumbled off. The other rider shouted, "My apologies! Are you all right?"

"Yes!" I shouted and spurred Stargazer forward, away from the stranger, scared by our near miss, and terrified that we might be caught so close to our beginning. But even as we raced ahead, something called me back until I reined in Stargazer, and turned, riding back toward the church.

"What are you doing?" The panic rose in Jeremiah's voice with each word.

"That rider. I think I know him."

"So what? We don't want to see nobody we know! Are you trying to get us killed? Turn around!"

"Quiet! It will only take a minute."

Fifty feet from the church we pulled into the woods and I climbed down. I handed the reins to Jeremiah and whispered, "Take these. I'll be right back."

"Robert! Don't do this!"

"Be quiet! I'll come back." I crept through the trees toward the church, drawn by the familiarity of the figure tying his horse to the post and slapping the snow from his coat. The church doors opened then and the man looked up. Light spilled onto the snow and across my father's face. Grandfather, proud and benevolent, his arm circling Ma, stood, framed by the open door. I saw Ma gasp, "Charles!" then run into his arms. This was the gift, the surprise my Grandfather had promised. How he had convinced my father to come I didn't know. But it was a Christmas miracle, and I wanted more than anything to rush into his arms, too, to give it all over to him and let him make things right.

I stepped back into the shadows, because I knew that time was gone. Grandfather would never back down. I'd made my choice, and Jeremiah's life rested in my hands. There was no turning back. I could only pray that one day they would all understand that I had to do this, for Jeremiah, for William Henry, for me. I was bringing disgrace to my family just when there was the possibility of uniting us all. "Give me liberty or give me death." Did the choice have to be so hard?

CHAPTER

Nineteen

THE MEMORY OF PA'S FACE and Ma's unbridled joy haunted me with Stargazer's every hoofbeat. I pushed the sadness and longing behind me and set my jaw for the job ahead.

Now that we'd ridden beyond the church, we knew that most people were either sitting in the congregation or at home for the night, keeping out of the cold and snow. We took courage and lit the lantern. Jeremiah held it behind me, and we made better time with its light.

Snow fell faster and harder. After nearly an hour the road forked. We'd started down the right fork when Stargazer shied. Jeremiah spoke in my ear, "Look! A light ahead!" Sure enough, a lantern bobbed toward us. "We got to get off this road!" Jeremiah shuttered our lantern and I reined Stargazer off the road, into some trees. We waited till the rider passed. "Think that a pattyroller?"

"I don't know, but we can't risk it. We'd best stay off the road." So we slid down the bank and hugged the river as best we could. Slowed to a walk, we turned the lantern shutter low, knowing that homes might be anywhere along the river.

"How far Granny Sara say this Mount Pleasant be?"

I shook my head. "She didn't! Did you come this way before?"

"Not this way." Two long hours must have passed as we

picked our way along the bank. We shivered through our wet and heavy layers of clothing. I shielded my face and eyes as best I could against the piercing sleet. Crusted snow inched upward from the ground and showed no sign of stopping. "Do you think we missed it?" Jeremiah voiced my own fear.

I shook my head and whispered, "I hope not. Dear God, please show us the way to take." We walked on for another mile or so—it was hard to tell how far in the dark and storm. Cold settled in my chest. My feet had long since gone numb, and I feared frostbite. What made me think we could do this alone? We'd gone only a few miles, and fewer hours. How could we run hundreds of miles and not get caught, or lost, or—?

That is when I heard the church bell, chiming somewhere in the night. At first I thought my mind had conjured it. But it came again and again, ringing the midnight, ringing in Christmas morning!

"Lawd A'mighty!" Jeremiah whispered it like a prayer, and I knew those were the perfect words for this perfect gift. We stumbled toward the bells, thanking God. Even Stargazer's spirits seemed to lift, and he stepped along more lively. When the tolling of the bells was directly above us and to our right, we climbed the hills and entered some woods. We stopped at the edge of the pines surrounding the church, peering through the dark, trying to see if anyone was there. The church was well lit, so we stepped back into the trees and waited.

After a time the doors burst open and carolers tumbled out into the night, their lanterns bright, their voices raised in "Hark the herald angels sing, glory to the newborn King!" My heart beat faster inside my chest. I had to pull back the reins on Stargazer and whisper into his neck. Even he wanted to trot up and join the happy scene. One by one the buggies and sleighs filled, rugs tucked around the travelers. The horses wore bells on their harnesses, stamping joy. Off they trotted into the night, the carolers singing and clapping in time to the music they made. The church bells rang themselves out. The last shining lantern slid through the door, carried by a tall man, wrapped so against the cold that I couldn't see his face. But he held his lantern up to the night and peered into the trees. Stargazer snorted. I muzzled him with my hands. We stepped back.

The man hesitated, then turned the church corner into the cemetery, and held his lantern high again. "Anybody there?" He swung his lantern twice. "I say, anybody there?" I wondered if this was a signal for us to come, or if he'd seen something in the trees and grown suspicious. Jeremiah must have wondered, too, because he crouched closer to me. We couldn't take a chance. We'd been told to wait in the bell tower. What if he wasn't the person we were supposed to meet? But what if he was, and we were missing our chance for help? The man walked among the stones for a time, then turned and took a path through the woods. We waited until we no longer heard the crunch of his boots in the snow, until no light bobbed through the trees.

Finally, we stepped from the shelter of the pines. Sleet picked our faces. I was afraid to leave Stargazer alone in the woods, unsure of where we could tether him that he wouldn't be seen. So we led him up the plank steps and into the church. The vestibule was still warm from the fire that had burned in the stove; we were glad to shed our wet clothes and huddle near its banked embers.

"It don't seem right, bringing a horse into church," Jeremiah said.

"We can't leave him outside. Somebody might see him. Anyhow, if the baby Jesus was born in a stable with animals, then it's all right to bring the animals into the church," I reasoned. Jeremiah wasn't sure. "Wish we could start up this fire. The cold's seeping in fast."

"Somebody might see the smoke and come to check," Jeremiah argued. "Too risky."

"I guess. Nanny Sara said to wait in the bell tower, but that's no good with Stargazer in here. And it'll be colder up there."

"When this sleet stops, every step in the snow will be clear as a banner, pointin' our way." Jeremiah hedged, then said, "Maybe Stargazer ought to wait in the woods. I could tie him to a pine and go check in the morning. Sleet's not so bad there, and he'd be sheltered from the wind."

I knew Jeremiah was right. I just hated to take the risk of him being seen, and it felt good to have Stargazer near me. But if anybody came into the church we couldn't hide in the bell tower with a horse in the vestibule. "I'll take him. No sense getting your prints out there, too. Just let him get warm through." After a time I wrapped up again and clumped out into the crusted snow. The sleet had nearly stopped. Four, maybe five inches covered the ground. I found a tight little den among the pines for Stargazer, and tied him to a tree. "I'll be back early for you. I love you, Stargazer. I'm glad you're here." I nuzzled his neck and left him with handfuls of oats taken from our bag, then crunched backward into my footprints toward the church, as best I could, with no light. Jeremiah and I huddled by the stove until the cast iron lost its last bit of heat.

"Maybe we ought to go to the tower, now. Somebody's bound to come." I said it, but wasn't so sure. Why would anybody come out on a night like this if they didn't know for certain they needed to? We pulled the hemp rope set in the paneling against the wall. A narrow door swung out on rusted

196

hinges. The smell of cedar filled our nostrils and we climbed up and around, up and around, our hands braced against the roughly hewn timbers. We pushed open the top door and, in the darkness, felt our way into the small slave gallery.

The bell tower sat between two sets of backless plank benches. I knew this was as close as slaves could sit to the white churchgoers or their preacher. In summer this gallery would be stifling. In winter it was freezing. Two small windows peered into the night. The snow and sleet must have stopped; we heard no "ping, ping" against the glass. Once inside the tower we pulled the door closed behind us and climbed the narrow ladder toward the bell. We could sit on either side of the ladder top's boxed platform, but the wind blew through the slats of the tower.

"We can't stay here long, Robert. We'll freeze to death." Jeremiah shivered so I could barely understand him.

"Maybe someone will come soon."

"We been saying that for an hour or more. Know what I'm thinking? I reckon that man with the lantern, the bell ringer, must have been the one looking for us. And since he thinks nobody here, he won't come again."

I shivered, too. This was harder than I thought it would be. "Let's go sleep on those plank pews. At least we can roll up in our blankets and stretch out, and eat some of that lunch Nanny Sara packed. If nobody comes soon, maybe we'd best go on."

So down we trudged to the gallery, huddling close in our clothes and blankets, shivering till I thought my bones might crack. I tried praying, but I couldn't keep my mind in one place. I kept thinking about Pa being there at the church, dancing with Ma at Mitchell House, and coming to Ashland for the first time since he and Ma had eloped. And how I wouldn't be there. What would he think? And then I remembered the note, how I'd said I was going home to Pa. I pulled my fingers through my hair, wishing I could turn back time and know all this before we ran. But even if Pa had come sooner I didn't see how he would have been able to help Jeremiah. I didn't see how we could have done anything else but run.

I tried praying again. I didn't feel the power that I'd felt on my knees beside Rev. Goforth. I was grateful Rev. Goforth wouldn't know about me until he got back from Rev. Cleary's. By then they'd all know I'd gone, they'd all have read my note, and they'd know that Jeremiah had run. I wondered what he'd think about it all. I wondered if he and Pa would take to each other. Sleep must have beat out my wonderings because the next thing I knew, bright sunlight streamed through the gallery's windows and danced in patches across my face.

"Wake up, Mr. Robert! It's full daylight! Wake up!" Jeremiah shook me till my teeth rattled. I tried to push him off, but I was so cold nothing worked right.

"Quit!" I finally blurted. "I'm awake! And quit calling me Mister!"

"We got to get out of here. It's Christmas Day and somebody's like to come by the church for sure."

"Okay. Okay, but we don't know where to go."

"Anyplace but here. I'm gettin' the willies settin' here. We shoulda made tracks before daylight." We rolled our blankets and were about to pull on our shoes.

"I hope Stargazer's—" The latch clicked downstairs. We froze.

"Hello?" A voice called from below. We didn't move, but motioned each other toward the bell tower. The heavy church door closed. "Anybody here?" Silence. We picked up our bags and crawled backward toward the tower. "Hello? Anybody leave a horse outside?" My heart caught, and I knew in that moment that whatever happened I'd lost Stargazer. Jeremiah jerked my sleeve. We pulled open the tower door, praying it couldn't be heard below. Jeremiah crawled in first. We heard feet stomping the snow off boots below us, then footsteps shuffling toward the front of the church. We pulled the door behind us and held the latch, afraid to set it into place. "Don't look like anybody's here." We couldn't tell if the voice was talking to itself or to someone else.

The footsteps came back on themselves. We dared hope they would leave the church. But they stopped too soon. The downstairs door to the slave gallery swung open on its rusted hinges. "Hello?" Jeremiah flew silently up the ladder in his bare feet and pulled up the saddlebags. I couldn't be so quiet but tried to match my steps on the ladder to the steps on the stairs below. As the upstairs door to the gallery opened, Jeremiah and I curled ourselves tightly into the eaves on either side of the bell's platform.

The footsteps searched the slave gallery, and then the tower door swung outward. "Anybody up there?" The ladder creaked and I knew we were done. I closed my eyes. One rung, two, three, four, five. Suddenly a voice spoke right next to me. "Why didn't y'all answer me?" My eyes popped open and a boy, not more than eleven, stared in my face, exasperated. I tried to make my tongue work, but it felt tangled inside my mouth. "Are you all deaf that you didn't hear me calling?"

"We was scared." Jeremiah found his voice first.

The boy grinned. "Well, there ain't nothing scary about me. Come on down. We've got to git."

"We thought it was a grown man that was supposed to come," I said.

"That'd be Pa. He did come, last night, but you wasn't

199

here. Y'all sure look white for runaways. Well, ya never know. Come on. Time's wasting." We scrambled down the ladder, and down the gallery steps, pulling on coats and shoes. Stargazer pawed the snow beside the hitching post.

Jeremiah and I looked at each other, chagrined that Stargazer had been so easy to find. "Nobody came last night. We've been here ever since the service let out at midnight."

The boy placed his hands on his hips. "Pa looked for you, but didn't see nobody. So he came on home. Trouble is, he fell in a gopher hole in the woods and broke his leg. He'll be laid up a while."

"Maybe that was the man with the lantern last night."

"Pa said he searched the cemetery—thought he'd heard a horse, but didn't see nobody, and nobody come forward."

"We saw him," I said, "but we weren't sure if he was the person we were supposed to meet. We'd been told to wait in the bell tower."

The boy looked fit to be tied. "Well, did you see him raise his lantern and swing it twice?"

"Yes."

The boy shook his head. "That's the sign! You could have been on your way last night! It's riskier now. But you can't stay over. Too many folks comin' and goin' at our house Christmas week."

"We didn't know." My heart sank.

"You two sure are green at this."

"It's my first time," I admitted. Jeremiah looked away.

"Well, don't worry none. I done it lots. You boys get on your horse so we don't have no more footprints than mine, and I'll lead. What's his name?"

"Stargazer."

"Does he pull sleigh?"

"I don't know. I never tried him. Where are we going?" I wasn't sure I wanted to trust this boy.

"Going home. Ma'll whip you up some breakfast, and then we'll go on. Would have been better to go by dark, but there's a way. It's Christmas Day so folks won't be surprised to see folks visiting one another."

We followed the boy through the woods, taking the same path we'd seen the man walk last night. Stargazer crunched through the frozen snow, maybe a half mile. As we neared the farmhouse, I drew images in my brain of a warm kitchen, a hearty breakfast, and a soft bed. But we never even made it to the back door.

"Y'all wait in the barn. I'll bring your breakfast out, and we'll get you on your way."

"Right away?" I said, smelling the wood smoke pour from the chimney.

The boy rolled his eyes at us. "They'll be out looking for you in no time if they ain't already. You're lucky the snow covered your early tracks."

"How did you know we were coming?" I asked.

"Didn't know who," the boy said. "Just got word to expect some Christmas packages from nearby. Christmas week's a good time to run, if you got to run in winter." The boy pulled open the barn door and slapped Stargazer on the rump. "Feed's in the sack. Help yourself."

"Thanks. Say, what's your name?" I asked.

"No names," the boy snapped, and closed the barn door.

"Well, we off to a grand start," Jeremiah said.

Tired as I was, I loved brushing Stargazer. The long brush strokes eased me as much as they soothed him. Jeremiah waited in the loft. It was one thing to explain a strange white boy in your barn, but a runaway slave was something else. It wasn't that

Jeremiah was black that made him noticeable—he was as white as the boy that had led us into the barn. It was the fearful cast in his eyes and the way he shied from the eyes of most whites that made him stand out, looked like he had something to hide. I wondered how it was possible to disguise such a thing.

Before I'd finished brushing Stargazer the boy brought back tin plates heaped with sausages, grits, stewed apples, and fried eggs. Maybe coming on Christmas Day was a good thing. We wolfed it down, every bite. The lady of the house even wrapped up lunches of bacon, apples, and a loaf of bread.

"Best not eat all that today," the boy cautioned. "Sometimes it's got to last a week. Just depends on how free you can travel or how long you got to wait till the next stop can take you on your way."

"Won't they give us food?" I asked.

Jeremiah knew more than I did. "Sometimes they don't got it to give, and sometimes they don't want to do no more than they're doing. Sometimes, it ain't safe to stop. Then, we on our own. We got to expect to be on our own, and just be glad if anybody helps." I had a lot to learn.

The boy harnessed his sleigh to Stargazer while we ate, then pointed to Jeremiah. "You'll have to ride on the floor. We'll cover you with bearskin." He pointed to me. "You ride with me, and if anybody stops us or asks, you're my cousin, Harlem, visiting from Rowan County. We're on our way to pay our Christmas respects to Aunt Matilda in Greensboro."

"I don't like making Jeremiah ride on the floor."

Jeremiah cut me off. "No. It's a good plan."

The boy sighed, like I was stupid. "Two white boys out joyriding on Christmas Day in a sleigh is one thing. Two white boys joyriding with a near white colored is something worth noticing."

I looked away. "What about Stargazer?"

"We'll black that star on his forehead and add a white patch on his rump. Then we'll see what they say at the next station. He can't stay here. Somebody must know where you got this horse."

"He's my—"

"I don't want to know!" The boy cut me off. "A body can't be made to tell what he don't know."

Jeremiah tugged me toward the sleigh. We made a pillow of our saddlebags, then Jeremiah curled tight on the sleigh floor. We tucked a bearskin rug over him, and tight around our legs. The sleigh made a smoother ride than a wagon, but I didn't envy him. The boy and I hunched our knees to keep them from smashing Jeremiah's face.

"How far?" I asked, when we'd ridden a good hour.

"Settle back," the boy ordered. "It's near thirty miles, all told. Be dark when we get there, I hope."

"We're not going to the mountains?" I'd heard that slaves sometimes ran there to hide and make their way north.

"Not now. Pattyrollers and bounty hunters on every pass. They expect runaways to take to the hills, especially since John Brown's hanging. They won't expect you to go east, then north. Besides, you could get holed up in those mountains for weeks if snow comes in deep."

Stargazer pulled true and smooth, like he was born to the harness, like he understood his role in all of this and would not let us down.

I must have dozed, for the sun moved across the sky. Jeremiah lay so still I wanted to check on him from time to time. Each time I did the boy with no name nearly snapped my head off. "Stop lookin' under that rug! You got to be careful!" I offered to drive for a spell, but the boy scoffed me off, even though Stargazer was my horse. We passed few travelers on the road. I held my breath each time we came close, but no one stopped us to ask about runaways. We forced cheer to call our Christmas greetings to every soul we met, pretending we hadn't a care in the world.

By midafternoon, some of the snow had melted. I wondered if the road would be solid enough for the boy to sleigh home when it came time. And when we took Stargazer on with us, how would the boy get home? But I knew better than to ask more questions.

The sun sank, our hands numbed with cold, and most of our food was gone by the time we reached Jamestown. We slid to a stop behind a hatter's shop. A single lamp burned in the back window. "Squat down and wait here." The boy jumped down and rapped softly on the window. The little man who opened the door took one look at the boy, peered nervously from side to side, then grabbed his coat and jerked him inside, slamming the door between us.

"WHAT'S HAPPENING?" Jeremiah whispered from beneath the rugs.

"Don't know. Stay down. Our driver just got yanked in the back door of a hat shop."

"Say what?"

"Hush," I hissed. The back door opened.

"Can't stop here. There's already patrols out looking for runaways, and bound to come back this way," the boy said, swinging up into the driver's seat.

"Us?"

"Don't know, but they ain't picky about who they haul off. There's another place, about a mile from here." We were on our way again. "Both of you listen good. I'm taking you to a Quaker farm." I thought of Mr. Heath and felt relief, knowing the welcome he or Miz Laura would have given, and they were only influenced by Quakers. "But don't think you'll get inside."

"What?"

"Quakers are stopped near every week now, and sometimes their houses are searched. Patrols suspect they help runaways but can't prove it. Quakers won't be caught in a lie, so you can't let them see you. That way they can say, 'No, haven't seen them.' But they'll help."

"How can they help if they don't see us?"

"I drop you near the woods by the river, then stop by their house and tell them you're coming. You'll have to give me that loaf of bread so's I can give it to them in case anybody's visiting, like it's a Christmas gift I brung. You follow the river, till you come to a barn. Go through the downstairs, where the livestock keep, and climb the ladder to the main floor. Look on the wagon seat. You'll find food and blankets. The Quakers leave it for you, but don't want to see you. Past the barn is a smokehouse and a springhouse, then a ten-foot drop. In the clearing at the bottom of the drop is a marble tannin' table. From the tannin' table walk directly back toward the bank, maybe ten or twelve feet. There's a brush pile. Behind the brush there's a cave. Stay the night there. Don't strike no light—it might be seen. Just before daylight go back to that wagon in the barn. Lift off the plank in the back, and—"

"And there's a false bottom!" I shouted.

"Hush up, you fool!"

The boy and Jeremiah both glared at me in the dark. I didn't need light to know that. "Sorry."

"Do you realize how many people be risking their necks to help you?" The boy pushed back his cap, angry.

"I'm sorry," I said again. "It's just that my pa uses one to help—"

"I told you, I don't want to know. And that's something you need to heed. If you mess up now you could get that whole Quaker family in big trouble. It might be a few days before they can move the wagon if the roads ain't clear. Just keep check for food and make sure you're in before daylight." He pulled to the side of the road. "Here's where you get out. Follow the river. Just past these woods is the barn. Keep low. Keep quiet."

"What about Stargazer?"

"Who?"

"My horse."

"Say good-bye."

"What do you mean? What do you mean, 'Say good-bye'?" Even while I argued, I knew I had no choice and that there was no time. Jeremiah dragged me from the sleigh. I reached for Stargazer's bridle, wanting to hold his head in my arms. "This is not the end, Stargazer. I'll—" The boy clicked the reins and Stargazer pulled away.

Jeremiah shook me, but I stood, rooted in the snow, staring after the sleigh. I wanted to chase after it, but my feet wouldn't move. Jeremiah grabbed both my arms and pulled me into the ditch. We stumbled down the steep bank, through the woods, toward the river. I bit my lip until tears blinded my eyes; their frozen streams stung my face. The rock in my throat burned like hot coals. I wanted to scream, to scream and scream. It wasn't fair! None of it was fair.

I fell. Jeremiah pulled me to my feet. I must have followed him. I know he pulled me into the barn. That's when I caught my senses and ran to the stalls, full of sudden hope. But there was no sign of Stargazer. I slammed my fist into the doorpost, angry with myself for not seeing this coming, angry for letting the boy take Stargazer, angry because I didn't know how to change it.

A basket of food, woolen blankets, and a warm pot of coffee sat just where the boy had said they'd be. "Bless they souls," Jeremiah whispered. But I couldn't bless anybody.

Crouched low, we felt our way downhill to the tanning table, then backward, toward the brush pile. It took some time to find the small cave opening in the dark. Our fit into the narrow tunnel was tight, but it kept us from eyes and wind.

It wasn't long before five gray-and-black-cloaked children

trooped in front of the cave, whooping and hollering as they dragged sleds and shovels over the snow, around the tanning table. They hung lamps on low tree limbs and chased each other by lantern light and moonlight, stomping and kicking paths this way and that from the house to the barn and along the lower meadow in front of our cave. Our tracks would never be noticed. They'd thought of everything. The sounds of their merrymaking took my mind from Stargazer for a time, like when you stop worrying a splinter in your eye. While they played we ate thick slices of warm bread slathered in butter and raspberry jam, then chased it down with sweet, creamed coffee.

A little one, not more than three or four years, peeked in the cave and hollered, "Is thee home?"

An older boy ran by and swooped the little one into the air, tickling him and laughing. "Thee is always home with me, Jedediah!"

At last a woman's voice called from the hill above us and the children stomped out of sight. We heard the farmhouse door latch. The laughter cut off, and the stillness hung heavy. My heart turned to Stargazer. Where was he now? Did the boy plan all along to take Stargazer, or was it just the way things worked out at the last? I wished I'd told him how Stargazer liked to be nuzzled, how he wanted his oats and mash, that he liked apples better than carrots, and a lump of sugar once a day. I wrapped my blanket tight around me and laid my head on my saddlebag. I thought of Pa back at the church, of William Henry, and Miz Laura, and now Stargazer, how the losses kept piling up, pulling me lower and lower. I wondered if there was any end to sadness.

"You asleep?"

"Huh?" I mumbled, nearly gone.

"Merry Christmas, Robert Glover." I heard the smile in Jeremiah's voice.

"Merry Christmas, Jeremiah." And then I knew no more.

It's a good thing Jeremiah was a light sleeper or we might have missed our chance to reach the wagon before daylight. "Wake up, Robert. We got to go."

"How do you know what time it is?" I tried to sit up but sleep called me back. Jeremiah shook me.

"Old moon's lower in the sky. We can sleep in the back of that wagon."

"All right. All right, don't push." But he did, and that's what got us collected and back through the shadows and barn. I checked each stall, just in case the boy had come back in the night with Stargazer, but neither was there. We climbed the ladder again, pulled up the plank in the wagon, and spread our blankets along the bottom. We each used a saddlebag for a pillow and climbed in side by side. I pulled the plank back into place as best I could. "What if they don't take the wagon out today? That boy said they might not if the roads aren't good."

"Snow don't usually last long in these parts. If we don't go we'll be spending another night in that cave."

"I guess there's worse things."

"They is," Jeremiah agreed.

Even though the space was hard and tight, at least we were out of the wind, and the lowing of cattle below comforted me. I lay awake for a time, staring at the dark planks inches from my eyes, wondering how they'd fill the wagon. Thinking on it, I remembered that Pa sometimes filled his with straw or apples, potatoes or corn or tobacco, whatever was in season or just harvested. I must have dozed.

"Coffins! They's coverin' us up with coffins!" The terror in Jeremiah's whisper grew, slapping me awake.

"Thee must drive this load of coffins to Petersburg, Brother Peter, and wait for the packages to be unloaded. There are two packages." The strange voice spoke from the back of the wagon.

"Should I expect more along the way?" A second voice spoke from the driver's seat.

"I do not know. Perhaps at the next stop. God will provide."

"I don't like this!" Jeremiah whispered. "What if they's dead bodies in those coffins?"

"Hush!" I didn't like it either, but that didn't matter now.

"Speaking packages could cause a great deal of harm if thee be stopped along the road, Brother Peter. It is a good thing that packages do not speak, would thee not say?"

"It is a thing I hope is true, Brother."

I stared at Jeremiah in the filtered light. We made motions not to speak again.

The barn doors opened and the driver, Brother Peter, clucked his tongue. The wagon lurched, found the frozen ground, and rolled forward. Icy wind bore its way through cracks in the sides and bottom of the wagon. We pulled our blankets over our heads and huddled back-to-back.

Hour after hour we rolled on. Brother Peter hummed tuneless ditties. Jeremiah and I talked in low voices when the wagon moved on open roads. He asked me about William Henry. I told him everything, about growing up together, about skinny-dipping and skunking and fishing and teaching him to read better than me, or that maybe it was reading that gave William Henry wings. He loved it so, he just took off. I told Jeremiah more about Miz Laura and how she loved William Henry, and how he was the best friend I'd ever had. Then I told him again about the night William Henry died, and why, how it was my fault. Jeremiah didn't say anything. I rolled over and let the tears fall silently onto my saddlebag. A long time passed before a hand touched my shoulder. "It weren't your fault, Robert. William Henry chose." I couldn't answer. I wanted to believe that, but I couldn't.

I thought about Stargazer, but pushed it away. The pain was too raw. I wondered what Ma and Pa were doing, and Andrew—Rev. Goforth. I wondered what kind of stir our leaving had made. I wondered what Ma thought when she read my note, and what Pa would say when he learned about Jeremiah, and Ruby, and Grandfather. I wondered if Ma would tell him, and if she'd tell him she'd refused to help Jeremiah when I'd asked her. I wondered if Pa'd stay at Ashland or go home to Laurelea, and if Ma would go with him. I wondered what Emily would say once she learned I'd run away with Jeremiah. I sighed. Maybe it was better not to know.

Eventually, even though we traveled north, there was less snow and more solid, frozen ground, making the ride bumpier. Even with the blankets, I ached all over, and figured we'd be black-and-blue by the time we reached our journey's end. Jeremiah never complained, and I thought well of him for it.

The first night we stopped just before dark. Brother Peter drove the wagon directly into a barn. Someone pulled the doors closed and began to unhitch the horses. "Thee will want a hot meal. I will care for thy horses. Mother wants to know how many packages?" It sounded like a boy, maybe nine or ten years old.

"Two," Brother Peter said. "Two packages could be stored in the loft, could they not?"

"They could," the boy replied. "Quilts are stored there, as well. Mother's basket will soon be placed above the manger."

"I need be on my way at first light," Brother Peter said.

"And I will be here to help thee harness. But thee will want to speak with Father. The patrols are combing the road north. Our house was searched earlier today."

"Are my packages safe here?"

"Father will know. He's just returned from town."

One pair of footsteps left the barn. The lighter pair led the horses to stalls. We could hear the sounds of feed and water being poured. The sound of water nearly did me in. I thought my bladder would burst before the boy finished and closed the barn door.

"Get that plank out quick!" Jeremiah and I made one voice. Traveling all day in a box has its drawbacks.

We slept well that night, despite the worry of the patrols. I was grateful for the loft, for the quilts, for the freedom to move around. The hot beef stew and apple pie from the basket filled and warmed us. Even my aches and pains didn't seem so bad. We woke in time to get in the wagon just as the boy and Brother Peter opened the barn door. The boy lifted the plank off the back of the wagon, shoving in a sack of food and jug of water. He grinned at us but didn't speak—just replaced the plank as though he hadn't seen four wide eyes staring at him from the dark.

Some days we traveled until nightfall, some days only a few hours. Once we stopped for five days. Then Jeremiah and I hid in the loft of the farmer's barn. It was hard to stay still and inside that long. At times I feared we'd been forgotten or that they'd gone to fetch pattyrollers. I didn't tell Jeremiah my fears, but I think he had his own. Brother Peter came out to the barn then, at least once a day, and talked to himself about this or that, I think so we'd know he was there. And we'd see the farmer's wife, who would bring us food. Not everyone minded seeing or talking to us, and that helped our spirits. Sometimes we'd begin our journey by night, along back roads.

Jeremiah and I talked as we rolled along open roads. I talked about Laurelea and begged Jeremiah to tell me about his life at Ashland. He told me about Nanny Sara, and how she raised him, about the nights they spent telling stories to each other in their cabin when Grandfather would let her leave the big house. But he clammed up when it came to talking about Grandfather, or his mother that he never knew, or what it was like to be a nearly white slave—the son of the owner—and live in the quarters. "Someday maybe I talk about that. Not now. Not while it nips at my heels." So we speculated on what freedom might be like for him, what kind of work he might find, and where he might live, building the hope in our minds that we'd make it.

Brother Peter spoke aloud to himself if he had something to say to us, like, "Rider ahead." Then we'd know to hush up and lie still.

I couldn't guess how far we'd come or how far we had to go. At first I'd kept careful count of the days. But soon, with all the starts and stops, the pulling off the road to hide until patrollers went by, and the sleeping at odd times, I lost track.

I began to wonder if we were really going to Petersburg. I feared Ma and Pa might give me up for lost or dead. The only sure thing is that we were always cold, always sore, and always afraid. If I had any doubts how dangerous our mission was, they were crushed late one afternoon, in what might have been the third week.

Sounds of a town surrounded the wagon—people talking, horses and their buggies rattling past us in the street. We glimpsed folks' feet through cracks in the wagon. A couple of times we crossed cobblestone streets that rattled our bones. We knew to keep still.

"Where you goin' with that load, Quaker Man?" The voice was surly and slurred, edged with whiskey.

"These coffins are to be delivered to Mr. O'Leary and Sons, Undertakers. Dost thee know the way to their establishment?"

"Their establishment?" The voice scoffed. "You got business for them, Quaker Man?"

"They have business of their own. I only supply the coffins."

"Say, Sheriff, wasn't one of those O'Leary boys jailed just last week? Somebody seen a runaway slinkin' round their 'establishment.' I 'spect all those O'Learys was helping him. Can't have that, can we, Sheriff?"

"No, sir. Can't have that." The crude voice laughed. "You wouldn't happen to have runaways in those boxes, would you, Quaker Man?"

"My coffins come empty. I have seen no runaways. Thee may search if the law requires it."

"Might not hurt to open up one or two—make sure." The new voice must have belonged to the sheriff because Brother Peter stepped from his seat into the back of the wagon. We heard him pry up a lid.

"Art thou satisfied?"

"Open up that other one." We heard the lid come up. Jeremiah and I held our breath. I chewed the sides of my cheek.

"Where you from, Quaker Man?"

"South—a goodly way."

"Why would O'Leary send south for his coffins?" the sheriff asked.

"Because mine are fine and sturdy. Because a tight coffin is the last bed of a good man and fine craftsmanship is to be desired, even though the price be dear. Would thee not rather be buried in a tight coffin than a loose one?" We'd never heard Brother Peter speak so much or so long.

"He's got a point," the sheriff replied.

"Hogwash," the slurred voice said. "I say we tip the whole kaboodle out and—"

"Leave him alone, Lester. Go on, Mister. Deliver your coffins. O'Leary's is just down the street and turn left onto Treemont. Best tell those O'Leary boys we're watching them."

"Godspeed, then," Brother Peter said, and clucked his reins. We drove on. Brother Peter pulled his wagon to the back of a shop—O'Leary's, I guessed. Heavy doors swung open, grating on hinges. The wagon backed just inside its opening. Jeremiah and I clutched our saddlebags, not daring to breathe. Brother Peter and someone above us unloaded the coffins. Scrap wood was thrown onto the empty wagon bed, crashing above our faces.

Somebody raised a ruckus farther up the street, drawing a noisy crowd. In that instant the plank was yanked from our hiding place and Jeremiah and I were hauled out, feet first, and shoved face up into open coffins. The lids slapped shut. Wagon wheels rumbled away. Heavy doors grated again on their hinges, followed by the sound of a heavy bar falling into place.

HOURS PASSED BEFORE all the voices and footsteps died away. We knew enough to keep quiet, to trust the people hiding us. But the coffin was cold and, after all, it was a coffin. I hoped Jeremiah hadn't fainted. I tried to turn over, but the space was too tight.

The clock in the room had long since chimed nine when I heard a door open and a cheerful Irish brogue whisper, "I'm here to let you out. Which coffin are you in? Give a knock."

Jeremiah banged louder and was let out first, then it was my turn. Fresh air never smelled so good.

Our rescuer grinned in the faint lamp glow. "A grave experience, eh?"

"Not funny," I said, but returned the grin. Our rescuer's tumble of red ringlets stood out from her cap, and even in the dim lamplight, her green eyes danced with mischief. She didn't look much older than me.

"That's as close to Old Scratch as I want to come for a long time." Jeremiah's color was returning.

"Well, I'm ever so glad you enjoyed yourselves, gentlemen. Because you may not fancy your next little jaunt. Or, then again, you may!" Her eyes twinkled. "How would you like a train ride?" Our faces lit like Christmas trees aflame until her next words. "As girls?" Our mouths dropped and she laughed so hard she had to slap her hand across her face.

"You're not serious! Are you?" I had the worst feeling she was.

"Very!" She smiled. "But not both of you."

"Oh, that's a relief!" Jeremiah breathed again.

"Just you." She pointed to Jeremiah.

"Me? Why me?"

"Because you're the one we're trying to hide. It makes it easier that you're—"

"Light-skinned—I know—but I'm not a girl!"

"No, I meant that you're slight. We'll dress you up so no one will ever know you're a lad. Mam sent me down to see what size you might be and if we've anything to fit. We'll have to veil you over; you're not very pretty." She grinned again. "Now stand to my back. That will tell me the height." Miserably, Jeremiah stood. "Ah! Not much taller. That's a good thing. Skinny enough to fit in most anything, I suppose." Jeremiah didn't like that. "Let me see your hands." She inspected Jeremiah's hands. "You'll need gloves, for certain. And perhaps some other shoes. I don't suppose you've ever walked in heels?"

Jeremiah couldn't decide if she was serious. "No, ma'am."

"Hmm. Perhaps a hoop would hide your feet. I think Mam has a mourning dress and veil that will do." She brushed her hands together as though it was settled. "Let's get a hot meal on your bones and a pillow under your heads. You can keep in the storeroom. 'Tis not a grand hotel, but you'll be safe." She ushered us along. "Me brother will be by later. He's out trying to raise the train fare."

"I have money," I blurted out.

"Have you, now?" She seemed intrigued. "A runaway with money—it's not the usual! Did you steal it?"

"It's my mother's," I confessed. "I took it."

"Well, it's a good thing. Hand it over." I must have shown

my thinking. "I'm not trying to lift your money, by Jim. A train ticket costs a pretty penny."

"How much?" After losing Stargazer I aimed to be more careful.

She colored. "I don't know. If you've enough for two, buy it yourself."

"I'm sorry. I didn't mean—"

"No. It would be grand to buy it yourself—in the morning, before the train leaves. Then it puts none of us in the light."

"I'd meant to leave something for Brother Peter, for all he did for us. Will we see him again?"

"Who?"

"Brother Peter—the Quaker man that drove us here."

"Brother Peter!" She laughed. "That's not his name! He'd never tell his real name! You've got a lot to learn!"

That was not news to me.

"Come on to the storeroom, then. Hot food and a proper sleep will mend you." She lit a candle, placed it on a low shelf, and handed us a cloth-covered bucket, still warm. "You'll stay here tomorrow. There'll be no workers in on the Lord's Day. But you must keep quiet, and don't strike a light, in case it's seen. I'll bring you food when I can. Use the chamber pot in the corner. I'll be back before dawn on Monday with your costume. We'll have to get you changed quickly then, and out before the workers come. Not all of them know that some of our customers still breathe." Not a trace of a smile passed her lips.

She was barely out the door when she turned. "I almost forgot! Off with your clothes! Mam said we'd need to wash and press them after all the time you've lived in them. You can't be traveling on the train looking like runaways—or smelling like them, either. I'll bring you wash water in the morning, though what you need is a proper bath! You're both a wee bit too fragrant."

She closed the door. Shamefaced, we undressed, wrapped ourselves in quilts she passed through the door, and handed our clothes out to her. If ever I'd had a swelled head, the women of this world cured it.

Alone at last, Jeremiah and I tore into the lamb stew and soda bread, not speaking to each other until the last bit had been licked from our fingers.

"I never knew what it was to be so hungry," I said.

Jeremiah stared at me. "You're lucky."

I felt ashamed, then angry. It wasn't my fault that I'd been born free or into a family that could afford enough to eat.

Exhausted as I was, I had trouble falling asleep. I heard Jeremiah's regular breathing long before I drifted off. I'm not sure where remembering left off and dreaming began, but it started with Stargazer, roaming the meadows of Ashland. My mind drifted to Rev. Goforth, and our talk about the Good Samaritan helping someone straight through until the need was met. I woke to the sounds of buggies in the street, but the dream stayed with me. I knew it meant that I must see Jeremiah's need through to the end, but I didn't know where that would lead us. When we got to Laurelea, maybe Pa or Mr. Heath could help, if Pa was there.

We spent the day wrapped in quilts in the storeroom. It was dark, but at least it was a change from the rattling wagon, and we could stand, and stretch, and walk a few paces back and forth. Best of all, it wasn't a coffin! The girl, good to her word, passed us a lunch through the door late in the morning, but hurried away again, afraid she'd be seen. Monday morning came before we knew it.

"Up and out, you lazy loggerheads!" The Irish cheer was too much before daybreak. "It's nearly five! Here's a bucket, for washing, and your clean clothes." She tossed me my bundle, then triumphantly shook out great folds of black fabric. "And here's your gown, my Lady!"

"Oh," was all Jeremiah could say. It was a monstrous thing, with stockings, black gloves, a black lace-trimmed shawl, and a heavy, veiled bonnet to match.

"Don't look so glum, my lass. You'll be lovely!" She enjoyed Jeremiah's misery too much. "Look sharp, now! There's no time to dally! I'll be just outside the door while you're changing. Call if you need anything! I'll help you with the hoop when you're ready—unless you've experience in such things."

The door closed on her laughter, and Jeremiah carefully avoided my eyes. We dressed in silence. I rolled up our bedding. Jeremiah rolled up his pant legs, and fumbled with the buttons of the dress. "Do you reckon you could give me a hand with these?" he asked.

Between the two of us we got him pretty well put together. Then the red-haired girl waltzed in, set us straight, and redid all the buttons. By the time she'd tied a hoop beneath the dress and Jeremiah pulled on his veiled bonnet and gloves, he really could pass for a woman. But one word or one step, and I knew there was something wrong with the picture. "It's certain sure you mustn't open your mouth!" The girl minced no words. "And you mustn't walk more than absolutely necessary. No one would believe you're a lady." She puzzled, chewing on the tip of her little finger. "I've got it! You are this boy's mother. You've recently lost your dear husband, God rest his soul, and it's given you such a turn that you fell down with the apoplexy. You haven't walked properly since, and you can't speak at all! Delicious!"

Jeremiah and I looked at each other, not at all convinced. The girl grew peevish. "Would you rather be sold South? There are slave traders right here in Petersburg, willing and anxious to sell anybody—slave or free—to turn a profit! And you!" She pointed to me. "Would you rather be jailed or tarred and feathered? That's what they do to people who help runaways, don't you know?"

Nothing sobered us faster. "Tell us what to do," I said.

She straightened. "You—" she pointed to Jeremiah— "practice walking and looking frail. And you," she said, pointing again to me, "practice acting as though he's your widowed mother. You are her protector now. You're a wee bit down in the mouth yourself, both for having lost your Da, and because your Mam is sick. We'll tie a mourning band around your sleeve for all to see."

Jeremiah and I walked up and down the narrow storeroom. "Wrap your arm around her!" the girl ordered. "And you—stoop a little when you walk. Lean on your son."

We practiced and practiced. We must have finally passed muster because the girl stopped ordering us, at least about that. "Come on, then, eat your breakfast, and you're off to the train station."

We washed down the buns with tea. I pulled a gold piece from my pocket. I didn't want to miss my chance to thank her and her family for all they'd done and given us. "Please take this, and give our thanks to your ma and pa."

Her green eyes widened and lit in delight. But she sobered quickly and shook her head. "Keep it. You'll be needing it." She looked at Jeremiah. "Or he will."

"But the dress, and food, and—"

"It's what we do. This is what you do. That's all there is." She tied the black mourning band around my sleeve. "Now, don't be flashing gold pieces 'round or you're sure to be robbed blind as bats. Something you should know: There's a new reward bill posted for a runaway male slave, chestnut hair, nearly white, in the telegraph office already, from North Carolina. It says he may be traveling with a white boy. You don't want to be noticed, so you've got to keep your wits about you. Gold tastes good on the tongues of the greedy, and they'll not be feeling sorry for either of you."

Jeremiah and I both colored with the certain fearful knowledge that we were hunted. Images of Jed Slocum and his whip sprang into my head.

"The train?" Jeremiah reminded her.

"Get off the train in Washington. Find a boardinghouse on Booth Street, two streets south of the station, marked McPhearson's. If there's a light in the front window by the holly tree, go to the side yard. There should be an old quilt hanging on the wash line. If both those signs be there, knock on the back door. Ask for Mrs. McPhearson—Mrs. McPhearson only! Tell her that Miss Ida Shirley sent two boxes on the train and does she want you to fetch them 'round. She'll take care of you from there."

"What if there is no light in the window—where did you say?"

"Booth Street! The front window by the holly tree! An old quilt hanging in the sideyard! Mrs. McPhearson's! If the light's not there, don't go in. If the quilt is not there, don't knock. It means that it isn't safe. Wait until you see the light burning and the quilt hanging—even if you have to meander about the city a day or two. If they never show, something's gone wrong, and you're on your own."

I looked at Jeremiah but couldn't see him beneath the veils. I wondered if he was as worried as I was.

"Good. Then follow me by twenty paces. Walk slowly as though you are really a sick, widowed mother with her son. There's plenty of time. The train doesn't leave until half past ten. I'll dally about the shop windows if I think you've lagged too far behind and are likely to be lost. When I pass the station I'll keep going, not looking back. Don't let your eyes follow me. Come on, then."

"Wait! Thank you. Thank you, ma'am," Jeremiah said.

She smiled at him and reached for his hand. "Godspeed to you, young sir. May your life be lovely and long, and as free as the birds of the air."

"Thank you—for everything," I said.

She smiled at me, too. "Perhaps I'll see you again." And she slipped through the door.

We followed slowly, practicing our disguise all the way. There was no telling who might be watching. When the train station came into view she quickened her step, turned a corner, and was gone. I wanted to catch the last glimpse of red curls escaping her bonnet, or the swish of her skirt, but I remembered her warning and kept my eyes fastened on the street.

"Two tickets for Washington, please." I tried to keep my voice confident and steady as I spoke to the stationmaster.

"Ten dollars," he said, stamping the tickets. I slid a gold piece beneath the barred window. He looked Jeremiah up and down, tipped his hat, and handed me the ticket. "New around here?" Jeremiah froze.

"Just visiting. My mother's been sick. We're going home now." My voice squeaked and I feared I'd said too much. The stationmaster raised his eyebrows. We took our seats outside on the platform, around the corner, where the stationmaster couldn't see us, and tried to breathe. I closed my eyes a moment and tried to imagine Ma sitting beside me. How would I act? What would I do if Pa had died and Ma had been taken with the apoplexy so she couldn't speak, or if she was frail like Miz Laura had been?

"Sure your mother wouldn't prefer to wait in the ladies' waiting room, Son?" I jumped, opening my eyes to see the stationmaster standing over us.

"No, sir. Thank you, sir." I took him by the sleeve and led him aside. "My mother's suffered the apoplexy and I need to look after her. She can't speak and has trouble walking by herself. Thank you for asking."

He tipped his cap to Jeremiah, who turned his head away. "I'm sorry to hear it. Let me know if you need any help getting her on the train. I'll tell the conductor to keep an eye out for you. Train'll be ready to board soon."

I swallowed hard. "Thank you, sir. I'm sure we'll be fine. We just want to get home again. It's been a hard trip."

He nodded, then walked away. I couldn't read his mind. I looked back at Jeremiah, trying to see him through the stationmaster's eyes. Jeremiah wobbled as he leaned forward and fumbled with the folds of his dress. His shoes were tucked well beneath the skirt, and he appeared for all the world like a frail woman.

I wondered who he reminded me of and I realized it was Grandfather, while he was recovering, soon after Ma and I had arrived at Ashland. Jeremiah must have watched his father every chance he got. It pained me to know that Jeremiah had never known the feeling of his father's arm around his shoulder, or a father's smile that made him feel he'd done a good job. It pained me more to know that this same man, who could have given Jeremiah everything, and had given him only misery, was my own grandfather.

"All aboard!" the conductor called. I helped Jeremiah to

his feet. I tried to think of him as Miz Laura. That made me sad, and helped make me more natural. We climbed the steps just before the conductor came to lend a hand. I was afraid that if he felt Jeremiah's hard muscled arm we'd be discovered. We found seats near the front of the car. I sat beside Jeremiah but couldn't block the seat directly facing us.

A plump little woman with white hair and a black bonnet sank into the seat facing Jeremiah. She placed a large hatbox on the seat beside her. "Good morning, my dear," she said to Jeremiah. Jeremiah turned toward her and nodded feebly.

"My mother's not well. She's suffered the apoplexy and can't talk just yet." I pushed between them.

"Oh! That's such a shame, and so young. Well, that's all right, dearie, I'm sure you'll be well in no time." She patted Jeremiah's knee. "Your legs feel strong. You'll mend quickly."

"She just needs her rest, ma'am."

"Well, of course she does. What does your father say?"

I looked at Jeremiah. "Father died last month."

"Oh, I wondered why the mourning. I'm so sorry, for both of you."

"Thank you, ma'am."

"But the Lord works in mysterious ways, His wonders to perform. You never know what strength you have until you're tested. Remember that, young man."

"Yes, ma'am."

"Tickets! Tickets!" The conductor walked through the car, punching tickets. I handed ours over. "Anything you or your mother need, young fellow, let me know."

"Thank you, sir."

The conductor tipped his hat to Jeremiah and to the lady opposite us. The plump little woman rattled on and on about the weather, her arthritis, the cold, the heat, and things I didn't hear. Jeremiah leaned his head back against the seat and feigned sleep. But I knew he had to be just as keyed up, and wouldn't likely fall off his guard. "I wonder where your mother found such lovely black lace?" The woman fingered the edging of the shawl Jeremiah had draped around his shoulders.

"I couldn't say, ma'am. It's one my father gave her before he died."

"Oh, how sweet. It looks for all the world like a pattern my mother brought from Ireland! But you don't sound Irish!"

"No, ma'am. But my father was Irish."

"Really! My mother was a Dunnagan, from County Clare. Of course, she married a Snow when she settled in America. What was your father's name, my dear?"

A name! What name? My eyes fell on a newspaper held by the man across the aisle. The back page advertised DuBock's boot blacking. "DuBock. Henry DuBock. I don't remember what county he came from."

"Henry DuBock? But that doesn't sound Irish!" The woman's eyes narrowed.

My throat went dry, and I felt my face flame. "Yes, ma'am, that's true. My father's father wasn't Irish but my grandmother was Irish and that's where my father grew up—in Ireland."

"How very odd."

"Yes, ma'am."

"How ever did your mother and father meet?"

This was getting too complicated and I wished with all my heart that I was the one with the apoplexy. "I don't know. My father never told me and now my mother can't talk." I swallowed hard. "It's a mystery."

"How very odd," the woman mused again, still squinting at me. "Your mother certainly sleeps a great deal. How anyone can sleep like the dead on a train is beyond me. You should remove her veil so she can breathe better. It's getting quite warm in here."

"I don't think she'd like that. She's fine."

"Oh, fiddle-faddle! What do boys know about the needs of women! The poor dear can hardly breathe in such trappings!" She reached across the aisle and took hold of Jeremiah's veil.

I lunged for her hand, but was too late. The veil was nearly to his chin.

"Arrrrgghhh!" Jeremiah poured out a high-pitched scream that would wake the dead and reminded me of Aunt Sassy's keening when William Henry died. Startled, I fell back in my seat. The plump little woman jumped straight up, matching Jeremiah squeal for squeal. She fell, missing her seat and upsetting her skirts so that half the train took in a full view of her plump, black-stockinged legs. Jeremiah scratched at the air like a weak cat. I held my breath to keep from laughing. The man across the aisle reached for the old lady, pulling her to her feet. The conductor came running down the aisle.

"What's this? What's this? Madam! Are you hurt?"

The old lady couldn't catch her breath.

"Mother! Mother! It's all right! She didn't mean any harm! Nobody will bother your veil, I promise!" The story missed my brain and poured from my mouth. "My mother didn't mean to frighten you, ma'am, but you can't touch her veil."

"I only wanted to help her breathe! It's stifling in here!" The old lady gasped. She grasped for her seat, red-faced and flustered, trying hard to divert attention from her legs.

"One side of her face is drawn up bad from the apoplexy. She doesn't want anybody touching her veil." That made everybody stare first at Jeremiah, then at her. I think we deserved a medal for not laughing. I felt as sharp as William Henry.

"Well—she shouldn't frighten a body to death like that!"

"Madam, perhaps you would prefer another seat?" the conductor pleaded. "Yes! Yes, I think that would be best." The old lady stood, gathered her skirts, and led the conductor away.

The man across the aisle heaved a sigh. "I thought that woman would never stop talking!" He leaned forward, concerned. "Son? Is your mother all right? Is there anything I can do for either of you?"

Jeremiah held out his gloved hand. The man leaned over it, and smiled up into Jeremiah's veil. If it wasn't so risky I might have burst inside. Instead I coughed. "We'll be fine, sir. Thank you." I pulled Jeremiah's hand away. "It's just too much excitement for my mother." But the man across the aisle couldn't seem to take his eyes off Jeremiah.

A dozen or so passengers left the train on the stop before ours, including the white-haired lady. She passed us on her way out of the car, stopping to pick up her hatbox. I tipped my cap, but she ignored me and squinted accusingly at Jeremiah. Once off the train I saw her clustered by a group of greeters. From her wagging finger and puffed face I knew she was carrying on over the scene aboard the train. I turned away, praying the train would roll on quickly, praying we could make it to Washington and lose ourselves in the crowds.

CHAPTER

Twenty-Two

IT WAS DUSK WHEN THE TRAIN finally rolled into Washington. Lamplights surrounding the station glowed a yellow welcome to travelers. The man across the aisle offered to help us find a carriage.

"Thank you, sir. We'll be fine."

"But I insist! Your mother can't be walking dark streets in her condition. We'll just get your luggage from the boxcar."

"We don't have any." I bit my tongue.

"No luggage?"

"We sent it on ahead."

"Oh. I see." But he didn't. "Just let me find mine and I'll be there to help you."

We stepped gingerly off the train. Jeremiah leaned heavily on my arm, keeping up our sham. Two police officers stepped toward us. We turned and walked in the other direction, trying to keep Jeremiah limping, and our steps measured and calm.

"Just a minute! Just a minute there!" The policeman's shout sent shivers up my spine. Jeremiah's grip clawed into my arm. We kept walking, pretending we didn't hear.

"That woman must have telegraphed ahead." Jeremiah whispered my fear.

"Wait! Stop!" The two policemen were running now, overtaking us. My heart stopped. To come so far and to be caught so near help and freedom! I froze, knowing that to run might get us both killed. From the corner of my eye I saw a man leap across the tracks. The policemen were on us now and I turned, ready to give myself up. But Jeremiah bent over in a fit of coughing, leaning heavily against my arm. "Pardon me, Madam! Out of the way, Boy!" And the policemen charged past, chasing the man across the tracks. My knees quivered. Jeremiah braced me.

"Let's get out of here," he whispered. We turned a corner and quickened our step, trying to weave unnoticed through the groups of passengers. Horse-and-carriage taxis waited just ahead. If we could just get past them, we'd be lost in the crowd of hawkers, passengers, and well-wishers. "There you are! I thought I'd lost you. What a commotion!" It was the man from the train. "Did they catch that pickpocket?"

"I don't know." I was shaking. "I had to get my mother away from all that."

"Good judgment. I'll hire a carriage. Taxi!" he called.

"Sir! We're fine on our own."

"Nonsense. It is my pleasure. Where are you going?" I couldn't think. "Yes?" The taxi pulled up beside us and the driver hopped down. "Where shall I order the driver to take you?"

"We haven't made our plans, exactly."

"You need a hotel?"

"Well—" I began. Jeremiah nodded weakly, gripping my arm. "Yes," I stammered. "I guess we do."

"I can recommend an excellent hotel. I've booked a room there myself. I'm sure they will accommodate your mother with a downstairs room."

"Thank you, sir," I said, as Jeremiah patted my arm. The man spoke to the driver, who loaded his luggage. "What are you doing?" I whispered to Jeremiah.

"Just go along. We'll slip out when he goes to bed."

I helped Jeremiah up the carriage step as the man placed his valise in the buggy. Jeremiah's skirt caught on the carriage handle, lifting the hem of his dress just enough to show a boy's black shoe, worn and muddy. I covered it, but too late. The man from the train stopped short, staring at us, as though seeing us for the first time. He stared into Jeremiah's veils, then straightened and stepped forward. His voice turned cold. "Unusual shoes for a lady."

I don't know if I would have done anything on my own. But Jeremiah hurled the man's valise at him, causing the stranger to stumble backward and sprawl against the driver. He shoved me back into the seat, jumped to the front of the carriage, and grabbed the reins. Jeremiah whipped the horse into a frenzy, and we charged down the cobblestone street.

"Stop! Stop that carriage!" the man bellowed behind us. Shrill police whistles blasted the night. Two taxi drivers stepped out and tried to grab our horse. The horse shied, then reared, nearly upsetting the carriage. Jeremiah shouted above it all, cracking the whip a hair above the horse's back. The horse reared again, pawed the air, then tore away, pounding down the middle of the lane. Jeremiah drove like a crazy person, the very ghost of William Henry in a dress. The carriage clattered and reeled, careening behind.

"Where are you going?" I yelled, soon as I could catch my voice.

"How would I know? I never been here before!" We twisted and turned down streets we'd never seen, taking the sharp corners on two wheels.

I pulled myself forward and shouted, "We've got to get shed of this buggy. They'll be all over us for stealing!"

"You got any ideas?" Jeremiah yelled. "We sure could use some!"

"Look! Up there!" I pointed far ahead to a well-lit square.

"Whoa! Whoa, there!" Jeremiah pulled the horse back. He clattered to a trot, then dropped to a walk. We heard the whistle blasts in the distance. "That's it. That a boy. There, now. You take the reins. Best if you be driving and not some widow woman."

We switched places. I pulled the carriage to a stop behind a long line of taxis flanking the square. Drivers ahead of me helped ladies from their carriages, then the couples, decked out in ball gowns and coats with tails, linked arms as they climbed wide stairs to some kind of theater house. Their drivers lazed against lampposts, ready for a long evening. I nodded to the driver ahead of me, then helped Jeremiah down. We took up the sham again, dropping the limp. But instead of climbing the stairs, we crossed the street and stepped into the shadows.

"First alley on the right," I whispered. We walked back the way we'd come nearly half a block, praying no one watched. Police whistles and the clatter of horse hooves grew louder. How I wanted to run to that alley! But we steadied our steps, turning in just before the horses rounded the last corner. We tore down the back street, then dived behind a stack of crates. Policemen on horses rushed past.

"I'm comin' out of this skirt now!" Jeremiah tugged at the buttons.

"Don't tear it! We might need it later!"

"Then you wearin' it! A body can't run in such as this! And run is what we got to do!"

"Calm down, Jeremiah!"

"Robert, I know what they do when they catch me!"

He was right. I helped him pull the dress over his head. "We've got to find Booth Street."

"Good thing you didn't give that McPhearson name to that man. They be all over that boardin' house by now."

I nodded, but didn't know what to do next. I was too tired to breathe, too tired to drag myself from behind those crates.

"Just a while longer, Robert. We gonna make it." Jeremiah placed his hand on my shoulder.

"I know." I swiped at the sweat trickling into my eyes. "We've just got to get to that boardinghouse." I tried to stand, but sank down again. "We'd best bundle that dress. They'll be looking for a widow and boy now." I leaned my head on my knees and asked the Lord to get us out of this mess, to give us the strength to keep on.

We waited another ten minutes, then crept from the alley and made our way along cobbled side streets, back toward the train station, keeping shy of the gas lamps. We walked and walked, checking signposts, ducking into alleys or behind shadowed stoops at every sound. We passed a church and heard the bells chime ten. We counted ten blocks, then took an alley to the right, guessing that was a little less than we'd driven by horse and carriage. But we came up against a dead end, and had to backtrack. We searched surrounding streets and alleys for what seemed hours—no Booth Street. So, we hiked back to the main street, and turned left. We searched four blocks over and still saw no sign for Booth Street. I worried that the red-haired girl might have been wrong.

I don't know when the fog first crept into the streets behind us. But when it swirled its thick cloud around our feet, and over the steps of houses, when it filled the alleys, something inside me began to break. How would we ever find Booth Street in such muck? We'd nearly run out of lampposts, and most of the lights shining from windows had been snuffed.

I had no idea where we were, or how far away the train station was, or Booth Street, let alone the boardinghouse.

"Robert," Jeremiah whispered.

"What?"

"We can't quit now."

"I'm not quitting. But I don't know where we are. I don't know which way to go."

"We can't ask nobody now. We just got to keep looking." I followed Jeremiah, who seemed to grow new strength. We felt our way along, reaching for corner signposts and shingles at the end of each block. Finally we came upon a shingle we could not read.

"You got any more of them lucifer matches Granny Sara packed?"

I dug in my pocket for the tin case. I rattled it, and it sounded like there could be two, maybe three left. "It might not strike in this damp. I'll have to hold it near the shingle."

"I lift you up," Jeremiah said, and hoisted me as high as he could. I don't know where he found the strength.

I struck the match but the head flew off. I struck another and the flame sparked, but wouldn't take. But in that instant, in that tiny spark, I saw the letter "B" on that shingle—plain as could be. I shook as I scratched our last match, cupping my hand round it. The match head glimmered, then sparked, growing brighter. I lifted my makeshift lantern hand to the shingle. "Booth Street," I read out loud. "Booth Street!" No two words ever looked so good. "Which way now?" My voice broke as Jeremiah set me on my feet.

"Just try till we find it. Good thing you can read."

"Yeah. Good thing."

"Maybe William Henry was right, Robert. Maybe you gettin' around to bein' a genuine scholar." I laughed. We both laughed.

We picked up our pace and made our way along Booth Street, searching for a candle in a window. The fog was thicker now and we had to get pretty close to the houses to see. I began to hope again, to think that maybe we'd make it. I wondered, as we walked, if Jeremiah might want to live at Laurelea. I wondered how Aunt Sassy and Joseph would take to such an idea, or if he could be safe there. Could Mr. Heath do anything about the law that would send him back to North Carolina? No, he couldn't the first time. It would be no different now.

And then it was before us. "McPhearson's Boardinghouse!" I dug my elbow in Jeremiah's side. A candle burned in the front window, next to a tall tree. We edged into the yard, crept toward the tree, and reached for its leaves. The prickles of the holly felt holy in my fingers, and I breathed, "Thank You, Lord. Thank You." We crept to the side yard, hugging the shadows. A damp quilt hung on the wash line. We tapped on the back door and waited. A minute later we knocked again. The door opened. "Mrs. McPhearson?" I asked, my voice shaking. Hands reached for ours, pulling us into a dark room. The door latched behind us and a lucifer match struck stone, springing its small flame before our faces, then rested on a candlewick.

"Packages?" The voice was deep for a woman, and direct.

"Yes, ma'am, two, for Mrs. McPhearson, from Ida Shirley. Should we fetch them for you?"

She nodded. "This way." We followed the flickering candle flame and the squat woman in nightdress and cap to a pantry behind the kitchen. "Sit here a moment and let me bring you a bite. You must be famished." Her voice took on softer tones.

"Thank you, ma'am. It's been a long day."

"I should say! You two caused quite a commotion at the train station—policemen tearing hither and yon all night, banging on doors, combing streets and houses from cellar to attic!" Jeremiah and I stared at each other. She pointed to our bundle. "You'll not be wanting that dress again. Everyone's looking for a boy in a black mourning dress and veil. No proper widow will be safe in Washington for weeks!" She toddled away, chuckling, and closed the door behind her. She'd left the candle with us, and it was all we could do to keep our hands off the apples and potatoes. She was back within minutes bearing hefty bowls of chicken soup, steaming and swimming with carrots and turnips.

"This be the best soup I ever eat!" Jeremiah nearly cried as he tasted it.

The woman smiled and brushed Jeremiah's hair back. "I expect it is, young man. I hope it is the beginning of many good things for you." Jeremiah seemed startled by her kindness, and I wondered at the change it made in him. "I hate to have to say it, but we'll need to move you quickly. You can't travel together."

"What?" I was not prepared for such an idea.

"It is far too dangerous. There are posters and newspapers for runaways all over the city. There's an advertisement from a plantation owner in North Carolina that answers your descriptions in detail. After your show at the train station, it is a good guess that you two are in Washington now and likely to take on disguise. And the two of you evidently stole a horse and taxi. The police have checked boardinghouses, hotels, taverns, alleys—anywhere runners might hide quickly. Bounty hunters are everywhere in Washington." She shook her head, frowning. "You've surely made yourselves noticed."

"As long as we stay together. That's all. I've got to get Jeremiah north. Just tell me how far north is safe."

The woman shook her head again and sat down on a flour

barrel beside us. "North in this country won't do now. The fugitive slave law saw to that. There is a thousand-dollar reward on this boy's head, and too many people are searching for two boys traveling together. I don't know how we could get the two of you out. Nothing short of Canada will be safe for this young man."

I shook my head. "I promised Nanny Sara. I promised his grandmother that I'd get him to freedom. If Canada is what it takes, then I'm going." The soup had raised my strength. I stood up. "If you won't help us go together, ma'am, then I'll do it myself."

"Wait. Let's hear what she got to say." Jeremiah pulled at my hand.

"Sit down, young man, and save your strength and your temper. You'll need both shortly, and you'll need them mightily. The point is not to get you out together. You have done a fine job so far. But now your traveling together is a danger to you both. You don't have to go to Canada to ensure—what are your names?"

"Our names? Everyone's told us that they didn't want to know our names."

"Well, I do. There's nothing anyone can do to drag them out of me, if that's what you're afraid of. I'm Effie Burton. McPhearson is the boardinghouse name."

"My name be Jeremiah." Jeremiah spoke first. How could he trust her? "And this be Robert."

"Where are you from, Robert?"

"Maryland." I swallowed. She waited. "Elkton, Maryland."

"And you've family that will take you in there? Even if they know what you've done?"

"Yes. At least, I think so."

"Then that's where you'll go. And Jeremiah will go to Canada."

"But I have to get Jeremiah to freedom!"

"You've done your part. The point is not to be a hero, Robert, but to get Jeremiah safely on his way to Canada, and you home safely to your family. I'll contact another conductor to start Jeremiah on his way by a western route. A few days later you'll take the train to Baltimore and Elkton. Separating you might slow your trackers."

"I'm not trying to be a hero! But this isn't what we planned!"

"Maybe she be right, Robert. Maybe this for the best."

"No! I can do it! We can do it, Jeremiah! Don't quit now." I'd promised Nanny Sara, and I'd sworn in my heart that I'd do this for Jeremiah, and for William Henry, and for me. And it was the only way I could help make up for Grandfather's cruelties and his selling of Ruby, the only way I could protect Ma's half brother, my own uncle. "I'd let them take me before I'd let them take you. You know I would."

Jeremiah looked at me like he was trying to decide who I was. "I don't want either one of us taken. I don't want either one of us dead or beaten or our feet cut off. I been caught once and I mean never to go back. I want to be free, Robert. I taste that freedom already. This lady risks her life helping folks find it. She knows. We got to trust her."

"Haven't I risked my life for you? I gave up Stargazer, my family, everything. We made it so far. Don't do this, Jeremiah." Jeremiah looked away.

"What both of you need right now is sleep. Jeremiah, I'll pull a cot in here for you. It will be safer, away from the eyes of my boarders. You'll be up before my help arrives. Robert, come along. I have an extra room. Sleep helps everything."

Sleep sounded so good. I had no more arguments. I followed her without a word or backward glance. I guessed

Jeremiah was as worn out as I was. We could talk more tomorrow. I'd make them both see, then. I fell on the bed and slept in my boots.

THE SMELL OF SIZZLING BACON and the bell from a peddler's wagon in the street woke me. White winter sunlight danced in patches across the rag rug of a room I couldn't place. All my bones ached. I rolled over, wanting only more sleep. But my eyes focused on the clock sitting on the mantel. Nine. What was it I needed to tend to? Nine. Where was I? Nine! How could I have slept so late? Why didn't Jeremiah wake me? I pulled myself up, hating to leave the comfort of a real bed. I slicked back my hair and straightened my clothes as best I could, then peeked out the door. Effie Burton was just coming up the stairs with a pitcher of steaming water.

"There you are, Robert! I thought you'd sleep the day away! I've brought you warm water so you can take a wash. As soon as you're ready, come down and have some breakfast." She smiled and brushed past me into the room, setting the pitcher in the china washbowl.

"Is Jeremiah up yet?"

She hesitated and brushed her hands down the front of her apron. "Jeremiah's—gone."

"Gone? Gone!"

"He left this morning with a conductor, someone who can see him all the way to Canada, where he'll be safe—and free."

I turned away from her. In that moment I hated her.

Despite all her kindness and generosity, I hated her. "How do I know you didn't turn him in for the reward money?"

She sat down on the bed. "Because you know better than that."

I did know, but I argued with myself. Why should I believe her? She'd tricked me. "Jeremiah wouldn't leave without saying good-bye."

"There wasn't much time at the last. Robert, sit down, son, and let me talk with you."

"I'm not your son." I kept my back to her and a full minute stretched between us.

"I don't risk my life to lose it, Robert. I don't risk the lives of those I help."

Still I stood, facing the window, and pushed back the sting in my eyes. "You tricked me."

"It wasn't a trick. It was a decision, and ultimately, it had to be Jeremiah's decision."

"How can I know that? How can I believe it?"

"Because I'm telling you the truth." I heard her smooth the covers on the bed. "He told me you both had a friend who died helping to protect conductors of the Underground Railroad. He said that he thinks you feel responsible for your friend's death. Jeremiah believed you needed to help him in order to set things right."

"Jeremiah said that?"

"Yes. How else would I know? Robert, you can't take on the whole world alone. Sometimes helping people means leading them to others that are willing to help and trusting that they will care as much as you do. Trust is an act of faith. Jeremiah chose faith when he trusted you, and again when he trusted me. Perhaps it is the step you need to take now." Something in what she said reminded me of Rev. Goforth, but

I pushed it away, because I didn't want to let go of Jeremiah. It was like letting go of William Henry all over again.

At the door she stopped, still speaking to my back. "Oh. Jeremiah said to tell you something—something he said was very important. He looked so odd when he said it. He said to tell you that you were right. He said to tell you, 'Jeremiah Henry is a fine name.'" My heart stopped. "Do you know what he meant?"

"Yes." I breathed. "Yes." I knew then that Jeremiah had made the decision to go on without me himself. He was on his way to freedom in the way he figured best.

"Breakfast will be waiting downstairs when you're ready," Miz Burton said on her way out the door.

"Miz Burton?"

She turned. "Yes, Robert?"

"Thank you. Thank you for helping Jeremiah."

She smiled. "It is what I do."

I washed my face and brushed my clothes. I felt like I'd been robbed, both of things I wanted and things I didn't. I didn't know how to explain it better than that.

The fresh eggs and bacon fried in onions tasted good, and reminded me of Aunt Sassy's cooking. Suddenly I wanted to go home. I knew it would be different than before. Miz Laura was gone, and most of all, William Henry was gone. But I hoped Ma and Pa would be there, and Aunt Sassy and Joseph would be there, and Mr. Heath, and—home.

I stayed on at the boardinghouse another week, to throw off anybody searching for two boys running north. Nobody came busting in, but we sensed the boardinghouse was watched, and were careful to keep our habits regular and the quilt off the line, the candle from the window.

I chopped wood, built fires, swept hearths, and ran

errands for Miz Burton. She told her boarders that I was her sister's son, visiting from Virginia. Miz Burton reminded me a little of Aunt Sassy—good-hearted and quick to take things in hand—and we took to each other soon as I stopped blaming her for Jeremiah's going on without me. I told her about Ashland and Laurelea, especially about William Henry and Jeremiah, Mr. Heath and Miz Laura, Aunt Sassy and Joseph Henry. I told her how I was both anxious and fearful of facing Ma and Pa.

"You mean your parents don't even know you're alive?" Miz Burton's eyes went wide.

"No, ma'am. There was no way I could get word to them, not without risking Jeremiah. We never stayed anyplace long enough to write a letter. If I'd tried to send a telegram we'd of been caught, sure."

"Yes, I see that. But now that Jeremiah is safely on his way you can write to them, just to let them know you are all right and on your way home. They must be worried sick! I would be."

"Except I don't know where they are. They might be home, but they could still be at Ashland, or looking for me. And I'm not sure they'll want me back, especially Ma."

"I'm sure your mother loves you, Robert. How could she not? Why not write your Mr. Heath and ask him to get word to your parents? Surely he is at Laurelea."

That seemed a good plan. Besides, maybe Mr. Heath could soften Ma and Pa, or at least Pa. So I wrote him that day, and posted the letter. I didn't tell him what I'd done. I figured Pa would've told him already. But I wrote that I was safe and coming home near the end of the week. I didn't get too particular about when or how. I didn't want anybody looking for me, putting Miz Burton or the boardinghouse at risk. I asked him to get word to Ma and Pa. And though I might have sounded the coward, I finished by saying that I hoped they'd take me back.

After early breakfast on that last day, Miz Burton slid a boxed lunch across the table toward me. "You'll be wanting this, come noon. There's a fresh set of clothes and a coat in the parcel I left in your room. You'll want to look nice for the train, and for going home to your mother and father." I didn't know what to say. What she'd already done was more than enough. She squeezed my hand. "They'll be overjoyed to see you, Robert. If you were my son, I would be." Her smile warmed me through and made it hard to keep my face clear. I just hoped she was right.

It was eight o'clock when Effie Burton sent me off with directions to the train station, wearing my new suit of clothes. I hugged her at the last, and promised to write when I could, letting her know how things fared. I left a gold piece on the pillow in the room she'd given me, knowing that she wouldn't have taken it any other way.

At the station I slid my money across the counter and looked the stationmaster in the eye. "One ticket for Baltimore."

As the train pulled out of Washington, the conductor worked his way through the car, punching tickets, and calling, "Tickets! Tickets, please!" When he came to me he said, "Traveling alone, son?"

"Yes, sir." And I was. For the first time in a long while I was just a boy traveling alone—no longer running, no longer hiding, not afraid of Grandfather or Jed Slocum or pattyrollers or anybody. I was Robert Leslie Glover, thirteen years old, standing on my own feet, free and clear.

And that made me think of Jeremiah. I prayed that he was

safe, on his way to Canada, and that people were helping him until he, too, could stand on his own feet, free and clear. I knew I had to put one foot in front of the other, trusting that it would happen for him, that the Slocums of this world were fewer than the Miz Lauras, the Andrew Goforths, the Effie Burtons, and the William Henrys. I knew that the power to trust like that was greater than anything in me.

I wondered if William Henry would be alive today if he had trusted someone stronger to help him, rather than taking on Jake Tulley alone. I'd always wanted to be more like William Henry. But maybe there were things William Henry hadn't known. It was no good trying to guess. William Henry had made his own decision. Jeremiah had made his.

I changed trains in Baltimore, and for all my worry and eagerness, slept some of the way home. I never saw when we rolled over the Susquehanna River. It was nearly dusk when I stepped off the train in Elkton.

I walked up the tracks by Eberly's General Merchandise. I nodded to old Mr. Wheeler as he clipped dead and frozen blooms from his hydrangeas. "Been away a spell, have you, Robert?" he asked.

"Yes, sir," I called. "But I'm home now."

"Good. That's good." And he went back to his work. Mr. Sellers lit the lamps along Main Street, the same as he did every night. Nothing had changed, and yet everything looked different—smaller, maybe.

By the time I'd walked out of town I wondered if I was the same person that had lived here last summer; it seemed so long ago. My hands were the same color, like sand at the bottom of the run—just a little bigger, a little stronger. The world was bigger than I'd imagined, but I'd made my way through a patch of it.

I thought of Rev. Goforth, and how he'd said our choices determine who we are and decide the path we walk for a very long time. I felt proud of the choice I'd made, glad of the path I'd walked. I'd helped Jeremiah toward freedom, toward liberty. Liberty, for me, I'd decided, is the freedom to make my own choices, to live with their consequences. Grandfather would never welcome me at Ashland again, and I'd thrown away my inheritance with both hands. I didn't mind. I just hoped Ma would one day forgive me and that Pa would understand. I regretted losing Emily's friendship. Those were the consequences of my choices.

Night fell before I reached Tulley's lane. The hounds snarled and barked, lunging against their pen. I cut through their fallow field and around their pond, the pond William Henry and I had fished in just last summer. My heart beat faster with each step that brought me nearer home. I made my way through the woods and over a log in the run, planting my feet, at last, with a shout, on Laurelea soil. Stars gleamed by the time I passed Granny Struthers's cabin.

Running through the stubbled fields, I rounded my house, almost afraid to look. I couldn't bear it if no light burned in the window. For all I'd said about Ma and Pa maybe not being home, I believed in my heart that they would be, that Mr. Heath had told them I was coming, that they'd be sitting in the parlor with the fire burning and all the lamps shining, waiting for me. I bounded up the front porch steps. But no light burned through the parlor window, not one. I closed my eyes, and opened them again. But it was still the same. My head went light, and my arms and legs felt heavy burdened. I pushed down the lump in my throat and stepped back, dropping to the porch step. I'd hoped. I'd so hoped.

I don't know how long I sat there. I just knew I couldn't

stay in my house without Ma or Pa. I couldn't do it. Maybe, I thought, Mr. Heath or the Henrys would take me in, at least for a time—at least until I knew where I stood.

But first, there was something I needed to do. I walked down the lane and around the barn, through the orchard behind Mr. Heath's house. Miz Laura's old quilt was hanging on the wash line in the yard. I pulled it from the line and buried my face in it. It smelled of wood smoke and sunshine, of snow and home. I marveled how I'd seen it almost every day of my life, never knowing it was a sign for runaways, letting them know it was safe to come for help. Then I wondered if the quilt Jeremiah'd set on Jacob's marker was left for that reason. I wished I'd asked him.

I turned to head over the hill to the colored church. That's when I saw a light glimmer from the Heaths' side window. Keeping to the shadows, I crept closer, hoping for a glimpse of Mr. Heath. My heart jumped in my chest and I nearly cried out. For there was Mr. Heath, just sitting down to supper at the head of his table, with Pa at the foot. Joseph and Aunt Sassy sat on one side, with Ma on the other—an empty plate and chair beside her. On the back of the chair hung my old coat, like I'd just stepped out and would be back any minute to take my seat. I blinked back the burn in my eyes. I wondered how long Ma and Pa had been home, and if Ma meant to stay. I wondered if they'd set my place every night, hoping I'd come. I wouldn't disappoint them long, and I could hardly wait. Still, there was something I needed to do first.

I walked to William Henry's grave. The moon skittered in and out behind a lone cloud, but I knew my way among the plots and markers. I ran my fingers over the carved letters in William Henry's name, wrapped Miz Laura's quilt tight around me, then sat down on the frozen ground. While that moon kept us company, I told William Henry the whole story, about Ruby and Jeremiah, about Nanny Sara, Old George, and Rev. Goforth. He already knew about Slocum. I told him he was right about my grandfather and slavery, more right than I'd ever imagined. I told him about the boy that found Jeremiah and me in the bell tower, and our Christmas sleigh ride, and about losing Stargazer. I knew he would understand what that meant to me. I told William Henry about the night Jeremiah and I spent in the cave, and the ride in the false-bottom wagon with Brother Peter, and how we ended up in coffins. I figured William Henry'd get a hoot over that, and especially Jeremiah's dress and veils. I explained to him about Effie Burton, and taking that leap of faith, and that Jeremiah was on his way to Canada.

I told William Henry all that he meant to me, and to Jeremiah, how I missed him and would never forget him. Finally I told him about Jeremiah's last message. I knew he would understand that, too.

Epilogue

PA HELD OUT FOR A TIME, I think for Ma's sake, but in the end it was Mr. Heath that convinced him I should be given the choice of helping slaves run north, that a boy who could do what I'd done deserved that much. I wanted it more than anything. So Mr. Heath took me with him on one of his trips north and introduced me to Mr. Thomas Garrett, an Underground stationmaster and his old Quaker friend in Wilmington, Delaware, the very man who'd influenced Mr. Heath to free his slaves all those years before.

Mr. Garrett said he believed I was sent by God for this great work, and that same day he sent me on the train with two disguised runaways to a colored safe house in Philadelphia—to meet up with Mr. William and Miz Letitia Still. That's when I learned that Mr. Still kept records, stories, of all the slaves who'd passed through his hands on the freedom train. He was tireless, and careful, and counted each head precious.

Mr. Still made me think of what William Henry could have grown into more than any person, white or colored, I'd ever met. I admire to say we became fast friends.

It was after that first trip to Philadelphia that two letters came for me the same month, the first letters I'd ever received.

The first one was from Ma, whose inner war and sharp tongue had raged all winter, and taxed Pa to the breaking point. Pa had finally agreed with her that maybe a visit home to Ashland would do her good. And that's what we both thought, that she'd only gone to visit. But in that letter she wrote that she could not consider returning to Laurelea for a long time, that without Miz Laura, life there was just too harsh, too lonely, and that Grandfather needed her. She wrote that she loved Pa and me, but trusted that we'd understand.

Pa told me to keep loving her, to think well of Ma for staying as long as she did, as long as she could. He prayed that she'd come back when she felt ready, and urged me to write to her. I did love Ma, but I did not understand her, and sometimes, though I knew it was wrong, thinking well of her did not come easy.

The other letter came from Canada. There was no return address. It was short. The penmanship was nothing to brag on. It read, "Dear Robert, Haven't worn any dresses lately. Are you a genuine scholar yet?" It was signed "J. Henry." It was the best letter I ever got.

So I helped Pa and Mr. Heath, and Joseph Henry, and Mr. Garrett, and sometimes Mr. Still on the Underground Railroad regular, for a time—as long as there was need. And every time I returned to Laurelea I gave my report to William Henry. I knew he'd want to know.